Blood Cells
By
Phoenix Andrews

P P Andrews Publishing
Bognor Regis
West
Sussex
England

www.phoenixandrews.com

This paperback edition 2023

First published by P P Andrews 2023

Copyright © Phoenix Andrews 2023

Phoenix Andrews assets the moral right to be identified as the author of this work

ISBN: 978-1-3999-5126-5

To steve,

Hope you enjoy the book!

Best wishes,

Phoenix Andrews :)

26/04/23

This book is dedicated to my mum who is my absolute rock; to my brother who had the courage to reconnect (for which I am so glad); to my beautiful friends who help me keep the light burning through the dark, but especially to my friend Peter, for helping me get the story to this point.

I love you all. X

Prologue

David hadn't slept for three nights in a row. Fear kept him awake, fear that if he closed his eyes, even for an hour, tiredness would grip him and he wouldn't be able to wake up again. But more than that. Since arriving at HMP Stafford, more and more of his fellow inmates had been disappearing. "Lock up!" came the ritual sound of the officers, as cell doors banged shut. Then "Lights Out!" would next echo around the block. And that was it for some, for too many recently. They just weren't there the following morning when the cells were unlocked for breakfast.

No one said a thing, no one dared ask the question "Where the hell have they gone?!" No one wanted to know the answer.

Of course over the relatively short time he had been banged up here at HMP Stafford, David had seen inmates, people he had come to think of as friends (in here anyway) finish their sentences and leave or get transferred to another prison. But this was always during the day, and they all knew it was coming. No, disappearing at night, now that was something else entirely and it scared the hell out of David. But damn he was tired!

He and Billy had been playing Backgammon, as they always did, over a night-time brew in their cell. On the top floor and in the corner, it was a cell that no one else wanted. It got very cold in winter, despite the heating pipes that ran around the whole block. It was the only cell where inmates were allowed an extra blanket each, but both David and Billy still slept wearing their prison clothes. David had purposefully put aside a set for sleeping in. Most of the others walked around in the ceremonial grey jog pants and sweater with white trainers that they had either stolen from some other poor sod, swapped for tobacco or had brought in with them. A Lot could be said about a person by what they wore inside, as I guess could be said also of people on the street. This was a micro universe in itself, a world within the world, managed not by officers, but rather by pockets of inner hierarchy. And what you wore helped to place you.

During the day, David preferred to wear prison-issue blue jeans, which were normally the wrong size and so held up by a belt made from a ripped strip of bedsheet, a pale blue or peppermint green T Shirt under a plain purple sweater. He also wore the grey sweater sometimes, but he had no white trainers to wear. He had stupidly come to Park Road Crown Court, London to be sentenced in a black suit and fancy black brogues. *Maybe making an effort will make a difference,* he thought at the time. He knew he was going down for a stretch and so brought with him a bag of essentials such as toothbrush and toothpaste, pants and socks, some notebooks so he could write a journal and some of his favourite novels to read. But those shoes! What was he thinking? To walk around wearing those just advertised N.O.N.C.E to everyone else on the wing, no matter what you were in for. Interestingly, it was during his first bit of outdoor exercise that he learned what it stood for, Not on Normal Circulatory Exercise. Going back to the early days of some prisons, basically everyone would walk clockwise around the exercise yard. But if you were in for any kind of Sex Offence, you were made to walk round anti-clockwise. At least this is what David was told. Luckily for everyone he was in with, most reasons for being inside were kept hidden unless it served a purpose to divulge it or be outed by someone else in order to get something in return.

David was in for Aggravated Assault, or ABH (Actual Bodily Harm) as people here referred to it. He had long since surrendered to the fact that it was his fault. The first week or so after being sentenced, David blamed everyone else for his mistakes. Being on his own, shoved into an orientation cell in Bristol Holding Prison and afraid to leave it during social hour, he would just lay on his single bed brooding. It was such a different environment from what he had been used to, his mind became distorted to the truth of events as the long, lonely hours totted up. But now he had surrendered to his guilt. He didn't have to hit the bouncer that had thrown him out of the club.

An IT Specialist in his former life, David had gone out to celebrate an old friend's promotion when they had decided late into the night to go to a local club. The bouncer had let his friend in, but refused David entry, calling him a Specky Twat and a waste of space, before pushing him to the ground. The rest happened so fast. The bit of old pipe was just lying there in the road next to his hand and without thinking, with a blind rage that comes with copious amounts of alcohol, David had grabbed it, got up with a sense of clarity and purpose and smacked the bouncer around the side of the head with the pipe. He didn't remember much else, only the wet crunching, cracking sound the pipe made as it struck the bouncer's head, followed by the heavy thumping sound his body made as the unconscious brute of a man hit the pavement. Then the echo of the pipe hitting the floor. A fleeting moment that put one man in a coma and an otherwise very respectable young IT Technician in prison for 18 months, his life over just like that. He knew all too well how hard it was to rebuild a respectable life once you had something like this hanging over you.

But in here, he did not want to be known as a thug, for that would have put him in with the wrong crowd. He had seen these types having to try and prove themselves all the time, forced to bully and manipulate others. No, he was happy being with the intellectuals. Okay so most of them were more than likely in for Sex Offences, but as so much as anyone said, they were all in for fraud. And David had managed to get hold of a pair of black trainers after a few weeks of being in.

And so here he was, lying on his top bunk and counting once again the cracks he could see on the ceiling of the cell through the light of the moon that shone particularly bright on this night. He had started to eat coffee granules mixed with sugar as a way of keeping awake. It left his heart pounding like a steam locomotive, but anything to keep him alert! They had eaten particularly well that evening. It was Ramadan and the Muslim inmates were given some amazing food. David was convinced he would get the same over cooked shit everyone had become used to. Hey, he wasn't complaining really. They had a menu given to them every Wednesday on which they could choose from three possible options each day for both lunch and dinner, planning for the whole week. They simply had to tick the boxes next to the meals and nine times out of ten everyone was given what they wanted. Okay, so it wasn't exactly the Ritz, and most of the options were very heavy on the carbohydrates, supposedly in order to keep the inmates subdued in a state of lethargy. But after a few weeks it became one of the few highlights, getting that menu.

But this evening was different. So as to not cause massive unrest and a sense of favouritism between the Muslims and everyone else on the wing, the cooks had decided to provide a full roast dinner for anyone not observing Ramadan, followed by Apple Crumble and custard. To David and, well almost everyone else, this was absolute heaven! Slices of processed chicken (probably Bernard Matthews), proper roast potatoes (that even had that crispy edge to them), cabbage and cauliflower. Then a smear of chicken gravy and a stuffing ball. And the Apple Crumble! Lack of sugar in the over-cooked apples and crumble mix was more than made up for with the generous helping of thick custard poured over. *Oh happy days!* thought both David and Billy as they cradled their plates and bowls carefully up the two flights of stairs back to the cell. By the time they had sat down, Billy on his bunk and David at the table, the food was only lukewarm, but it didn't matter. This was such a special treat on a Tuesday. Once finished, the blue plastic plates and bowls washed up in the bathroom sink, both David and Billy sat by the table to play their ceremonial game of Backgammon. The small plastic kettle was filled and switched on; two blue plastic cups were laid out and filled with coffee and sugar and the games board was set up ready.

Routines were so important in prison, if anything to break up other, more mind-numbing routines such as work detail. As well as having the meal sheet each week, inmates also received a 'Spends' sheet with items they could purchase with earnings saved up from work and education. For the majority of people in here, tobacco was the most bought item. It was used as currency as much as for personal use. But for David, chocolate and other food items made his and Billy's week.

David was sent first to a more general sort of employment in the main warehouse-type building on site. His job entailed screwing in the housing on the brake lights you see on those trailer light boards for caravans and, well, trailers. Yep, that was it for 4 hours each day. Ushered into the warehouse in single file as if entering a slaughterhouse, David had to collect his screwdriver from a large tool board, all of which had a number on them, and then go to the same bench as a pile of trailer boards awaited to be assembled. People chatted and joked, pranks were pulled and even a few inmates that were clearly lower down on the evolutionary ladder would start on each other, before being pulled apart and led away onto different areas of the job, or in some more serious cases where tools were involved, straight to segregation.

David would have gone insane, if it hadn't been for Billy telling him of the possibility of joining the "A Team". This was a team of only a handful of inmates whose job it was to clean the gum and glue

off old PVC window frames ready for recycling.
Now at first, David thought of this as an even worse
job than screwing down bloody trailer board lights
day in, day out. But then Billy told him of the
camaraderie between the inmates in this area, of
the officer that brought in biscuits sometimes and
made the group cups of tea. It seemed wonderful to
David as Billy told of it. And it was. Within two days
of working on this detail, the officer had indeed
brought in some rich tea biscuits for everyone and
the group could stop working for 20 minutes or so
while having a break with a brew. The one thing
Billy didn't mention however, was the way in which
every couple of days an inmate would leave and
another would join the fold. Again, no questions
were asked. No one had appeared to have done
anything wrong, for not one inmate assigned to this
team would want to jeopardise their role. But it
seemed like some kind of system was happening.
Apart from Billy, David didn't see any of these "A-
lister" inmates outside of the work detail. But during
these 4 hours, they were like a small family, a
secret club. Each day they were led to a separate
building, where they were given a scraper by the
officer and they got to work scraping the sealant
and glue off the white plastic frame pieces. David
thought of it as quite meditative really.

Then one day, they arrived at the work building to
find a pile of old furniture laying on the floor and the
officer asked for volunteers to sand them down and

give each piece a new coat of white paint. Both Billy and David were chosen before putting their hands up. Not all of the furniture could be saved and it was then that David had the idea of making a games board for the cell. He was afraid of asking the officer at first, but with a bit of egging on from Billy and a few others, he plucked up the courage. The officer simply said that just as long as the main job was done, he couldn't see a problem. It didn't take long, cutting and sanding down a piece of wood for the board and slicing sections of an old broom handle to make the backgammon pieces. They were given total trust in using the saw and David even got to paint one half white. The board and pieces were checked by the officer and then taken back to the cell at the end of the shift.

Then something strange happened. The following morning, they left their cell as normal after breakfast and made their way down the two flights of stairs to wait in line for work duty, only to be taken to the main warehouse, to the main work detail again. Both David and Billy were utterly crushed and confused, wondering what they had done wrong? Was it that they had somehow taken advantage of the privileges given to them? But if so, why did the officer allow it? David was put back in the same spot on the same bench as before, at the far side of the warehouse, back to screwing in the brake lights. Whilst Billy was put on another bench with some rather rough-looking guys. David couldn't see what they had got Billy to do, but he certainly didn't look very happy. And why would he? They both soon came to realise that life was about giving and then having it taken away in prison. It was a way of control, of power. And nothing hammered this home more than the numerous disappearances happening of late.

The threat of David or Billy being next, the ominous air of possibility that this may be their last night left David staring at his ceiling with a sense of dread, his hyperactivity starting to give him the shakes and cramps.

It must have been almost early morning when he heard a key being inserted into the lock of his cell. It turned so quietly, making the faintest of clicks as the door was unlocked. Strange, as during the day and when there was an incident, the locks on these doors were incredibly loud and clunky. But not this time, this time it sounded like that mechanism inside a grandfather clock turning the cogs to make a midnight chime. But no chime this time, just the door slowly opening, the dim yellow lights of the corridor flooding into the cell. Billy was still fast asleep and there was barely a sound from outside apart from an intermittent beeping from somewhere below. Three shadows moved seamlessly into the room, blocking out the yellow glow momentarily and instead bringing in a chill that filled the space around them. David had stopped breathing, gripped with a fear that encased his heart and stomach. He didn't move and couldn't think straight. Was it the lack of sleep? The chemical injection of caffeine and sugar running through his veins? Or just that fact that there was an overwhelming sense of dread that something sinister had just entered the cell? They seemed to bring all of the shadows of the space around them together, merge with the night and yet the light of the moon didn't seem to touch them. And they were tall and hooded, like a trio of Grim Reapers ready to take souls from this world. *SHIT!* David thought in near delirium, *is that why they are here? Is Billy dead? Have they come to take him?* In a blind panic, he seemed to come quickly to his senses and shouted out "Oi! What's the problem here guys?" He had no idea if they were indeed men or women, or human in actual fact "We haven't done anything".

Unfortunately for David, he should have remained quiet, for they had only initially come for Billy. But now both inmates were to be taken from this cell.

With reflexes defying logic, one of the shadows rushed forwards, grabbing David and throwing him out of the bunk and across the small cell. He rebounded off the wall and landed heavily onto the table, scattering books and drink-making items onto the floor. He was momentarily stunned and unable to move, as the other two shadows leant over the body of Billy. *Why wasn't he moving or screaming or something?* David thought. But that was all he had time to think of. A black, gloved hand clasped over his mouth and nose. All thoughts slowly disappeared and David drifted into a sea of blackness.

The three shadows silently carried the still forms of David and Billy out of the cell, across the corridor and through a door at the end. Just as quietly as opening their cell, a key gently clicked and the only noises left were a snoring sound across the way and the intermittent beeping from somewhere below.

One

Adam Vaziri needed time. Time to think, time to reflect. Every hundred years or so it was the same. When you had lived as long as he had, it was important to disappear from time to time so that the weight of events unfolding around the world could settle down. Of course, they never really settled down, not really. But the world didn't need to see a man that never aged, a man that seemingly couldn't die, a man that was not really a man, not anymore. At least, not in the conventional sense for over 800 years.

Vampire. Every time he heard the word he would chuckle to himself. Stupid made up word to make sense of yet another thing people couldn't understand or explain; a box to put someone in to make people feel better, safe. In all honesty Adam didn't really know what he was. His memories were becoming ever blurrier and more unfocussed of late, all except one. The final moments of his demise all those centuries ago. The broadsword that had pierced his belly on the battlefield during the war of Jaffa back in 1195 should have killed him there and then. He was a general, a Persian masquerading as a Muslim and fighting for their ruler, Saladin. Standing right next to him when the fatal thrust struck his torso; lying bleeding in the red dirt, he had made peace with his God. But then a stranger, a bannerman to King Richard the First, decided for some reason to make him above others immortal. He could still feel the searing heat and pain in his dreams after all this time. The sharpness of the long teeth biting his wrist; the venom working its way rapidly through his whole body; the ice cold feeling as his wounds sealed themselves and his strength and health returned. Then became more, much more.

But Adam hadn't appeared to change physically. At just under 6 feet tall, with dark brown hair cut short and olive skin accentuated by dark stubble framing his chiselled jawline, he was a handsome man, with an air to him that spoke of a wisdom belying his 35-year-old, athletic body. His accent now had a soft, well-spoken British tone to it. Although he could speak many languages, Adam had long since preferred to live in England. He seemed to fit in here. It felt like home and he couldn't help but wonder now and again whether this was because it was the birthplace of his maker all those centuries ago.

But now, here he was on a prison transport van on his way to a holding cell somewhere in England. Most people would have been nervous, scared even, but he felt at peace. This was a deliberate act. Something sinister was happening to the lowest rungs of society. Prisoners were disappearing and he needed to find out why.

Getting put inside was not a problem for Adam. In fact, he had to be extra careful to attract just the right amount of attention whilst still being able to be invisible to more watchful eyes higher up in society. For he had also been given other gifts that fateful night on the battlefield. It was all too easy for him to make an error of judgement in the heat of any given moment, kill a man with almost no effort.

Over the centuries Adam had focussed on honing his skills. Unlike the fairy tales, he did not need to stick to shadows. He could walk in the sun and his skin did not glisten. *Shit, how cool that would be though, right?* He often thought amusingly. His hazel eyes did have a tendency to glow slightly orange when under heightened emotion though, or when he was hungry. To most, he was just a regular good-looking man in his thirties. He breathed, had a heartbeat, but then most people only tended to see what they wanted most of the time. Misdirection was easy when you knew what you were doing and Adam had been awarded more than enough time to learn.

He had acquired a few contacts over time, friends he could share his secrets with. At first they would seem so jealous of his 'powers', as they called them. Some even wanted Adam to make them the same as him, but in all these years he was so careful not to create anyone else like him. Although Adam had no choice but to come to terms with immortality, most of the time he hated who he was. If he could have taken his own life he would have done so a thousand times over, but as yet he had found no way. It was not for the lack of trying though. For all the wonder that came with this existence, there also came a terrible curse too. And Adam could not, no, would not give this curse to anyone else. Actually he didn't even know if he was able to turn someone anyway. His kind had some sort of hierarchy system of its own and the power to make more like him was something normally left to the top tiers. But he had also learned that over the years most of his kind had since gone into hiding, disappearing from the world completely. His maker, Leofric, was one in particular. And Adam had made finding him at the top of his list. In fact, he was thinking about travelling to North Spain to follow up on a recent lead when word had come his way of strange killings in certain prisons.

Although he could eat and drink the same as anyone, Adam's body needed more. It needed blood to survive. Well, plasma to be exact. Killing and feeding off animals did not provide the right balance, it had to be human and he had contacts behind the scenes in hospitals across the country and in Europe. It was the only way to get blood without drawing attention. This of course was also becoming increasingly difficult as there was a national shortage, had been for years. And more and more eyes were watching everything everywhere, despite the fact that people were also becoming so self-absorbed of late, stuck with their eyes glued to whatever the latest trend, influence or Tweet was. But before Instagram, Twitter and bloody Facebook, it was all about looking like the models in magazines and possessing whatever was photographed at the time. And before that, well, people actually socialised and so tried to "one up" with whoever it was they were befriending. And so it went on, right back to when the most important thing in daily life, was to try and not die before you were thirty years old, coughing up your intestines onto a dirty pillow filled with straw.

And so, as technology advanced and social media spread everywhere, there became less and less opportunity to feed. Cameras now patrolled the darkest corners of the globe and even his lightning reactions and overwhelming sense of caution couldn't stop people from finding him, recording him and thus outing his true existence to the world. And that was why he needed contacts watching his movements. They could help to erase what he needed erasing, from both the internet and other more archaic forms of media, stopping him from being exposed.

He currently had a couple of IT specialists on hand, youngsters really, millennials that loved the distraction from their normal, mundane routines. They were geeky hackers spend their days patrolling every aspect of the Web, as well as traffic cameras, street CCTV, media and chatrooms. Adam loved these geeks. So harmless, but at the same time so positive and full of energy. They loved the romance that came with helping someone like him, it made them feel like superheroes themselves. It gave Adam hope in Humanity. And then he had heard that one of his geeky friends had recently been incarcerated. A young, smart, non-assuming lad called David who had been sentenced to 18 months for assault on a brute of a bully bouncer outside a club. This wasn't like David, not like him at all. But this was the least of this lad's worries, for if Adam was correct, David had been sent into the heart of evil itself.

So here was Adam, bouncing around on a plastic moulded seat that seamlessly flowed into the plastic wall, floor and ceiling of his particular compartment in the prison van. Only one small black square window gave a teasing impression of what was outside during the journey. But Adam wasn't interested in the outside, only what a group of wannabe gangsters were arguing about in the other cubicles.

"Nah, I tell yer bruv, honest to Christ. MY solicitor told me. There's a right weirdo on this van wiv us. He's got something wrong wiv im, init".
"Bruv, that doesn't say nothin, does it? Wot you goin on about? Is there a N.O.N.C.E. in ere or summit?"
Then another "highly intellectual" being piped up "Ah, I fuckin ate kiddie fiddlers bruv. Wait till we get off, then we'll know for sure, init?"

Why had this ridiculous way of talking been allowed to evolve in recent years? Adam thought

to himself. The parents of these little shits should have had their legs sewn shut before they could procreate and produce kids that wanted nothing more but to live off the wealth of other hard-working people. Like leeches they were, sucking society dry!
Adam couldn't help but chuckle at the irony of that thought. He had no right to quibble really. Any anyway, back in the Medieval times the poorer classes could be understood by others even less! And they were even more opportunistic to boot.

"Hey, who's laughin'? You think it's funny do yer?" Came the squeaky voice again from the first kid. These were clearly very low on the ladder of the underworld, the fall-guys if you like for people much higher up. The scapegoats who would freeze like rabbits in the headlights as soon as the blue flashing lights stared them down. Or maybe they were just too high smoking the merchandise they were meant to sell to really care what happened. They were young and probably knew more people inside than out anyway, learning some new skills every time they had their little 'all expenses paid' package holidays inside.

It was the turn of one of the officers now to step in. "Oi, keep it down you lot. We have a long way to go and I don't want to be hearing you all the way there, giving me a headache".

"Miss we just wanted to know who it was that is wiv us, init?"

"None of your business. Now shut up, stay seated and you might get something to eat shortly, alright?"

"Yes Miss, sorry Miss". *Oh*, thought Adam, *treat them mean to keep them keen eh?* At least they showed some sort of respect.

"Hey bruv, still fink we should batter whoever comes out of the van at the end though, don't you bruv?" the first kid whispered loudly.

"Sssh bruv, you thick or what?"

These kids mean me, I know it, Adam thought. He had asked his solicitor to quietly pass on false information about why he was in the van, in the hope that they would give up some kind of information about what was happening in the prisons. he didn't mind what his solicitor said to the other legal beans, as long as it sounded convincing, making Adam out to be more vulnerable than he of course was. Adam had stupidly forgot that there was actually a wing called the Vulnerable Prisoners Wing, which mainly housed old people and Sex Offenders. So, as Adam wasn't old (to look at anyway), Ta

Dah! Sex Offender it was. *Oh well* thought Adam. It was a way in, no matter how much he despised men and women who took pleasure in hurting children and those more vulnerable than themselves. He chuckled again at this second piece of irony, considering he had killed his fair share of people over the centuries for food, sport and justice. In the early days he had taken great pleasure in the thrill of the chase too. But not now. Now he tried not to hurt anyone, at least not kill them anyway. A rule with a slightly grey area used for certain situations.

It was roughly an hour into the journey and these brats hadn't shut up about what they wanted to do to Adam once they got inside the prison. He was getting quite tired of their style of banter and craved some sleep as the van rocked gently from side to side along the motorway. They were heading North, the sun slowly starting to sink somewhere to his left on what was actually a rather nice day in the middle of April. The clocks had only just gone back a couple of weeks ago, giving that extra delicious hour of daylight. Adam figured this meant they were maybe on either the M6 or M1. Interesting. But also good for Adam as it was in the North that most of the disappearances were taking place, not to mention it was also where David was being held.

Adam had started to get hungry. He hadn't fed for what must have been a good eight hours, what with the court scene, waiting in the holding cell underneath the courtroom and then this journey in the van. The young louts were also clearly feeling it too, as they started changing their incessant whining to that of demands for food.

What he assumed was the female officer slid a pack of sandwiches under the door of Adam's cell along with a bottle of water and without seeing what kind they were, he hungrily demolished them in just a few bites, downing the water without taking breath. It did a lot for his energy, but he still needed some blood plasma in his system to keep his thoughts straight. He just hoped they would stop soon. He also secretly hoped that the youths would try something when they were off the van.

Two

Around 100 miles away, in an old, abandoned barn, David crouched in a corner, shivering both from the early evening cold, and fear. His thoughts were running wildly around in his brain. Normally he was able to focus on at least six things at once, compartmentalise, analyse, and then make a sensible hypothesis as to the best course of action based on the current variables or evidence available to him. But he had no point of reference, no research or previous experience to help him deal with this. This was far, far beyond him in every sense of the word. He started crying again, sobbing like a small child, curled up, alone in the dark of the barn, dressed in nothing but a blue hospital gown which gave him even less dignity than the way in which he was almost murdered. Slaughtered like his cellmate Billy.

He had been taken unconscious from his cell to another part of the prison. He could only remember coming to and seeing his friend dangling upside down in front of him. Swinging slightly in the gloominess of an old brick building, Billy looked like he was very wet. Liquid was dripping from him onto the floor. No, not onto the floor, into buckets or containers. A dark liquid. David was not a fan of horror films and had never really seen one before. Of course, as part of his unpaid job, he was tasked with trolling the internet looking for sightings and accidental and non-so-accidental images taken of Adam which had to be erased, and then erased again more completely, entirely in fact. This would occasionally drag up all kinds of disturbing photos and videos from the depths of the Dark Web, but nothing had prepared David for this scenario. And now, as he slowly, groggily came to his senses, seeing his friend dangling in front of him and being drained of his blood like some kind of halal meat in a Jewish butcher's backroom, he was terrified. He lost use of his bladder first, urinating over his thighs without knowing until the warmth oozed across him. *How long have I been unconscious?* Was his first thought. Then his second came screaming at him *Find a way out now! They are going to kill you!* But of course he was frozen, sitting in a puddle of his own terror and shame, in near pitch dark in an unknown part of the prison. It was definitely not a well-used part anyway. The only light seemed to come from a few thin, wide windows high up, which at least told him it was a round building. He heard strange voices somewhere ahead but couldn't quite make out which direction they were coming from; high-pitched, wheezy voices that were really more of a whisper than anything else.

It felt as if it had been hours since Billy and he had been snatched from their cell and dragged here. Poor Billy! He had been sent here for being caught up in a local gang. He had an addiction, which had started with a bit of occasional weed now and had then got harder and harder. Most recently he had got himself hooked on meth and just couldn't seem to get himself out of it. Having been embarrassed to talk to anyone about it, by the time his family had noticed what was going on, it was really too late. Billy had got himself mixed up with an unsavoury group of friends who stole to feed the habit, living in an abandoned warehouse as squatters and he had ended up living there too, high as a kite most of the time. Then things escalated. They had tried to hold up a small off licence in town. Unfortunately it wasn't well planned, stupid actually. But they were high and not really thinking. Just a street away from the local police station, a group of officers practically bumped into them as they left the shop. Showing their true colours, Billy was pushed to the ground as bait for the officers, whilst the other so-called friends scarpered. And so Billy got the full wrap. He never gave up any names, well as far as David knew anyway. He had promised Billy that once he was out he would use his skills to hunt down these bastards and have them arrested on something which would not implicate Billy at all. After all, Billy had been a good friend to David when he arrived at Stafford prison. David had no idea what to expect when he arrived here, wearing the wrong shoes and just screaming of someone to be used and abused at the first instance. Then Billy had introduced himself, at first looking as if he was going to be the guy to do it first. But he just wanted a friend it seemed. Unlikely fellows that just seemed to click in a place that was far detached from the outside world.

And now he was dead, and David was soon to follow. But not yet!

The shadows at the other end of this strange, cold, damp building seem very preoccupied with something and David was starting to collect his senses. His eyes were adjusting to the gloom and his smell and hearing were sharpening. He wished not to have his smell back though, what with the metallic sweetness of blood mixed with the acrid warmth of urine filling his nostrils.

The hardest part was trying to take his eyes of Billy's gently swinging corpse, which appeared to have stopped dripping. Then David saw it, a door to his left that was slightly ajar and spilling in the thinnest slither of green-tinged light. It would be now or never and with a strength and speed that defied the horror of the situation, he rose to his feet and staggered slowly towards it, his limbs stiff and sluggish. Pushing the old door further jar, just enough to slip through, David took the slightest of glimpses back into the darkness behind him. He could just make out the faint silhouettes of the shadowy figures, still busy at a table with their backs to him. Unless his mind was playing tricks on him, something highly likely in this situation, David was convinced that they seemed to be feeding on something.

 He pushed the door closed behind him and turned around to see that he was in some kind of boiler or maintenance room. It was warm in here, very warm and quite stifling. But there was a strange buzzing coming from above him. A small flight of stairs over to the far corner caught his eye, but David knew that to go upwards meant certain death, for he would be found sooner or later. Instead, he continued to the other side of the room and to his relief spotted a small door, similar to that of a fire escape. Indeed, the green tinge he had spotted came from a glowing sign above the door. Without hesitation, David pushed down on the release bar and was met with a blast of cool night air.

Through the door and out into the courtyard, drizzle was falling at an angle and there appeared to be no one around. He expected those massive searchlights that you see in the films to quickly shine on him along with a loud siren and the snapping sounds of shotguns being prepared to shoot. But nothing, only the drizzle pattering on the cobbles. And then he thought to himself, *why would anyone be searching for a missing person anyway? I'm a dead man walking*.

He scanned the courtyard as quickly as he could, finding a door, again to his left which was embedded in the high brick wall. But this wasn't the prison. Those walls were not as tall as the ones circumnavigating his incarceration, with no such razor wire on the top neither. Where was he? How long had he been out of his cell? It was impossible to tell and he had no time to figure such things out.

He raced for the door in the wall and it gave easily. He was through and out into the night. The ground was soft against what he now realised were his bare feet, like some kind of field. David ran and ran, not daring to look back, until he came across an old barn. He quickly ducked inside and this was where he was now, crouched down in the mud wondering what in God's name was going on. No one had followed him; no alarms had sounded and no helicopters or sniffer dogs were on his trail. But what David couldn't fathom was whether this was a good thing, or the horrific realisation that no matter what he did next, far worse people were now after him. After all, he was friends with a vampire and his cellmate had just been drained of all his blood. *Will Adam come and rescue me? How will he know where I am?* David started to panic. All of his options from this point seemed totally unfathomable.

It felt like an eternity crouching there in the dark corner of the barn. His feet were scraped and cut from the barefoot running in the night, across fields and gravel tracks. He couldn't stop himself from shivering but was it from the bitter cold or just the fear coursing through his veins right now, he was unable to ascertain. David seemed to recall running along a train track as well, but nothing was making sense to him, all of his thoughts muddled as he tried to make sense of not only what had happened to him, but also what to do next. A couple of large dogs barked somewhere in the distance and everything suddenly sharpened. Had they sent dogs after him? No, of course not. Not in England, surely? He slowly got to his feet and stretched out his tired limbs, limbs not built for physical exercise. David knew he had to get to a payphone or internet café, but first he had to find some clothes. The dogs barked again, this time closer, or was it his imagination? He started to panic again, rational thoughts escaping him once more. *Shit!* He thought. *They are actually coming after me with dogs!*

Edging his way slowly into the moonlight, David tried to look past his immediate vision into the distance. And sure enough, there to the right he was convinced he could see torchlights flickering on the horizon. They seemed far away, but the sounds of those dogs certainly didn't. He knew he had to act fast. The only thing was to strip out of the gown, hide it in the corner of the barn and then run as fast as he could to some housing estate where he had any hope of finding clothes. The dogs would at least go to the scent of the gown, buying him a little time. This was something had seen many times in films. The main thing now was to compartmentalise his actions. *Yes,* he thought, *think in easy steps, not too far ahead, just enough to keep going forward.* David took a deep breath, reluctantly shedding himself out of the dirty green gown and throwing it far into the corner of the barn. He then ran in the opposite direction to the strobes of light and the increasing sound of the barking dogs. Feeling the fierce bite of a chill wind trying to penetrate his insides, he just hoped that it was late enough in the night that no one would be on the streets to see his naked form charging down the road.

Three

It was dark by the time the prison van turned right into a main courtyard shrouded from the world by a high brick wall, the top of it lined with razor wire. The ground was glistening from a recent shower, an eerie orange glow that shimmered like some old gothic scene. There were several other vans also parked up, which meant he would have to wait a while before disembarking. This gave Adam a little time to think.

All he knew at this stage was that David had been sent to the Vulnerable Prisoners wing, a place he needed to get into. Unfortunately he looked far from vulnerable himself and so in order to get into this wing he had to portray someone far from savoury in the eyes of society. This was where Xion, another of his Geek Squad, had done wonders. He was now seen in the eyes of the system as an alcoholic and drug addicted city boy. He had apparently bitten off more than he could chew, trying to procure Class A drugs and as such had been arrested after an anonymous tip off. His medical records had been altered to show a history of mental health issues, time in rehab and a string of misdemeanours, all related to drink and drugs. All he needed to do now was keep his head down, find his friend and formulate some kind of plan to get them both out.

Ordinarily, his nerdy comrade would have been put straight into the main wing of the prison due to having been convicted of assault. But his sheer demeanour (thin, skinny, and scared of pretty much everything) meant he would be torn to shreds unless put where others could look out for him. Of course in the main wing he would probably also be taken under the wing of one or two inmates. How glad he was that this did not happen. He would have spent many days and night continually having to drop and then pick up the soap. Although dangerous in their own way, Sex Offenders were more often than not quiet people who preferred to keep to themselves. Any kind of Sex Offence, in particular looking at kids, was a real taboo in society today and certainly not something you went shouting about. In fact, in Adam's long experience through the centuries, it had also been seen as taboo, but the last century had wanted to make a real example of those caught abusing pretty much anyone or anything less powerful than themselves. *Too bloody right,* thought Adam. So, it was protocol not to put such a convicted criminal in with rough inmates. No one needed to have to deal with the mess and paperwork of an unnecessary murder on the wings.

And so, knowing he would be put in the right wing at least sorted out the first problem of getting close to where David was reportedly being housed. The second issue, of course, was to figure out how to get him out without drawing too much attention. Now Adam knew something was happening in the prison system, a scandal if you like. People were disappearing, inmates and petty criminals that society wouldn't truly miss. Of course, relatives and close contacts would make a bit of a fuss at first, trying to raise attention to the disappearances, but these were quickly quashed, making way for far more important matters happening in the world; matters such as celebrity marriages and people being utterly offended by tweets about the misuse of pronouns. *How society changes it priorities will always baffle me, when death, starvation and poverty always stays the same*, he thought bitterly, *but then, I guess this doesn't sell half as much press.*

People were quick to forget, easily misdirected. There was a time, long ago, when, whilst living in Paris, he had uncovered a sinister scheme to kidnap the homeless, chop them up and sell their organs on the black market. Body Snatching was a common occurrence back then, but with accelerating scientific advancements at the time came demand for fresh subjects. He had helped the police catch most of those involved, but not all. The crimes went as far up the political chain as they could possibly go. And now, it seemed something just as sinister had started up again in England.

This has become a truly massive conspiracy that reached into the justice system and travelled right up to government itself, but for now, Adam was just focussed on getting his friend out, if he could. Suddenly, the door of the van made a lock creaking sound as it was opened. The first of the cells was unlocked and Adam saw through his window a short, stocky, middle-aged guy in jeans and trainers being led through one of the doors at the other end of the yard. The two young lads in neighbouring cubicles jeered and whistled as this scared individual was led from the van along the courtyard to the processing room. It looked like they had found their nonce, which took eyes away from Adam at least. The less attention drawn to him the better.

Next, the two youngsters were led from the van and Adam was certainly not mistaken in his judgement of them. White trainers with no laces, baggy jog pants hanging halfway down their buttocks and puffer jackets, with baseball caps completing their ridiculous ensembles. They clearly wanted to portray personas that screamed "I am all powerful and you should not mess with me". However, they had such baby faces, Adam could only snigger as he imagined them soiling themselves at the first sign of real trouble. In a true battle, like the many he had been involved in, they would only have been good for emptying chamber pots and fetching the wine or mead.

Then it was his turn to be processed. The night air was much colder up here in the North of England, fresher somehow. And as he was taken to an officer in a small room, Adam got a real sense of the age of the prison building. It didn't look as if it had changed much at all from the Victorian times. Peeling pale blue walls and a chipped dark red concrete floor, the officer sat behind an old wooden counter with a desktop PC flickering like something out of a 1980s film. It seemed clear to Adam that this prison had been left alone, both in attention and finances.

"Name?" he said gruffly, clearly tired and drawing to the end of his shift, or career. Even sat at his desk, Adam could sense his arteries tightened to the point of cardiac arrest. He smelled of 40 a day washed down with cheap whiskey and bad choices. This was a man who needed to make a few life changes, and quickly. "John Jones" came his reply, as meek as he could make his accent, trying hard to give a slightly Northern twang to it. "Well, Mr Jones, welcome to HMP Stafford, where you will spending the next 2 years of your existence. My name is Officer Barns and I will be taking you through processing, after which you will be placed in a temporary cell for the weekend as we run on a skeleton crew during this period. Do you understand what I am telling you?" this script seemed to roll of his tongue with no emotion. He had spurted out the same spiel time and time again for the past 25 years. "I said do you understand Mr Jones?" he repeated.

"Yes Sir" replied Adam. Barns looked up from his PC "Ooh, Sir, I like that! You taking the piss?" Adam breathed hard at this sudden act of aggression, calming himself. "No Sir, err, I mean Officer". *Shit,* he thought, *what does this angry bastard want to be called?* "You call me and any other staff member Officer, OK son? You start saying Sir or Madam with other inmates listening and you'll be in trouble, understand?"

"Yes Officer".

"Good. Now, I'm going to take your photo, both front and side view, then your fingerprints. Understand?" Adam was very much wishing this jumped-up officer would stop asking if he understood! Barns proceeded to take his photos with a smartphone, which he then downloaded onto the system before pressing his fingers, one by one, into an inkpad. Interesting, thought Adam, that they still did this method instead of using a scanner. Once this was done, Adam was told to strip down to his underpants and then sit on a kind of chair. Barns looked again at his PC before coming round, putting on latex gloves and running his finger along Adam's hair, ears and inside his mouth. Satisfied, Barns then led Adam through to another room where he was given grey jog pants, a pale blue tatty T-Shirt, a grey sweater and his shoes back. A clear bag was thrust into his arms containing a couple of bedsheets, pillowcase and basic toiletries and he was led out into another courtyard. "Right then Mr Jones, Officer Parker here will take you to your temporary cell. Keep your nose out of trouble and you'll be collected on Monday and taken to your Wing. Understand?" *No, you prick, please can you repeat in Swahili,* is of course what Adam thought but didn't say as he followed the Officer Parker across the courtyard towards his "temporary cell". To his left, Adam spotted a shadow, darker than seemed possible, moving silently along the wall and through an old door at the far end. His hackles suddenly rose on the back of his neck, and he felt his eyes glow as they tried to focus on what he was seeing in the dark. But even his superior sight failed to catch any kind of evidence as to what was casting the shadow. Before he had a chance to think more on it, he was through a door into what appeared to be the main wing of the prison, precisely where he didn't want to be.

Four

They were desperately thinking how to tell The Master. As yet there was not a version of the events that had just unfolded which would satisfactorily conclude the evening. Not one single version.

How the small, unassuming man had managed to slip away was the worst part of it. They had been doing this for so long now without any problems or questions, the mere thought of this occurring seemed beyond comprehension. And yet it had happened. On their watch no less. Dressed in long black cloaks that seemed to increase the sense of darkness around them, they were pacing up and down the old hanging house that stood almost dead centre inside the grounds of the prison. For the first 100 years it had been used for just that, the systematic hanging of prisoners. Then, in 1913, the last inmate had been hanged here, a woman who had strangled another to death. Now the history books will have it that the law for Capital Punishment was abolished in 1965 in England. But what they fail to mention is that by the mid-1900s, hanging rooms in prisons across the country were being used for something far more sinister, but ultimately far more profitable for everyone concerned, from prison staff right up to the Government itself, and above even that.

And they had just potentially ruined everything. Or this little sack of flesh had. With an angry swipe of a pale, skeletal arm, one of the shadowy figures lashed out at the corpse swinging in front of them, forgetting the vicious looking curved blade in its grip and amputating an arm, which hit the ground with a soft, wet thud. There was no arterial spray from the stump as this corpse had been totally drained of blood. At least they had done this one right. They had never meant to take both of the inmates, but the little weasel on the top bunk had stayed awake. They had worried about leaving witnesses behind so were forced to take both inmates. The room wasn't equipped to have two bodies strung up at the same time, and it took a good hour to fully drain a body of fluid. And then they got busy feeding off a few bits and pieces they had kept aside. Livers and kidneys were the tastiest parts, as the rest got incinerated. They had Forgotten about the skinny little runt on the floor for just a moment. And he was gone.

The cloaked shadow bent and picked up the severed arm, placing it in a large wheelbarrow. It then proceeded to mutilate the rest of the corpse, piling up the parts in the wheelbarrow before motioning the other to take it away. No words were passed between them, as they had done this so many times no words were needed. Then, once the second shadow was gone, it started pacing again, thinking hard as to what to say when the phone rang. It didn't have long to wait.

The shadowy figure waited an eternity staring at the ringing phone on the table, afraid to answer. Then, finally picking up the receiver and placing it to the side of the hood, the voice on the other end spoke quietly, patiently. "This is disappointing news I have just heard". It was a rasping, hissing voice that sounded as though raw meat was being thrown onto hot coals "I must emphasise my disappointment in your…incompetence". The spectral figure thought carefully about its response, "My Master, we did not expect that this small, skinny runt of a man would be able to slip away so easily, but we do apologise profusely for our tardiness. It will not happen again and we will deal with this man as soon as he is returned. Every drop is sacred. Every drop is Life". There was a long pause, before the voice on the other end simply repeated "Every drop is indeed sacred. But an example must be made. I want you to use that knife in your hand and remove one of your fingers. Only one. I still need you to function. As you can see, I am watching". and the Master hung up. There was a creaking sound as the second figure returned with the empty wheelbarrow. They nodded to each other and started decanting the vats of blood into small bags ready for transport. Then the first cloaked figure hesitated before laying out its left hand on the table and with a swift chop, sliced clean through the pinkie finger. It barely gave a yelp. All sense of pain and emotion had long since been drained from its mind body long ago during the transformation. Looking down at the stump, which did not draw blood, the cloaked form brushed the finger to the floor and looked up at the second figure, who simply nodded.

Five

Charles McNeil was concerned. That last phone
call was not the kind of news he wanted to hear at
all. It could seriously put a spanner in the works,
that was for sure. As Minister of State for Prisons,
he had only recently been made permanent in his
role, and news like this could really mess things up
for him. Especially after the disappearance of his
predecessor, Dame Charlotte Fitzpatrick. God she
was a hard bitch and governed the prison system
with the kind of stick that could cut through anything
with a single swipe. But the system was working
brilliantly, and that was definitely down to her, no
doubt about that. Numbers of inmates were kept at
a steady flow, which kept costs down and the
taxpayers happy. No one asked any questions on
how his could be possible when crime rates and
prosecutions were at an all-time high. No one
worried on the finer details as long as pockets were
lined and everyone in parliament sat pretty. Those
that did ask honest, uncomfortable, probing
questions were soon got rid of anyway, one way or
another.

Oh yes, Charlotte had set up her own Alaskan radio
towers or desert outposts in unmarked areas of the
UK where MPs and nosey bastards could be sent,
no questions asked. Of course, families would get
emails and other correspondence from them, but
mobile service was always a bit sketchy in these
places. And these placements were long-term, very

long-term. But Charlotte had got greedy. He didn't know the details, but word on the street, so to speak, was she had tried to threaten the wrong people, trying to punch above her weight, higher up than the Prime Minister himself. And that had led to her disappearance.

As far as the media and public were told, she had been tragically killed in an accident on the M25 on her way home from the office. Her car, chauffeured by some poor sod being paid meagre pounds to protect her, had exploded on impact with a truck and by the time police and firefighters had got to the scene, there wasn't much left to identify other than a charred number plate amidst black, twisted metal. The truck too was completely wrecked, the driver taken to hospital where he died of his wounds. Charles suspected he had actually died of other wounds inflicted, but he didn't ask questions. Charlotte was not in that car, she had been abducted much earlier before leaving the office and driven off somewhere, according to whispers and chatter within the Chambers. But it meant that the following morning, whilst Charles was watching the news in utter disbelief, his mobile rang, and he was immediately promoted. He was but a cog in a very large wheel. Pieces to be moved around, and removed when no longer needed, from a large chessboard.

So, when Charles got this particular call from his weasel of an underling Farling, Acting Director

General of Prisons, he wasn't happy at all. In fact, maybe he would think about finding an opening for Farling in one of these outposts. *No*, thought Charles, *not necessary at this point*. More important was to find out how an inmate that had been selected for the Dark Scarlet Program managed to escape and remain at large!

This particular inmate was a nobody, according to his file. Just some young, pastie geek of a kid who had been in the wrong place at the wrong time, defending himself and landing a bully in hospital. Nothing to suggest he would have been a problem for the system. But now he was a big problem. This subject had seen the inner workings of the program. He knew what was going on behind the scenes of this particular prison. If he wasn't caught soon, the whole thing could be blown wide open and he would lose his opportunity to expand to other institutions, a dream he had to give him a great legacy.

Charles took a deep breath before finishing the last drop of his favourite Lepanto Gran Reserva brandy and gently placing the bulbous crystal glass on his shiny walnut desk. He stroked the surface of this exquisite wooden piece, bought at an auction a few years back. It had belonged to some captain from the Spanish Armada and had been beautifully restored. The pattern of the grain that snaked seamlessly around delicate knots always seem to calm him down, draw him in and away from his temper so that he could think clearly. *Ah, what you must have seen during your service aboard galleons all those years ago,* he thought to himself. *I wish I could be there now rather than having to deal with this shit show.*

After a moment, he sighed again. Farling was just doing his job by relaying messages to him, amongst other business. But he did need to have a talk with him, ensure every security was in place to keep ears and eyes as far away as possible from the truth. His desk phone rang, catching him off guard and making him jump. He started at the flashing red light, beeping in time with the shrill of the ringtone. Gingerly, he picked up the receiver and listened. At first there was no sound, then he heard a rasping breath on the other end. "Is it at hand? Is it being dealt with?" came a voice that was almost inaudible. Charles had noticed the red light had gone out, and yet this person was still speaking to him through the phone. "I have people out looking, as well as teams scouring the internet and CCTV as we speak. We will find him, do not worry". Again, a pause, followed by another high-pitched breath and the voice "If you need assistance, speak with your man. He will pass on your request to us. The young man is not all he seems. He has contacts that can hurt us. They must be dealt with as well". Then the phone went dead.

The office had got very cold all of a sudden, despite the brandy in his belly. Charles shivered despite himself. He had never met this person, and from the sound of the voice which was neither male nor female in sound and tone, he really didn't want to. The last thing he wanted was to involve 'them' any more than he had to. He had a good thing going, with strategically placed people at every level of the prison system to ensure things went without a hitch. The number and frequency of inmates were selected based on what the need for product at the time. Then they were quietly taken, disposed of and no one said anything. But of late, he had been requested to make regular selections. And the initial concern that this could lead to unforeseen problems was clearly presenting itself. "Shit!" he muttered, picking up the brandy glass as if to throw it across the office. But he realised where he was and quietly placed it back on its coaster on the desk.

His peers were generally happy with cleverly altered and fabricated statistics when he met in the House of Lords and he had even got quite close with the Prime Minister himself, playing golf once or twice a month at his personal request. No, this was bad. If one of the thousands of cameras out there got even a snippet, a whiff of this escape; if this little blood sack squealed to anyone, there would be devastating consequences for Charles McNeil MP. And he would find out quite intimately what had happened to his cold-hearted bitch of a predecessor. And then there was his wife Julie and little Alex. *No,* he thought, *failure is not an option*.

Six

As David approached the residential area, his heart sank. There were still people milling about here and there. Naked as he was and frozen to the bone, there was no way David could pass by unseen. He ducked down the first alleyway he found and to his luck, the back gate was unlocked to the property. Trying to make as little sound as possible, he lifted the latch and just hoped to God that they didn't have a sleeping dog in the back garden. Again, luck was definitely on his side, as not only was the rear garden quiet of pets, but also they had left out a load of washing on the rotary line! David rushed over to it, just as a bright white sensor light suddenly flashed on, illuminating the whole garden, and his pale, skinny frame. Without thinking, he grabbed at the first pair of jeans and jumper he could get to and ran for the alleyway again. He could hear muffled noises coming from inside the house and the alleyway light switched on. David threw himself into the jeans and jumper, both a couple of sizes too big, and ducked round the corner to the front of the house. An elderly gentleman sleepily opened the side door and staggered out, making his way into the back garden to see what had triggered the sensor. David found a bit of courage, knowing that it definitely seemed like an elderly couple lived here. He quietly sneaked back into the side alley and tried the side door to the house. With no idea what he would find, he was amazed to see a pair of old work boots right inside. These also looked too big for him, but it had to be better than bare feet! His soft soles ached so much with the scrapes and small cuts of this desperate escape from certain death.

He also grabbed a black jacket that was hung up and ran back out into the street. Once fully dressed, David felt much better, albeit a bit like a homeless man in his oversized wares. He put up the hood of the jacket, hands in his pockets and made his way towards the city centre. He had to find a phone somewhere to call his friend, Xion. She could get a message to Adam. She was his only hope now.

Seven

Luckily, Adam's eyes had muted their colour to a less intimidating chestnut brown shade, as he proceeded along the main corridor of the wing, opening out onto the ground floor space. There was a distinct scent of bleach hanging in the air, along with a slightly metallic taste on his tongue, a scent that made his heart skip a beat involuntarily. Blood. Well, more precisely, blood that had been spilled but had then been mopped up as best as could be done using an old, dirty string mop and lukewarm water. But whatever drama had occurred on the floor, there were undoubtably still drops of it seeping into the grouting of the tiles somewhere and it only fuelled Adam's need for food. His energy level was seriously low, and this could be dangerous, for everyone else as much as him. Centuries of living had given him a superhuman level of control over his emotions and cravings, but Adam could feel a heat building up inside him. Like an itch under the skin that couldn't be scratched; ants crawling through his veins. If he didn't feed soon, his other, more predatory side would no doubt show itself and the whole plan would be blown wide open.

The officer leading him climbed the first flight of stairs which were situated right in the centre of the ground floor space. The walls were painted a soft peppermint green, with paint coming away here and there, revealing history and secrets of the prison's past in various shades of magnolia and dirty white. Their footsteps echoed with an eerie clanging sound as they ascended, rebounding off the walls as if to notify the other inmates of fresh meat entering the building. A rhythmic dinner bell had been struck and Adam could feel the energy of this place shifting, the smell of testosterone hanging in the air as if to challenge this newcomer. *This place is so feral,* thought Adam as they turned back on themselves at the top of the first flight of stairs, moving up a second flight. There was black mesh stretched across the opening that separated the ground from the first floors, and Adam looked up to see that each floor leading up also had a metal net. This just made him more nervous. Clearly, they had a pattern of inmates either jumping or being pushed over the bannisters. Or thrown. Maybe the nets gave the officers a feeling of safety too. Then he realised that no inmate was making a single sound. That was why their shoes sounded so loud! He thought he would at least get some kind of heckling as he made his way to his cell. but no, there was an unnerving silence which in itself felt louder than any scream. *Interesting* thought Adam.

The officer stopped halfway along the left corridor and unlocked the cell door with a loud click, almost like a boom sound. "Here you go Jones. This is you". He said with no emotion, a bored employee of this failing system that just wanted to go home to his family. Or to a pizza, beer and mission six of Call of Duty. Who can say? The officer gestured for Adam to go in first and then walked in after him, which left the cell feeling slightly cramped. But an opportunity had suddenly presented itself and it was over in a flash.

Eight

David, walking with a sense of purpose along the main high-street, was well aware of the need to look as if he belonged out at this hour, just a young local guy walking from A to B as quickly as possible. Not too fast as to look suspect to any passer-by or but also not slow enough to make people look at him too closely. His mind was still reeling from what had felt like an eternity of horror unveiling before him. It was as if David had started questioning his own sanity and sense of reality. Maybe his cell mate had slipped something into his coffee and he was having a proper trip. Or psychotic breakdown. I mean, it's possible right? After all, surely all this monster stuff happened only to his friend Adam and not to a mere mortal like him? Come to think of it, has far as he had known him, Adam hadn't had to flee from monsters who wanted to drain him of his blood. David suddenly shivered despite the warm jacket. *No*, he thought, *Adam would have been the one chasing*. David stopped for a second as a realisation hit him. What if Adam knew what was going on? What if he was a customer? He shivered again against a chill in the air and David started on again.

A faint dampness had started to envelop him, he noticed, like a thin fog or early morning dew. The sky was also starting to lighten slightly. This made

David super nervous as now his chances of being spotted were increasing exponentially. If he had just been slaughtered back at the prison his disappearance would probably just have been covered up. Like a suicide in his cell after having had an argument with and then stabbing his cellmate. It sounded far-fetched, but he had spent a number of years creating stories and erasing footage and documentation for Adam, so he knew how easy it was to do if you had the knowhow. And now he would either be erased entirely, or he would be the talking point of every TV channel for the next few days. And he suspected the latter, as having a witness to a terrible blood business running around was just too dangerous. Even he knew that.

Just then a food delivery van pulled up almost alongside him and David jumped as if stung by a taser. He carried on walking as the van slowed down and then quickly ducked into a side alley as the deliveryman stopped outside a small Eastern European food market. Peering around the corner of the alleyway, David saw the man get out and, after a few moments of waiting by the door, saw the man enter. Then something took over David's brain and body and without any conscious thought he dashed back to the van, opened the driver's door and there, on the passenger seat was a mobile phone! Apologising silently for his actions, David snatched up the mobile, gently closing the door again and darted as fast as he could down the street and round the corner. He carried on going, before turning into a side street, down a residential passage and then squatted silently behind some bins. All he could hear was the pounding of the blood in his ears and the shallow, painful breaths as he tried desperately to calm down. Adrenaline was making him feel nauseous and he thought he was going to throw up. Then his mind slowed down, his breathing regulated and he started crying once more. What has my life come to? He thought miserably. How did it come to this? I know I was playing a dangerous game being connected to a vampire, but still, did I really deserve this? David wiped his eyes and berated himself for such foolish and childish thoughts. *This is not the time!* He shouted in his mind.

The mobile wasn't even security locked, probably because there wasn't anything on it worth hacking. It looked just like a phone the deliveryman used for his business, not his personal phone. Which meant he may have a bit of time before it was disconnected or logged as stolen. It was also Pay as You Go, even better. Harder to trace. In his current predicament he could honestly say he now had in his possession a stolen burner phone. The thought of him being some super spy made him giggle dryly. He was always the man in chair, not the one running and shooting.

There was only one number he knew off by heart, his best friend and fellow geek Xion. At this hour it was doubtful that she would even pick up, but David had no other choice. Praying silently, he dialled the number. After just a few rings it went to voicemail and the sweet yet edgy tones of his secret sweetheart sang in his ears "hey, you know who this is if you've dialled right, and you know what to do if you're listening to this, so do it now, cheers" then the beep. "Hey Xion" breathed David, trying unsuccessfully not to sound like a man in a trench coat answering an 0898 number "It's Dee. Shit I'm in so much trouble I don't know where to start! You might even have thought me dead. Please call me back on this number but use just two rings and then hang up. Then ring again after 10 seconds, that way I know it's you. I need your help so bad Xi, everything is so messed up!" and then he ended the call.

All David could do now was hope and pray to whatever sadistic God up there that he got to Xion before the monsters caught up with him. He drew his hood up as far as it could go, totally covering his face. Before he knew it he had drifted off, like a dog with one ear ever so slightly cocked, listening out for the smallest hint of danger.

Nine

The prison guard had been sitting on the chair in Adam's cell for just a few moments, but it must have felt to him like an hour. His head was spinning for some reason, as if he had suddenly been overcome with a seizure or funny turn. All he knew was that in the blink of an eye he had been unlocking the cell door, pushing the door open and then as if he had blacked out, had found himself sat on the chair with his head in his hands and with Jones, or prisoner 29461 by this side asking if he was ok. Eddie felt giddy to the point of wanting to throw up and strangely tired as if he had just worked out for a good 30 minutes.

"Do you want me to call another officer? Are you OK?" he could hear the prisoner ask, but it sounded like it was coming from the far end of a tunnel. Then he was handed a cup of water, which he gulped down without even thinking if it was spiked or not. Normally he would never accept anything from a prisoner, not even sealed. It only took a smallest of needle pricks in the foil top to allow a substance to mix with the drink. *Maybe this is what had somehow happened!* He fumbled at his belt to check that his radio and keys were still there. Thankfully yes, and his key fob too. He slowly stood up and edged toward the door of the cell, wobbling slightly. Taking a few deep breaths, he turned to the prisoner "Well, that was weird. No idea what that was, probably just low blood sugar or something. Keep this to yourself, ok? Or more to the point, between you and me". He made sure 29461 knew it wasn't a question before leaving him to get settled in, closing the door, turning the key and ensuring that the sound of the double click echoed throughout the landing. *New fish, lads,* he thought smugly to himself. Eddie would have to keep an eye on this one, something odd about him, something he didn't like at all.

Adam felt bad for the officer. With his speed, it had only taken a few seconds to drink a small amount of blood from the guard's neck, using a few drops of his own to heal the puncture wounds and then sit him down on the chair before he knew what had happened. Time worked differently for Adam, and he had been so hungry. Most of the time he functioned with the same level of agility as every other human. But he had the ability to move ten times faster, should he have need to do so. All of his other senses, especially sight and hearing followed suit. He understood this to be the case with most predators. That moment just before a strike, when all the senses became heightened in order to make a successful kill. Predator. God he hated that word, but he had long since given up trying to deny who he was. He just had more control. It had taken so many years to get to this stage, and as far as he knew, there were not many others like him with the same restraint. Until situations such as this presented themselves, that is. His metabolism needed nourishment regularly to counteract the rate it burned. This was the downside. The upside was his enhanced speed, strength and senses. And so by the time the guard and come to his own senses, Adam felt better. Most people will never admit to or believe something that they can't rationally explain, and so will automatically come up with a more 'sensible' explanation. As far as the guard was concerned, he had just had a funny turn. Low blood sugar, he called it. *Well, he's not entirely wrong*, thought Adam, *not now anyway.*

But there was no way he could get used to feeding off people in here, regardless of how easy it was. There was something going on, a bloodletting business that had to involve other vampires somehow, or something worse. There were creatures hiding in both plain sight and in the depths of shadows that even Adam did not want to come face to face with. And he had to try and blend in and remain inconspicuous. Just another guy trying to do his time. Nothing to see here. With that, he switched on the meagre light, giving the pale blue walls an eerie green tinge. The bunk bed was a slightly rusty metal frame, coiled mesh bases and thin, dark blue plastic mattresses. The frame was bolted to the wall and Adam saw where other inmates had tried unsuccessfully to dig these bolts out. He chose the top bunk and made up the bed, before filling up and switching on the plastic kettle provided. Also in the clear bag were a toothbrush and small tube of toothpaste, as well as a spare set of jog pants, T Shirt, sweater, boxer shorts and socks. A food ration pack fell out too, enclosing sugar and coffee sachets, teabags, powdered milk, a plastic plate, knife, spoon and fork.

All in all, it was much better than other institutions he had been sent to in the past, so Adam really didn't have many complaints. There was also a cheap disposable razor and a bar of soap, along with a towel. Within 10 minutes there was a loud knock at the door, the double clunk of the lock and a creak as it opened up to reveal another officer holding a bag. "Well, not sure what you did Jones, but my colleague has had to take a breather. Says he had a funny turn in your cell. I'm Parker. As you came in late, you must be starving…" *Not anymore*, thought Adam dryly "so I've brought you a lunch pack. Sandwich, crisps, yoghurt and a juice. That should see you through until breakfast. It'll be lights out soon, then you switch to just the table light. Your door will open at around 7:30am where you'll head down with the other inmates for breakfast. All meals are eaten in your cell. You get it done quickly, no lingering. Here's your meal sheet for next week" Parker handed Adam an A4 yellow sheet with days, choices and tick boxes.

"Fill this in tonight and hand it in to one of us in the morning. As for this weekend, speak to the officer on duty at the canteen counter and he will inform the servers. Then you can choose what you want. You get a canteen sheet every Wednesday for delivery on the Friday. Each day you work, you get £1.60. This then gets added weekly to your prison account. You can use this to purchase things from the canteen sheet. Any money you have transferred in will also be added. Be careful John…"

Strange that he used my first name, thought Adam, "…there are people on this block that will want you to buy things for them, even do things for them. You'll get to know who these are soon enough. We don't have superpowers, so can't be everywhere at once. Just keep out of trouble for a few days and you'll be moved to your proper wing".
The officer closed the door hatch and Adam heard his footsteps disappear down the landing, metallic rings echoing as he made his way down the stairs. *And so starts this little journey,* he thought. *David,*

you better be where you're supposed to be, you little shit!

Ten

Charles McNeil was in the middle of his delicious Toasted English muffins, topped with crispy smoked bacon, perfectly poached eggs (could he smell and taste a hint of oak smoke?) and a petite jug of Hollandaise sauce, which he poured generously over the dish, when his mobile rang. Normally he wouldn't feel nervous about his phone ringing, but his current predicament was far from the norm. This little twerp, David Jennings he had since learnt, was still at large and he had been up all night trying to ensure that the press had got no wind of it. So far he had been successful, but Charles also knew that it was only a matter of time before this was blown wide open to the public. Well, if the escaped prisoner ended up on a front page of some tabloid, it was an easy spin to make him out to be some paedophile or a lonely and desperate loser that had knifed his grandmother. That should at least put a couple of million extra eyes on the streets.

He gingerly answered the phone, seeing that the caller was unknown. "Charles McNeil MP speaking" he pronounced. The other end gave a faint hiss as if steam was slowly being released, and the phone seemed to feel cold to his ear all of a sudden, or what it his imagination from lack of sleep? "Charles McNeil MP, for now at least", came the rasping response. "Do you have any more news for us? Your man has failed to pass on any message since you and I last spoke and we have been forced to contact you again directly. This displeases us somewhat". His ear was definitely cold, as were Charles' insides as he hastily thought of the correct response. "I do apologise for Farling's tardiness in not getting back to you sooner. I will certainly be speaking with him, I assure you".

"And the update?" spat this rasping snake-like voice "McNeil, you don't need to try and climb inside my posterior like the small insignificant worm that you are. Keep it brief, always brief and succinct. Do you understand?" It was rhetorical. "s...sorry" he stuttered "we are still searching for him, but I have just had word that the search dogs are on his trail. They have found where he has rested, an old barn, which has given a fresh scent heading towards the town centre. Now that daylight is upon us, it will be so much harder for him to avoid the CCTV cameras".

"Our people can no longer help you. It would draw too much attention to our operation. It may be time to alert the police. Also, use the media, but be smart McNeil. He is a dangerous individual remember. A Threat. Make the public afraid of him. Make him a monster".

With that, the line went dead and Charles quickly threw the phone down onto the table, causing a few other MPs to look his way. He rolled his eyes at them, indicating infuriation and they just sniggered and got back to their own breakfasts and conversations. Parliament was starting to liven up for the day, despite the early hours. They would be back in session soon and he needed a new plan. He played with the remains of his food, picking it apart as he formulated a next course of action. He picked up his phone, happy that it had returned to room temperature at least. Searching through his contacts, he phoned Victoria Lambert, the Chief Commissioner for Scotland Yard. She answered almost immediately "Charles, what in two shits is going on?" He was so taken aback at the greeting, Charles was momentarily lost for words "Erm…Victoria, I'm not entirely sure what…" he tried to say before she cut in "don't try and spin all that politician bullshit on me McNeil, I've just had a call from the Management, informing that the project is in danger of being outed. Something about a subject escaping and being on the run as we speak. Explain to me firstly why I am just hearing about this now, and secondly why I had to hear it from *Them*?"

Shit, bugger! panicked Charles. "So sorry Victoria, I thought that, due to the slight physical nature of the prisoner, he would have been caught by now and the matter would be closed. In fact, I was just phoning you to escalate the situation, putting it in your capable hands and to ask whether you thought creating a rather unsavoury story for the media might be prudent now? Given the severity of the situation?"

There was a slight pause before Victoria spoke again, slow and deliberate. "Right. You come up with something, a back story for this little shit and I will liaise with local police officers. They can go through CCTV and we can hopefully get something on the news by lunchtime, should he still not be found. In the meantime, and on a more personal note Charles, we cannot let this carry on. Or it will be our own blood and that of our families on the market. Do I make myself clear?" Charles shuddered as he thought of his wife and young son swinging upside down from chains, throats cut and faces a wet, stained dark red. "Of course I understand!" he answered a bit too harshly than maybe he should have.

Eleven

It took an absolute age for Xion to answer, but then, thought David, she had probably got off to sleep when he left the message. "For Christ's sake Dee" she answered, "What trouble *have* you got yourself in, you dickhead!" For Xion, or Xi as David affectionately called her, this was about as much sympathy and warmth as he could expect, but he loved her anyway. She was brilliant at hacking and cloning identities. Two things David sorely needed right now. "Hey Xi, I have no idea where to start. I'm in desperate need of so much right now. They could even be tracking me as we speak. I know this is a burner, but I had to nick it off some poor delivery guy who's probably reported it stolen already to his work. Is there any way you could sort me out with a new SIM? You see where I am right?"

"Yeah, just calm down OK? I see you are in Longhurst Drive in…Hang on, Stafford??! Shit babe you're miles away from us! We thought you'd got sent to a prison in the South, like Devon or something. Why did they send you all the way up there?"

"I have no idea. I was sent to Bristol holding prison and the next thing I knew I was on a transport bus for bloody hours and arrived here. So you're saying no one knows I'm here at all?" His voice cracked as he thought of the possibility that his family would be trying unsuccessfully to contact him in Devon. Well, his older sister anyway. For now she would have to make up her own mind as to what was going on, too dangerous for him to contact her. "Sorry Dee, as far as we all knew, you were in the South. We've been scouting the news, CCTV, internet, but it seems like you just disappeared off every network. It's almost as if some people high up want to keep you a secret from the public. But this could also only mean they want full control of what and when to leak. But don't worry, I'll sort out a SIM pick up for you. Actually you're right, that phone you're holding could get tracked, so best dump it and I'll get another one for you to pick up with the SIM. There's a convenience store close to you. You may have passed it already. Just looking on Google and you're in luck boy! They sell cheap phones and SIMs. Did you do know where I mean?"

"Yeah, it was closed before" He looked at the phone display. 7:35am. Good, they would be open now. He mirrored his thoughts to Xi "I'll head back there".

"Do it. And use the name Robert Mitchell and the password Greenwich09. I used this guy's card details only yesterday, so they should be fine. I'll tell the person on the counter that you had your bag stolen which had everything in, wallet, keys, phone etc. That way they can't ask you to show him or her any other form of ID. Give me 20 minutes to sort it OK?"

"OK. Thanks so much Xi. I'll ring you in 30 minutes on the new phone".

"Cool, just ditch that burner now. You've been on the digital radar for too long as it is". And with that she hung up. David felt so much better having had a familiar voice to talk to. Adrenaline was still coursing through every part of his body. He had no idea who knew what, whether he was already on the news, in newspapers or what! *Shit!* He panicked, *what if my face was on the front page of the local newspaper? The convenience store staff would have seen me! And the delivery man who's phone I just stole would have seen it too! Maybe he delivered the sodding papers!* Taking a breath, David suddenly realised the obvious; newspapers would of course only show news as at printing, before his escape. Breathing heavily, David tried to calm himself down. Xi had mentioned that so far there was no digital trace of him escaping the prison, or even having gone up North. *Why was that?* He pondered. He could be on the news, on radio and TV. But there was nothing more he could do but to risk going to the store. He just hoped his stolen outfit would mask his appearance a bit. And so, with more than a little trepidation and a feeling of impending doom, he crawled out from behind the bins, out onto the main street and walked back the way he had come, towards the store.

Twelve

'Slippery' George Reynolds felt so incredibly lonely. He sat quietly in his particular spot with his back to the wall of the wing, but so that he could watch the comings and goings of the other inmates during the social time. Six till seven every evening, routine was important when so much was taken away from you. It had been robbed from George. No longer hooked on alcohol and drugs, he felt he had been rehabilitated enough these past 3 years inside, his body clean, although out of shape thanks to the new addiction to carbs they gave you in here. Stodge. Nothing but stodge to keep you docile.

Last week had been his Fifty Seventh birthday, but no one would have known. Not a second after he was arrested again for aggravated assault with a deadly weapon whilst under the influence of something or other (pick from a long list), what remained of his family immediately disowned him. What he needed was support and clear-minded people around him, who could help to show him the way out of this gravity-assisted spiral of addiction. But instead everyone had turned their backs, not wanting the association in their seemingly wonderful and picket-fenced perfect world. But that was a long time ago. Now it was him versus this institutionalised world, and he didn't trust a single person in here.

The usual suspects were busy playing pool on one of the two tables in the centre of the floor, whilst another group were chatting together over on the right, watching two youngish guys play backgammon. There was a noise from the far left where another small group were having a table football tournament. And the rest were just moping around, wanting desperately to fit in but finding all doors locked, metaphorically speaking. As for the cell doors, they were all left open, so inmates could socialise in their cells should they wish. Most people in here were either sex offenders of some sort or addicts that had pissed off more dangerous criminals. No one wanted trouble, for that meant they would be either put in solitary or sent to the main wing. You wouldn't want that. Better to slit your throat and be done with it than have to explain yourself to the real criminals, proper nasty they were. No, it was far better to just keep your head down, don't try and associate with anyone and just do the time.

And so 'Slippery' George sat on the chair in his designated corner, watching. And that was when he noticed something was not right. *Yes, that's it. Billy was missing, along with his new fish cell mate. What was his name again? Danny, no, David that was it. Maybe they were in the cell?* thought George. *But Billy always came out of the cell during social.* Then it dawned on him, *oh no, they've been taken!* And with that he did something totally against his normal routine. Slippery George stood and quickly made his way up the two flights of stairs to the top floor where David and Billy's cell was. Empty, door wide open. As if the guard had just unlocked it as a matter of course, without thinking. He spotted one of them walking along the opposite side corridors and started towards her, a lady in her middling years with a slim figure and greying blonde hair tied back in a tight ponytail. She turned as he approached, eyeing him up and down as if prepared for trouble. "What is it Reynolds?" she asked simply. Her tone was soft, as she knew this inmate was no threat once she had clocked who it was. "You're never normally up here on Second. Finally made some friends have you?" she smiled at this and George knew it was not meant as sarcasm. He liked this officer. One of the few that actually paid attention instead of just going through the motions until the end of shift, like it was a punishment for them as much as the inmates being in here. "Sorry to bother you Miss, as you know, I normally keep myself to myself. But I couldn't help notice Billy and his cellmate aren't out and, well, they aren't in their cell either. Is everything alright with them?"

Suddenly the officer lost her smile, her eyes became wide and intense and she leaned in close to George. "You are very observant Reynolds. But you know more than most here not to ask questions".

"Sorry Miss, I mean Officer. It's just I liked Billy. Just wanted to know that he's okay is all". The Officer looked at him for a moment, her gaze showing signs of what to tell him, sizing George up. She then sighed and said matter of factually "Nothing to concern yourself with Reynolds. But I must insist that you forget about those two, got it? They were transferred out late last night. Some kind of altercation in the cell from what I gathered. I've said far too much just saying this. More than my job's worth, you understand?" He nodded quickly. "Good" she continued "You've been here long enough to know not to go snooping around George. Just keep to your chair in the corner eh? Best not to get noticed". And with that the guard turned on her heels and continued down the corridor, leaving George standing rooted to the spot, baffled, slightly afraid, but more determined to dig deeper. *I know bullshit when I hear it*, he said quietly to himself.

Thirteen

Up by the ceiling of the second floor, on each corner as with all the floors on the wing, a small red light blinked intermittently. This was the only clue to tiny cameras mounted everywhere. There was nothing short of a hundred placed strategically around the prison. And these did not include the ones mounted on long poles or fixed to the external and internal walls of the grounds. Or the more basic CCTV cameras in the Processing room and offices. Data from all the cameras, terabytes of it every day, fed back to a dark, secret room above where an old storeroom used to be. Once housing bed sheets and other prison furnishings and sundries, all these were now brought in from outside companies. Legislation had changed years before, meaning no longer could bedsheets be washed and stored on site, for hygiene reasons. And so the storeroom had been forgotten by the staff, becoming a perfect place to hide massive servers. Of course, there were also a few servers in the main office capturing images from a few of the main cameras, but this data overwrote itself every five days. By then, any incident would have been logged and evidence saved if needed.

In the old storeroom, steel flue pipes fixed close to silent fans kept the room as cool as was necessary, but it was still fairly stifling in there. The silent blinking mixed with the heat to give an eerie feel of a thousand rats sculking in the shadows waiting for their next kill, red eyes watching en masse. It was on one of these that a key piece of information lay. The first was the escape of the inmate. Although grainy and unable to pick up any sharp detail, he could clearly be seen making his way across the courtyard from the hanging room, along the external wall and out of a side gate. There the cameras lost him. A long, bony finger adorned with a large gold signet ring housing a huge blue stone pressed a key on the laptop, pausing the last image. An equally skeletal thumb then joined the first digit on the pad, moving in sync to allow the image to enlarge until the escapee was filling up the screen. The finger then selected a digital program which beautifully enhanced the image so that, although still grainy, showed the features of this slippery little young man. More fingers rapidly worked now, saving the image and forwarding it to an email, which was then sent to an encrypted address with a simple message:

NO TRACE OF THIS HUMAN MUST BE LEFT ALIVE. SEE TO IT PERSONALLY. USE OF ALL MEANS HAS BEEN GRANTED. ENSURE NOTHING HAS BEEN COMPROMISED. EVERY DROP IS SACRED. EVERY DROP IS LIFE.

A long, yellow nail tapped *send* and this cloaked figure sat back and breathed deeply, a shallow, high-pitched rasping sound not unlike the death throes of a rodent, or a snake hissing with deadly intent. Then, the laptop flashed a call waiting. "Speak" came that whisper of a voice of inside the hood.

"Master, it has been brought to our attention that an inmate has been enquiring into the…err…last shipment. Shall I send through the feed?" there was no response and after a few seconds the screen showed a clear video of the second floor, time stamped less than an hour previously. An older man could be seen first making his way to a cell, then turn and head towards a female guard. No more needed to be seen. "We have already lost one. Fill the shortage with this one. In fact, take the female guard too. I will send through immediate transfer papers to the main office. Let her finish the shift, then wait for her to leave. She will have left the building first, you understand?" This was the most the voice at the other end had ever heard the Master speak. "Yes, of course. Blood is Sa…" but the laptop was no longer transmitting.

Fourteen

The delivery man had gone by the time David approached the shop. He had obviously been too busy to notice straight away that his phone had gone missing. And there was that familiar hum of a city starting to wake up, a thousand distant activities, morning routines all coming together into an almost soothing kind of white noise. It was a sound you either loved with addictive passion or hated so much that you would run for the literal hills. David loved the sound. It gave him a sense of calm, and then a sense of purpose. It had been his call to virtual arms when looking for what Adam had been up to and then erasing it. But now the sound was telling a different story. It was a noise conjuring up feelings of anxiety and apprehension, for he had no idea quite how infamous he had become. His heart drummed in his ears as he grabbed hold of the door handle and pushed. A two-tone beep rang out signalling his arrival to the cashier at the back of the shop. Long and thin, the store seemed to sell all manner of goods from all over Europe, but mainly Eastern Europe it seemed. At any other time David would have loved browsing in a place like this. He loved to cook and experimented all the time with what most Brits would call "unusual food". As a nation, he was embarrassed by how both naïve and stubborn we were when it came to trying different cuisines. Especially as England was pretty reliant on influences from other countries to make dishes more appealing to foreigners anyway, not to mention keeping the backbone of employment going.

Slowly, but as casually as he could muster, David made his way up the central aisle towards the pay point at the back, where a young lady was waiting, watching him with a smile that seemed not to touch her serious eyes. *Just be calm* he said to himself as he approached the counter. "Good morning. I believe my friend has just called you explaining my unfortunate situation. She said she would leave a phone and SIM for me behind the counter?" The lady nodded. "I thought it was you. Hang on, I put them out the back". And with that she disappeared.

"I thought it was you!" What the heck does that mean?! panicked David. He wanted to just run out of the shop, thinking that the damn cashier was dobbing him into the authorities this very second. But she almost immediately came back out with a cheap phone and a SIM card, both still in their packaging. He silently let out a breath, unable to hear a thing over the blood banging in his ears. "Here you are". The lady said simply. She put them both in a small white carrier bag and was about to hand them over when she suddenly stopped, staring at him "Oh, sorry I totally forgot. I was asked by your friend to request a password form you. That you would understand, seeing that you have had your ID stolen. Is this correct?" There was a sense

of testiness in her tone. *Of course!* David had totally forgotten that this was the story, the arrangement he had made. With his brain whirring, it took him what seemed like an age before remembering "So sorry, yes. My name is Robert Mitchell and the password is Greenwich09. Glad one of us is on the ball eh?" he laughed, trying to act normal. The young cashier smiled again as she handed over the bag. "So terrible you being mugged mate. Hopefully you'll be able get everything blocked quickly. Strangely enough, our delivery man literally just had his phone nicked too not half an hour ago. Crazy world right?" The colour drained from David's face. He quickly asked "what, from right here?" "Dunno. He can't remember when he last had it. Thought it was on his van seat, but then he thought he could have dropped it on any of his other drops this morning. Apparently this shop is number seven on his route. Bad news for him though, as it was a work phone. Anyway, better let you get to work. Have a good day". David just wanted to get the hell out of the shop as quickly as possible. So much so, he at first didn't register when the young lady called "Hey Mr Mitchell? Mr Mitchell?" he turned to hear her laugh. "Forgot your own name have you? I just wanted to say that you have £5 credit on the SIM, but you'll need to top it up as soon as. OK? I hope your day gets better. Oh, and I like your look by the way".

Is she flirting with me? David thought with a smile. He thanked her and left. He headed back to the spot behind the bins before popping the SIM card in the phone. Switching it on, he saw that there was only 20% power. He just hoped it was enough. The good thing about these cheap smart phones is that there isn't much of an operating system and as long as he was careful, the battery shouldn't drain much. Looking at the strange makers mark, he had no idea of the make either, which made it even more untraceable.

"Well you took your time, Dee", came the usual friendly greeting from Xion. "Listen, you need to hear this. The police have just issued a statement saying there's been a breakout. They haven't as yet taken it public, so you're good for now. But you don't have long. I only know from the police scanner and internal chatter on the West Midlands Police Mainframe. You have to get out of there as quickly as possible". David's heart sank even further, if that was possible. "Shit Xi, where can I go to get out?" He felt like he was going to start crying again at any moment. Xion had obviously clocked this from his tone, as her response was like that of a scolding mother "Get it together David! We do this for a living, YOU do this for a living! Finding solutions to problems, ways out of situations. You just need to calm the hell down. I know it's easier said than done, but if you are going to get out of this you have to think straight. Use that bloody Sheldon brain of yours. OK?"

"OK, sorry. Hey, thanks for the phone".

"No problem, it'll be coming out of your savings once you're back here". *Back here*. He liked the sound of that. "I think the train station is going to be monitored now, so I'll have to hitch a lift South. Can you see any truck stops around here Xi?" Xion fell silent, the sound of her fingers tapping the keyboard for a few moments before coming back. "Yes, there's one on the other side of the city, near the main roundabout that leads to the M6. And you're in luck, they have a greasy spoon there too. You can get that dirty fry up you love so much". David had completely forgotten that he hadn't eaten since the prison meal over twelve hours ago. The thought of a full English breakfast made his stomach growl like a mother bear protecting her young. "Oh my god, you are such an angel Xi. Any chance you could lend me some money on Smart Pay or something?"

"Oh shit, of course you don't have any funds. No probs, Dee, I got you".

David felt much better as he made his way across the city. Knowing that he only had to look out for the police at the moment meant he could act normal. A couple of times he heard sirens coming near him, but apart from an ambulance screaming by, they seemed to turn off somewhere in the distance before reaching him. Xion had helped him add a credit card to the Smart Pay app he installed on the phone. This would at least let him get back to London where he could meet up with her. They could attempt to hide him whilst he figured out what to do. He could then try and contact Adam. If anyone knew how to hide or just disappear, he did.

Fifteen

The dogs were pulling the officers frantically along the street, forcing people to cross rather than be growled at or worse. It was still fairly early, but the city was really starting to wake up now and they did not know how much longer they could go on with the search in broad daylight without raising too much attention. Scanton, the lead Sergeant on the search had just been informed that this little weasel's face was about to be plastered all over the media with the story that he was an escaped rapist and murderer. That would surely get the public riled up and wanting to report any sightings. But it would also drag so many attention-seeking Social Media addicts from out of whatever digital rocks they hid in, the lines more than likely being jammed with red herrings. If Scanton knew society well, and he did, no one really took an actual interest anymore.

In the 25 years of service to the prison system, he had seen it all and met probably every type of person you could think of. And they all had one thing in common. No matter what was going on around them, all anyone cared about these days was watching their own back and just trying to survive. No one wanted any trouble, not even the scum. Of course they orchestrated the trouble on the outside, but on the inside they simply used skills to make a living. A dead body, in most cases, was exactly the opposite of a cry for attention. Everyone thought they were better than the system, or the person next door. But that was only because they were so wrapped up in their own world, their own role-player game, they always failed to see beyond. The actions never seemed to define the person. Good people did bad things just as much as bad people had the capacity to do good. The cynical society merely failed to see beyond the carrot dangling in front of them, that was all. No, a story would be spun about this Jennings fella and the public would lap it up for two seconds before throwing it away.

"Sir? Sir!" came a harsh reply that snapped him back to the present. "What is it boy?" he answered not to an officer calling him, but to his faithful hound Boris "Are we close?" Boris stopped for a second and whined at Scanton, causing the others to halt their hounds too, a black suited and booted hunting party totally out of place on a sleepy looking street.

"Sir, the dogs seem to be taking us into this residential area. Are you sure we want to go? I mean, people are waking up now and we don't want to cause a scene right?"

"Fletchley, I've just been notified that a scene is exactly what's about to hatch over the Media as we speak. This twerp will be found, and he will be found soon. Now, I don't know about you, but I would prefer it was us that found him, don't you officer?"

"Yes Sir, of course Sir."

"Good answer. Right lads! Let's see where this bastard has gone eh?"

And with that, the party headed down the street, dogs pulling and sniffing the ground. It was only a few houses down that Boris suddenly made a beeline left and down an alleyway, stopping short of a gate and barking loudly. An elderly man opened the backdoor and almost fell as he leapt back from the sharp teeth and snout lunging at him with hungry intent.

"Bloody hell! What in God's name...?" He spluttered as he staggered back. "Sorry Sir, Boris here has been picking up a scent is all. He's harmless enough to most. But I have to ask, can I have a look round the back garden. Should only take a sec sir. We have an escaped convict you see. Dangerous individual and Boris here seems to think he may have gone round back of your property".

Before the old man had time to give an answer, another officer had unlatched the gate from over the other side and a line of dogs and uniforms were making their way passed. "Thank you Sir, should only take a sec as I said". Doffed Scanton as he too led Boris to obvious commotion in the back garden.

It was empty, but that didn't stop the dogs from going crazy as they sniffed and clawed at the ground below an empty washing line. The old man followed them around the back and quickly piped up "I left my washing out last night, forgot all about it I did. My night sensor flashed in the night while I were going for a leak and I came out but didn't find anyone. Thought it were just foxes".

"was anything missing sir? It looks as if our man was here you see. The dogs followed his scent right to this spot".

"It were dark and I were half asleep to be honest. I just gathered everything and hung them up inside. I'll take a look now". And the old man went back inside.

"Could've bloody invited us in for a brew Sarge", mumbled one of the officers. An early morning chill was still in the air and they were all tired and cold after having traipsed across town all night.

After just few moments, the old man appeared again with a worrying look on his face. "Well, unless I'm going doolally, which is a sure possibility, I think this man may have taken a few of my items. Jeans, hooded jumper, and I can't find my puffer jacket or work boots either. I normally keep those by the door".

Bollocks! Cursed Scanton to himself. The dogs wouldn't find a scent now. The little git had got one over on them. It was down to the cameras now to pick him up. "Right then, Mr…?"

"Barker, Stanley Barker".

"Right then Mr Barker, I'll need you to describe again in detail everything you think was taken".

"I'll pop the kettle on n'all. You officers look bloody frozen".

The officers silently high-fived each other.

 Scanton was seething inside.

Sixteen

David could smell that sweet, smoky scent of bacon even before the truck stop came into view. Daylight was fully up now and he could see maybe six lorries in the parking bays outside. The diner, as it was, was not much more than a large caravan that had been converted a number of years back. The pale blue paint and chrome finish that had once given it a feel of something from the film Grease had long since faded, succumbing instead to the more literal sense of the word. David chuckled to himself as the lyrics "Grease is the word that you heard" played in his head. He was feeling slightly dizzy from lack of food, the adrenaline that had been keeping him going slowly subsiding in his system. He struggled to get the sound of dogs barking from his mind and he felt awful for stealing a poor old man's clothes. But he felt hidden under this guise as he took the two steps up to the front door of the diner.

There were only four tables and three of them were taken. Stafford FM was playing rather loudly and a small TV filled an upper corner, perched precariously from a bracket that did not look suited to the task. But the whole place felt warm and cosy, in a rugged kind of way. David went straight up to the counter and ordered a coffee and a full English Breakfast, paying with the phone app as instructed by Xi. As he sat down, he took off the jacket, but decided to keep the baseball cap on. It didn't look out of place as he saw another trucker wearing his too as he sipped a cup of tea, his breakfast finished with. Of the two other customers seated at the other occupied tables, there was nothing seemingly out of place with either of them. David smiled, realising that his analytical brain was back, his nerves steadier at the thought of a full stomach.

The waitress that served him came over with the coffee and, despite his body screaming otherwise, David stirred three spoons full of sugar into it. He needed the hit and knew he would probably regret it later with a crash. With only a few minutes passed the waitress returned once more with a hot plate full of the most wonderful looking breakfast he had ever seen. And a round of toast to boot! He had got so used to prison life that he had totally forgotten what decent food looked like. And this breakfast was not at all swimming in grease either. With a slurp of the strong, sweet coffee, David tucked into the breakfast, trying hard not to draw attention by eating too quickly.

Halfway through, he suddenly noticed that the radio was no longer playing in the background. Instead, the TV had been turned up and was now showing a news article. And there, filling the screen was a poorly captured photo of him! Thankfully it was slightly blurry, but the reporter was describing crimes committed which included rape and murder of a young girl. *Holy shit, what?!* His mind went into overdrive again and he almost coughed up a mouthful of bacon and egg. *What are they saying about me? Why are they making up all of these lies about me? This must be a mistake, they are looking for someone else as well and put my photo up by accident.* Then the reporter went on to describe how this dangerous fugitive had stolen clothes from a frail old man and started listing what David was now wearing. Thankfully, unlike the movies, the other customers merely glanced at the screen before going back to whatever they were looking at on their phones. The waitress, however glanced his way and seemed to hold a stare for far too long. Then she took a look at the jacket slumped over the back of the chair next to him. All David could do was concentrate on methodically finishing his breakfast and coffee, one eye glanced sideways at her.

When the plate was clean and the mug empty, David slowly stood, but didn't put on the jacket. The reporter hadn't mentioned the colour of the hoodie, nor did he mention the baseball cap. With luck, he could pass as just another customer who happened to be wearing a similar jacket, that was all. He thanked the waitress as he went to leave. "Excuse me love?" Came her voice behind him as he opened the door. *Shit! Shit! Shit!* He repeated to himself. David turned, keeping his face slightly down. "Love, you left your phone on the table".

"Oh, right. Thank you so much. That was lucky", he stammered as he quickly went back to pick it up.

"Not from around here, are you love? Accent like that, you from London?" He racked his brain to think if the reporter had mentioned where he was from, but it came up blank, instead once again filled with panic. "Erm, yes, just here for work. Heading back today actually".

"Ah, I thought so. Just you be careful. It appears there's a nasty man on the run. Escaped from prison right here in the city. Had a jacket just like yours. Might want to keep it under your arm so you don't get nicked by mistake". She giggled as the last words came out and David simply smiled, leaving the diner and closing the door behind him. He walked round the back and sat down on an old empty wooden cable reel. He need to think. Suddenly his stomach did a complete flip and he wretched uncontrollably. Swallowing the remains of his breakfast back down without thinking, his stomach lurched again and this time half of what he had just eaten came out onto the concrete. Breathing heavily, David realised that his brain had wanted to eat something his body had not been used to. Mixed with this constant impending sense of doom, he should have just had some toast or a bacon sandwich.

Why had Xion not been able to stop his face from being posted? Was she in trouble too? But as good as these questions were, one thing now struck true in his mind. He couldn't afford to make himself known to anyone now, not even the truckers. Hitching would be too risky. For all he knew, they were reading all about him on their phones. If he went up to them asking for a lift, what's to say they didn't simply knock him out and make a citizen's arrest? The waitress may even have clocked by now and been making that phone call to the police. No, the only option now was to risk going to the train station and hope the police weren't waiting for him.

Adrenaline pumped in his ears once more and David wanted to sob again as he followed signs to the station, completely unaware as to the full extent of just how much danger he was now in.

Seventeen

Adam stood silently against the wall of the ground floor as if he was carved out of alabaster. At first glance it was difficult to spot anyone in particular amongst this rabble of human depravity as they moved, sat, chatted and squared up against each other during the social hour. But it didn't take long at all for Adam to realise that he had been put in the main wing, or Category B as it was referred. There was no way David would have been brought in here with these pigs, he would have been torn apart on the first night, mentally, emotionally and most likely carnally. *No,* thought Adam, *my source was right. He's definitely been put in Cat C, Vulnerable Prisoners Wing.* Which meant he would have to embellish his cover story a little more to get sent there.

Without realising it, a tall, skinny guy had come towards him through the throng. Adam's mind had been so elsewhere he had completely not noticed. Not something that normally happened. The stink of unwashed flesh was getting too much for him, as was the noise. He needed to think. On this wing, unlike Category C, inmates were not allowed to congregate in their cells during the social. It was too dangerous. These particular inmates were in for aggravated assault and manslaughter to mention just a few. Gangs and gangsters constantly on edge, waiting for one or the other to make the wrong move, thus giving an excuse to start something. Adam hadn't moved a muscle as the guy came right up to his face. "First time inside?" came a gruff, smoker's rumble of a greeting in a Scouse drool. "You need to watch that stare of yours mate. Looks like you're eyeballing someone with the intent on causing harm. Those eyes almost looked like they was glowing for a second". Adam caught himself. He had let his emotions get the better of him for a moment. That was all it took to show a bit of his other side. A bit was too much. He needed to get himself in check, for David. "It's not my first time. Well, in this prison maybe it is. As for my eyes, not sure what you think you saw. They've put me on some strong shit so I don't go into some sort of relapse. Side effects like you wouldn't believe mate!" Adam feigned a slight Northern twang to his accent. He had mastered this trick quite well over the many years. Mr Gruff didn't seem all too convinced, but obviously couldn't come up with another suggestion and so changed the topic "Good looking guy like you needs to watch himself in here mate. Some proper reprobates in here there are. You need anything, just find me, ok mate?" Adam nodded slowly and the Scouse wandered away, no doubt looking to see if there were any other newbies around to manipulate.

As he watched the guy go back into the throng, Adam made a mental note to look out for him should he need information, which he did. And lots of it if he stood any chance of getting transferred to Cat C. He was already well on the back foot. Just then, he spotted a couple of guards standing to one side above him on the first floor, one holding a clipboard whilst the other pointed at various inmates, as if selecting them for something. His hackles went up immediately, then he checked himself again. *Don't be stupid,* he chastised himself, *they're probably just choosing the work rotas.* But there was something else, a hint of malice in their eyes perhaps?

His attention was brought right back to the moment as a guard suddenly shouted "Alright, social's over. Back to your cells! Don't mess about dawdling. Get to it!" Adam waited to see everyone slowly disperse, clocking who was hanging around in groups, as well as snippets of chatter. Then he tagged on at the end of the line heading back up the stairs. Like Noah's Ark, they all went entered their cells in pairs, except him. A few others noticed this and stared at him a little longer than was necessary as he sauntered in. He wanted to look as confident as possible. With a fluid motion, Adam glided up onto the top bunk as a guard came to the doorway "Jones, I noticed you keeping yourself to yourself. That's good, for now. Keep your nose clean eh? Oh, and I've been asked to tell you an officer is coming to have a chat with you later".

"About what?" asked Adam a little taken aback "No

idea, above my paygrade mate". And with that he

slammed the door shut.

Eighteen

'Slippery' George knew that something was going to happen tonight. He could just sense it. The female guard had not been pleased with him asking questions, even though they appeared innocent enough. Everybody knew 'Slippery' George, he was the man who knew things, picking up snippets of information which he could pass on to interested parties for the right price. Of course, by price he meant chocolate or tobacco, two things very much sought after in here. Sometimes he would even ask for the odd sleeping pill, anti-psychotic or tranquiliser as these were also great currency for some. Keeping his head down and obeying the system for these last few years had amassed him a nice balance in his prison account. With savings he had never tapped into, there was no personal need for anything. His cellmate was definitely happy with having old Slippery share with him, as they ate very well, with being able to choose whatever they wanted from the weekly canteen sheet. Crisps, chocolate, biscuits, nicer coffee and even a cheeky hamlet cigar every Friday, which they would share by taking turns sitting by the open cell window. The thick metal mesh covering might stop most things from escaping, but not the wonderful scent of the cigar smoke.

George didn't mind people calling him 'Slippery'. He had grown to find it quite endearing actually, as it was far better than some of names other inmates in here were referred to as. And it was fairly accurate. He was an old thief and grifter, like that character from the old TV programme Minder, or the leader of the gang in Hustle. If there was a way to make a deal, which profited him in some way, George would pounce on it without question. And he was loyal to a fault, which was why he was in here whilst others carried on earning for him on the outside. They were making sure he was rewarded when he was released.

If he was ever released.

This was the thought he had now as he sat on his bottom bunk. The TV was blaring out some kind of gameshow where people humiliated themselves in front of an audience for a tiny cash reward. Tony, his cellmate was giggling as he tucked into a packet of crisps from the top bunk, but all this was just incoherent noise to George. His mind was whirring, thinking at a speed too fast to compute and making him panic. He looked at the clock propped up on the table next to the kettle, 9:10pm. Just then he heard the shout he had been dreading "lights out! Turn the TVs down!" and with that the corridors beyond the cells muted to a familiar dull, yellow glow. Tony turned down the TV while George switched on the table lamp and then the main light was turned off. *And so here we are* he thought to himself, laying back on his bunk with his hands behind his head, staring at an old photo pushed through the bed mesh of the bunk above. It showed a small girl laughing on a beach next to a beautiful young lady as they made a clumsy-looking sandcastle. It was a treasured moment in 'Slippery' George's past life. Nancy, his ex-wife and their daughter, Tammy. She would be 26 now, but he hadn't seen her in over 16 years. Both she and her mother had walked out on him after Nancy had discovered a bag stupidly hidden at the bottom of the wardrobe. Inside she had found over five thousand pounds and four kilos of marijuana, plus a few dozen stolen credit cards.

George knew that Nancy was aware of what he did, but I guess to actually see the fruits of some of his labours was a reality she just couldn't bear. And he never wanted her or his daughter to have to see any of it. He only wanted them to live the kind of life he never had growing up. He was living on the streets of Manchester from the age of fifteen after his parents' fatal car accident and the abuse he had endured in foster care.

But to separate him from his little princess was too much for George and he soon began to get himself involved in more and more risky ventures with his small gang of brothers in arms. They had just done their most successful score and were in high spirits. As they all went their separate ways from the local pub, George was staggering down towards his shit lodgings when he was picked up by the fuzz.

Turned out, after years of no contact Nancy had not only been advised to get a divorce by her new man, some nerdy dickhead who worked in the same office as her, but also to shop him into the police over that bag she saw! And once she had told them everything she had actually known about his previous dealings, they then implicated him in other robberies which led them to wait to search his digs.

He had been so angry at her for the first year, but not now. He wanted to try and make amends, at least with his beloved Tammy and that meant moving forwards. He never said anything about anyone else involved in his dealings and so took the full brunt of the sentencing. The heavy hand of the law they say. But he had made a few enemies along the way and so asked to be put here in the VIP ward for his own safety.

And now here he lay, wishing he was anywhere else but in this bloody wing! Of course he had no idea whether or not inmates were being snatched in the other wards, but that didn't matter to him. He had grown to know most of the people in here over the last few years, despite his seemingly introverted nature and was really starting to struggle with their frequent 'transfers' during the night.

George brought himself back to reality for a moment, suddenly realising that Tony had started snoring. He switched off the TV and lay back down, listening intently to the sounds outside. A few shouts could be heard from somewhere along the corridor, simple 'ribbing' and name calling. There was a faint bleeping sound as well, rhythmic enough that had he not been so anxious, concentrating on it would have sent him easily to sleep. Then he heard a slight scraping sound, as if something was sliding along the corridor outside, getting closer. It seemed to stop right outside their cell. Then silence. The yellow glow went out as if something was blocking the light and there was almost inaudible clunk as the door was unlocked. The guards made so much noise opening and closing the doors in this place, and yet this time it slid seamlessly open, revealing two shadows that seemed to fill the doorway.

A chill breeze entered the room and George couldn't help but shrink up and back, making him as small as possible against the far corner of his bunk space. He felt like a child again, afraid of the bad men coming into his dormitory all those years ago. He started whimpering uncontrollably, cold sweat suddenly covering his body and he then realised that he had involuntarily released his bladder.

Tony was still fast asleep and, had it been anything else but tall shadowy spectral figures, he would have shouted him awake and together they could have rushed these intruders. But George was frozen, and anyway, the last thing he wanted was to get his cellmate killed too. For he knew deep down his time was up. The shadows grabbed him with an unnatural strength, a bony hand knocking him on the back of the head and sending him into blackness. They then gently carried him out onto the corridor and away through a small door at the end of the wing. Once again, only small noises were heard throughout the wing, and the rhythmic snoring of Tony, totally oblivious as to how close he had come to death.

Back in the wing office, Janet wept silently into a tissue as she watched the monitors. Not much could be seen really, just black blurs moving silently across a black and white screen, but it was enough to know that she had just been party to the death of another inmate. Had she just ignored him during the social and told him to get straight back to his usual spot, maybe he would have been spared, but she doubted it. He had looked straight into the cell of Billy and David. He had also been spotted asking questions about some of the other transfers. *No, thought Janet, your time was up George.* Just then, her office door opened and an older officer came bustling in. "Woah Janet, you alright love? Look like you've seen a bloody ghost!" He came round and put a gnarled hand on her shoulder. Paul had known Janet for a number of years now and they had both been assigned to the night shift for what seemed like an age.

"I'm fine, sorry Paul. Just remembered a sad new article I had been reading earlier".

"I would have thought you'd have nerves of steel by now love, but I guess it's the motherly side of you eh?" he chuckled as he went over to switch on the kettle. "Fancy a brew before you go?"

"No thanks. Robert will be waiting up for me and my little Matilda will probably not be sleeping. She never does until I get home, bless her. No, I better sign off and head home". With that, Janet got up and clocked out, inserting her timecard into the archaic punching machine on the wall by the door of the office. She went to a row of lockers propped up against the far wall and retrieved her jacket, placing her radio, baton a few other items in and closed it with a click. None of the officers locked their lockers as they all knew each other. This was probably against protocol, but with things as they were at the moment, no one cared much. Janet could not actually remember the last time they had had a visitor from outside. She waved goodnight to Paul and exited through a second door which took her out into the cool night air of the courtyard. Janet always hated walking across the courtyard as she felt eyes watching her every time. That feeling that someone is walking over your grave, sending cold chills down the spine. *It is bloody cold tonight!*

she thought as, moving quicker than she needed, Janet made her way to a small par cark that lay through a small door to the side of the outer wall. Her blue Corsa had misted up on the inside and Janet cursed slightly. Unable to afford a new car, she had to use one of those plastic de-icer tools on the inside as well as the outside. Inserting a key in the lock, Janet threw her jacket onto the passenger seat and climbed in, shivering against the chill wind that had started to stir up. And then a cold blast of air caught her breath. There was a lightning motion from behind her in the backseat and everything went black as a hand, strong as steel grabbed her by the neck, choking her so fast there was no time to think before darkness came over her.

Nineteen

The blood room was quite cramped, as it was not built to house more than two bodies gently swinging from their ankles at most. The cloaked figures were hard at work. They had long since become accustomed to the dark. In fact, it had become a friend to them over the many years, enabling them to hide as they went about their business. Once daylight started to splinter the shadows of the work room through the tiny window slits dotted along the old, damp walls, they would disappear through a door at the far end, across to the maintenance room and then down some roughly carved spiral stairs and into a basement where they could rest and sleep. There was no questioning; no pondering thought about what lay outside during the day. They very rarely saw anyone else and if they did, they no longer liked to speak to them.

It had been throughout the fifty last years that they had been steadily picked from amongst the ranks within the prison. Two of them had been cleaners here, whilst the other three had been officers. During their routine shifts, they had been drugged and brought in front of the Master, where they had been blood let themselves, before being transfused with something more. This had not only ensured a prolonged life but had also altered their appearances. Skin had turned so white as to almost be translucent; muscles had withered down and yet bones had strengthened to a point that nails had become claws. Indeed, these beings, now known as Shadows, had become quite feral in appearance with a yellow glow to their irises. They were no longer comfortable with wearing regular clothes and instead preferring the long black cloaks they now wore. They were impossibly strong despite the muscle atrophy induced during the painful, otherworldly transformation. And quick, moving with deadly silence from one task to another. They had also developed a kind of telepathy with each other, although this could well just have been the many years of work here in the blood room. The voice of the Master was always present somewhere in the back of their minds, as he could control them with mere thoughts. Being filled with his demonic blood created this bond. They each had families that would never gain see their smiling, human faces. Friends and colleagues who would believe them to be victims of vicious, unprovoked attacks or freak traffic accidents. Stories involving injuries so horrific, they could only be identified through DNA testing, something that was always planted at the fabricated scene of their demise.

A pulley system had been erected up by the ceiling which enabled them to easily move the bodies around to where they could be drained and then disposed of. This was the only noise to be heard within the room. The bodies were still alive to ensure efficient blood flow, not to mention the right temperature and consistency prior to decanting and shipping. One of the Shadows pulled on a rope dangling nearby and one of the victims moved gently towards a table in the middle of the room. Since the recent and foolish escape of a victim – foolish on their part anyway -, the Shadows were taking no chances. All of the bodies were now bound tightly across the chest and legs, their hands by their sides and they were all now strung up, the leg ropes suspending them off of meat hooks attached to the pulley line. They were careful not to leave any inmate out of sight, especially on the floor behind them.

As the Shadow stopped at the nearest body next to the table, a bucket was then placed underneath the head. Suddenly this elderly male twitched as it started to become conscious. Quickly, a piece of cloth was stuffed in his mouth and tape wound round the face to hold it in. The twitching continued, more frantic this time and the old man's eyes widened so much, it looked as if they would drop out of his head. The Shadow moved quickly over to the table and picked up a length of surgical tubing with a large, 22-gauge butterfly needle attach to one end. The other end was dropped into the bucket while the needle moved with practised accuracy towards the jugular vein of the man. He was sweating so much at this point that the tape came loose, flapping down on one side and pulling out the cloth from his mouth. "Please, please don't do this! I won't say anything to anyone, I promise", came a plea that was so full of fear so as to be no more than a whisper. The Shadow simply stroked the old man's face with a cold, bony hand, clawed nails scratching his cheek. "Sssh George. It is done". Came the simple response, each S being slightly overpronounced.

With a fluid jerk, the needle pierced Slippery George's neck and he let out a short scream as the other bony hand clamped his mouth shut. The off-white surgical tube darkened with gravity as the blood flowed quickly and efficiently down, filling the bucket. The Shadow always liked to look deep into the victim's eyes, always wondering what their last thoughts might be as the light left them. Pupils dilated slightly as George's life slowly left him, his drained heart stopping a few moments before his brain, which silently captured a final, eery image of a smiling, almost reptilian face with glowing yellow eyes under a black hood.

The other body was pulled across the line and swinging slowly. Whilst this female remained dangling, the Shadows got busy piling up the corpse of Slippery George onto a hand cart that wouldn't have looked too out of place during the Great Plague. It only took one of them to lift and wheel out of the room and across the courtyard, a small distance to another door to where a fourth

Hooded and corporeally deficient figure waited. Again with improbable silence and grace, the Shadows carried the corpse through this small door, revealing a furnace which was to become the final sentence in the culminating chapter for George's existence.

Officer Janet Townsend was far too scared to use anything but her hearing to try and make sense of her surroundings, as she moved upside down from side to side. Her thoughts were total chaos in a brain desperately trying to work out what had happened. All she could remember was a cold skeletal hand clamped around her nose and mouth as closed the door of her Corsa, ready to go home to her family. She couldn't help but think again of old George. It was her fault he had been taken, and to hear him so close to her in this darkness pleading for his life just now, made it all the more anguishing for her. But now there was silence, mixed with a horrible scent in the air of human excrement and something else, something metallic but slightly pungent in itself. Shit, piss and blood. Her brain separated and translated the smells from memory. Back before she became a prison officer, Janet had worked part time as a paramedic, typically dealing with the Friday night clean-up operations in the local city centre. As is always the case right through history, drinking sessions often ended with a fight or six. Eager to prove their masculinity (or feminine predatoriness), drunkenness would replace rational behaviour and within moments of stupidity, one or more bloodied or unconscious form or forms would litter the vomit and alcohol-covered pavement. These were some of the scents Janet could discern now as the blood rushed to her head.

She heard herself whimper uncontrollably, struggling to keep her eyes shut and failing to keep the unconscious ruse going any longer. But she didn't need to. They were not going to slaughter her like the others. Little she did know she was destined for something far greater, far more important, far worse than death.

As the remaining Shadow finish decanting the last of the blood into pouches, sealing them and stacking them in a number of transplant boxes ready for transport, it slowly turned to face Janet. Bony hands steadied her pendulum like motion to a halt and Janet could feel a cold, intimidating breath on her cheek. "Sssh Janet, you are not to die. You are to be saved, to become a Shadow like us. It is a great honour to meet the Master. You will see." And so Janet started whimpering louder, ashamed of the trickle of urine running slowly downwards, passed her breasts and along the side of her face, it's vinegary aroma at least helping to mask everything other scent in the room. Suddenly there was a scraping sound as a door was opened, letting cool air rush in. A huge shadow seemed to

embrace the whole space, despite the figure
entering being quite small in comparison. It moved
as if gliding on ice as it floated to where the
Shadow and Janet were.
"Janet, I am The Master. I am here to give you a
wonderful gift. Do not think of it as death, but as a
rebirth into something far greater than this pitiful
existence. But we must first empty in order to refill".
Janet then felt a sharp prick as something pierced
her neck. This terrible figure then clamped its
mouth over the wound and Janet could only take a
quick intake of breath before feeling dizzy and
finally elapsing into sleep. She felt colder than she
had ever felt before, as if on the edge of a
precipice, being urged to jump. To stay felt like
pain, but to jump seemed to be far more soothing,
as if it would take all the anguish, all the fear and
guilt away with it.

Suddenly, she was brought back to this waking
nightmare with a piercing scream. It took a second
before she realised the scream was coming from
her as a burning fiery liquid poured through her.
Her skin felt as if it was going to melt right then and
there off her body and her bones seemed to stretch
inside her. She found it hard to breathe through the
agony. And then, as soon as it had started, it was
over. But more than that. She felt calm, an
emptiness washing over her that was intoxicating. It
felt amazing! She felt invincible. And yet, was there
something else? A void in her mind? The more she

tried to remember things, the more they seemed to disappear. For a second she was convinced she had a family, children. But that was crazy. She would remember right? Then she failed to remember her name. the only thought left was that she was in service of the Master, her master.

"Good", came The Master's voice out of the gloom. "It is done, she is now one of you. Give her a robe. Let her rest in the basement. Tomorrow night she will learn the tasks".

The Shadow that was once Janet was taken down off the pulley system and untied. Standing up, it shed the bloodied and soiled officer's uniform, dumping them on the cold concrete floor. Standing naked, this skinny, pale flesh could no longer be identified as either male or female. Ribs now showing through opaque skin and breasts reduced to a wafer-like consistency, lying flat against an extended sternum, the form was covered with a black hooded cloak and led down into the basement.

Twenty

Adam sat quietly on a chair in his cell, feeling the cold, slight breeze wafting in against his neck and upper back from the badly insulated but well barred window. The moon seemed to glide with an unhurried majesty across the night sky, a pearlescent waxing gibbous not far from being full. Although he gained no extra strength, power or transformation from such an event, Adam certainly felt more heightened across his senses during this period leading up to fullness. His eyes had that slight orange glow to them in the dim light of the cell. No other lights were on and Adam did not really need them anyway. The light of the moon was more than enough for his well attuned sight. His eyes could draw in in the smallest light from around him and produce an almost perfect picture of his surroundings which, along with exquisite smell and taste, gave Adam such an advantage over humans.

And so here he sat, waiting for this visitor to arrive. It was a little past midnight and Adam was starting to think he was being played with or tested. Maybe they knew his secret? Had he given the game away? If so, it was incredibly sloppy of him and could perhaps have been put down to him being so hungry earlier. He could not rule out cameras watching him in his cell, and so felt the best course of action was no action. Just simply sit here and hope this in itself did not rouse suspicion.

He had to get transferred. Every minute he stayed here could potentially mean more danger for David. Then an idea occurred to him. A few of the other inmates had looked at him as if marking him during the social. If he acted vulnerable, maybe even tried to score some gear from one of them, then they would surely try to intimidate him, perhaps even attempt to physically assault him. It would put a target on his back and with enough of a show, this could be his best chance of being transferred for his own safety.

The drugs were handed out every morning and just because he wasn't actually prescribed anything, it did not mean he couldn't make a bit of a scene with the nurse. After all, he was meant to be an addict right?

The hours slipped by and Adam remained in the chair, deep in thought. He was used letting time slip by. In fact, his sense of time had altered slightly over the centuries. Knowing you were damned to live possibly forever would do that to anyone. He thought back to the last time he was imprisoned, over 70 years ago in North Africa.

There was always a war going on somewhere in the world, normally started out of religion or greed, if there was a difference. People trying to seize more than they are entitled to, jealous of what others have and thus ending up becoming prey themselves. And so the cycle goes on and on, never ending. Adam had been working as a volunteer doctor out in a village between Dongola and Karima in Sudan. He had been travelling around Africa for much of the Second World War as a medic in the SDF (Sudan Defence Force), trying to keep out of the way, under the radar, whilst knee deep in the same shit that everyone was enduring at this time. There was no escaping the tyranny of the Nazis, but he had found that trying to flee just meant coming up against the Japanese or Russian armies. So it was better to have an element of presence.

The war continued at some level well after what the British called V-E Day. Land was there to be carved up and anyone who got in the way was butchered. Being a volunteer doctor gave Adam access to blood banks, but also meant he could do some good too.

Then one night, local militia came into the village in a blaze of gunfire and Molotov cocktails, destroying everything in their path. Adam tried to stop these senseless animals but ended up with three bullets in his chest, from a young boy waving an AK47 around wildly. He was high on heroin mixed with gunpowder, a substance they called Boom Boom, injected into the arm to make you seem like you were invincible. It took only 10 seconds for the bullets to make their way out of Adam's chest the way they had entered, his wounds closing up and the boy staring unbelievably at this figure rising from the dead. Then came the infantile scream, followed by shouts of "Devil! Devil! Demon is here!" But it was Adam that ran in the opposite direction and straight into the hard end of an axe handle, knocking him out cold.

He awoke in a small wooden shack with a metal roof made of corrugated sheeting. The heat was unbearable and he was dangerously hungry, or thirsty. There was little difference for him, as the outcome would have to be the same. The old chain that linked his arms and legs together broke with the slightest of tugs and the boards making up the walls of the shack came apart just as easily. As Adam stepped into the light of the afternoon, he did not recognise where he was, but there were jeeps and ammunition everywhere. Bodies were piled up on one side of the camp and he recognised some of the men and boys, including the one that had shot him. There appeared to be no one left alive, but also nothing had been taken. The bodies stank to high heaven and the sound of blowflies could have been heard for miles around. It was an apocalyptic scene for sure, and one that Adam had added it to the long list of things he would never forget in all his years. Even the last battle of the Crusades dimmed in comparison to this, for it was the senseless, mindless violence that rocked him as he surveyed the carnage before him. Then he spotted it, a message written in blood on the wall of one of the huts the militia must have used:

You may thank me another time, my love. Your secret remains. See you, L.

Adam knew who this was, but he could not believe it. Leofric, his maker had been there. But why hadn't he stayed? Things had not ended well the last time they had met. Calling it a difference of opinion was extremely mild, but they still loved each other and this was evident in the way Leofric had saved him from whatever torture and ritualistic sacrifice this militia had planned. Without waiting around, Adam had burned everything, including the jeeps and ammunition, making it look like a turf war attack. He then made his way back to England.

An owl hooted close to the cell window and he was suddenly brought back to the present. He realised he had nodded off, something he hated doing because he didn't really need sleep and they only brought back memories he tried to bury. And still there was no visitor to his cell. Adam gently rose from the chair and lay down on top of the bed. The moon had surrendered to the more prominent light of the dawn, a celestial battle that always ended the same way. Soon enough, the double clunking of the key sounded in the cell door lock and another day was to begin. But first, he would make his way to the medicine queue.

The Master watched Adam for most of the night, sitting there on the chair in his cell. He knew there was something different about this one, which meant he would possess a rare blood type. His eyes were like those of a cat and his posture was not that of a supposed addict, that was for sure. *Who was this John Jones?* he thought to himself as he tapped long, sharp nails across the table in a sinister, rhythmic pattern. One thing was certain, he would need a blood sample to test. For if he was right, this inmate could be something very special indeed and incredibly dangerous to the operation.

Twenty One

Xion stared at the plain brick wall of the small kitchenette as she thought hard about the kind of mess David had got himself into. Out of everyone she knew in her inner circle of specialist hackers, David was always the one least likely to want to go out socialising. He was in no way a rebellious character, preferring to sit in front of his screen looking for new ways to hoodwink some authority or large corporate company with his brilliant mind. It was no secret that both she and David had a kind of thing going on. They would joke with each other in ways that on the surface could easily be misled as more than a brother and sister relationship, but this subtly flirtatious behaviour was for her teasing steps towards something more one day. She would do whatever she had to in order to keep him alive, and free.

They had known each other for almost six years, working first out of the tiniest room behind an internet café on the outskirts of Brixton. Most of the regular punters would spend their time online looking at menial shit, but it helped mask the amount of juice she and David produced whilst undertaking their various questionable and quite often illegal activities. Of course they always used sophisticated VPNs (virtual proxy networks) which made it look as if they were hacking their way through corporations from random places such as

Georgia or some Eastern European back end of
nowhere. And that was when they had met Adam.
He just appeared in the café one afternoon and
demanded to see her and David. It totally shocked
the hell out of the owner of the café, a short, fat
balding Russian who happened to be heavily
involved in drugs and other unsavoury activities for
the Russian Mafia in London. He was merely a tiny
pawn, but Xion and David did online traces and
erasing for him in exchange for use of the
backroom. Better the devil you know right?

Anyway, it turned out that Adam had been told of
their particular skills by another IT nerd who had
helping him to hide from the online world as much
as possible. With London alone being one of the
most monitored cities in the world per square
metre, disappearing required some serious
hardware and skill to both understand and use it.
And even then, if you were on any kind of radar,
you would eventually be found one way or another.
But Xion was an expert at surveillance monitoring,
whilst David could hack into just about anything and
plant a bug that would disable the systems for
however long he wanted. He could then put
everything back as if he was never there. And so,
with the promise of tech that defied belief and a
budget that seemed bottomless, they agreed to join
him. At first they didn't really ask too many
questions as to why he needed such anonymity,

but then, who cared as long as the money was wired once work was completed, right?

Of course the Russian lowlife was none too happy about losing its criminal advantage and things got a little messy for a spell. It started with a dead cat being nailed to David's front door with a note pretty much telling him to come back into the fold or else. This was then followed by two burly chaps waiting for Xion as she left her apartment, trying to scare her into giving up on Adam and coming back to the café. But Adam had a way about him. Whether it was his relaxed but commanding stance or just the way he seemed to look deep into your very soul. Either way, by the end of the week, the café owner had disappeared along with a couple of the henchmen, the café itself had been closed down and both David and Xion were employed without further incident by Adam. What followed was the rather scary realisation at first as to what Adam was, but with the assurance that he would never hurt them. Instead, Xion was promised full protection from anything else that may inadvertently happen to her in the future just so long as she served him. David too. Weirdly, Adam's previous help had also disappeared shortly after they joined, but Xion did not have the stupidity to ask how or why.

A sharp whistling sound snapped her back to the present and she switched off the double camping gas hob, removing the small, steaming kettle. The smell of chamomile and fennel wafted up enticingly as she poured boiling water into the Hello Kitty mug (a birthday gift from David which she actually loved). The mix of aromas cleared her head a little from the sleepiness she always felt after a long night of work. Her reading glasses had that yellow tint to the lenses which helped ease the glare of the screen, but spending 13 hours straight online, well, it could make anyone zombie-like.

She took the mug and plate -piled high with buttered toast- back over to the desks, set them down and glanced once more over the 4 monitors which flicked between CCTV cameras from streets, shops, traffic cams and station platforms. All in real-time and showing pretty much the whole of the North of England, Xion could spot if someone, or something was hot on David's heels as he made his way back to her. For a second a lump was caught in her throat thinking of how helpless and alone he must be feeling. She had helped him as much as she could. But what really troubled her was the way in which she had not been able to decipher where he had been taken once his sentence had been passed. I mean, how could you possibly get from a terrible drunken accident in Brick Lane, to the Crown Court in Regents Park, only to be sentenced, sent to Bristol, before being unwittingly transferred to a prison over a hundred and sixty miles away?! It just made no sense.

Suddenly Xion froze and almost dropped the slice of toast in her shaky hand. What if it was not about David at all? What if this was some large-scale scheme to trap Adam and David was merely an opportunistic pawn that had fallen in laps just at the right time? And Adam had put himself in harm's way to go and get David out!

As if Mystic Meg herself had been listening, an alert flashed up on the far-left screen indicating a media spike. She had set up algorithms that would automatically notify her of media information posted or released depending on whatever criteria she filtered. In this case, as well as the usual <a href="#">Adam</a> </li> <a href="#">Vakaris</a>, Xion had also added David's name to the search. And it had just pinged. "Shit!" she shouted to herself as her mouse quickly clicked, opening up the news channels. And there he was, a prison picture of Dee, looking very worse for wear on the day he was arrested. There was then another image, a fuzzy black and white image of what really could have been anyone creeping out of the opening of what looked like a service or maintenance door. Quickly, she used her skills to remove the images from every social media site. But it was impossible for her to remove them from the bloody news on TV! All Xion could think to do for now was to try and plant a fake trail, digital breadcrumbs for the authorities to follow whilst

David made his way South. Quickly, she created posts using anonymous profiles which gave detailed sightings of David heading towards Liverpool. Each one used slightly different language or words which were just similar enough to point virtual sniffer dogs in the wrong direction.

Next, Xion erased the alerts that had been put out in the train stations and local police stations. This should buy him some extra time and allow him at least a chance of getting on a train. She just had to hope he had not already been spotted by anyone.

There were so many unanswered questions and Adam had also now appeared to have disappeared too. But then this was not uncommon. I mean, the whole point of having Xion, David and the others in the first place was to ensure that he remained invisible. But not too Xion surely? Since climbing into a prison van, she had not been able to catch the slightest digital whiff of him.

There was another ping sound as a second alert flashed on the screen. It was the same pictures of David showing on all the social media sites again! *What the…? How could this be possible?* she thought to herself. Someone was hacking her own algorithm, ensuring that David would be seen by everyone online. She checked the train station alerts and there he was, his scared looking face staring at her with his name and the words "dangerous prison escapee, do not try to apprehend. Call this number." Xion tried to back trace the number on the screen, only to be blocked. It was a dark site number for sure, not the police or government. A private, untraceable number. Should she ring it herself and pretend to be someone with information?

Without thinking, she dialled the number without switching on the blocking app installed at her own end. It rang once, then clicked three times before going dead. Xion knew what this meant. She had been tagged. Whoever these people were, they could well be on their way to her. If it truly was the Government or something equally sinister, they were probably already in the city! Xion only thanked whatever Lord is up there that she was not at their headquarters.

She grabbed a bag, filling it with some essentials, then clutching the smartphone she had been using to contact David, she promptly left her flat. Quickly walking to a coffee shop across the road, she ordered a coffee and sat at the bench in the window. If anyone was coming, she would see them first. And in the meantime she could rewrite her algorithm to continually block the resubmission of David's photos.

Xion was one of the best, but she had no idea that she had met more than her match.

As the trace ended abruptly, Farling made the phone call. Charles answered immediately "Farling, what do you have for me?"
"Well, it appears that we may have a lead on this fugitive David Jennings for a start. We set up a number which automatically activates a trace should anyone ring it with information".

"You mean a bloody information line, yes I know what it is you buffoon!"

"This one has no one on the other end, just an automatic trace, even if the number is blocked at their end. Anyway, we think we may have found one of his friends, or certainly someone he is contact with as the address traced comes from an area of London close to where this David resided. With your permission, I can get some of our people on it". Farling had actually already authorised this and they were on their way, but Charles needed to feel useful and powerful. "Yes, yes, of course, just get it done and find this slippery bastard, you hear?!"

Charles had a meeting planned for an update on various policies. But there was a meeting due on the current crisis in the NHS on blood donations too later in the afternoon. Present would be some of the Society, with others listening via cameras mounted secretly in the main conference room. He needed to bring his A game if he was going to come out of all this alive. *Or worse,* he thought with a shudder.

Twenty Two

His methodical brain had somewhat recalibrated as David approached the station entrance. Miraculously, there appeared to be no police presence at all. He had waited in the doorway of an old office building across the road for a good half an hour before plucking up the courage to step out of the shadows and make his way across the road. Having bought an E ticket for his journey to London, David had managed to get the next direct train which only a couple of stops. It was going to be a long and tense ride, but he had looked at the times into each station along the way, setting an alarm on his cheap phone to alert him should he nod off asleep. *Oh to just close my eyes for half an hour!* he thought to himself.

There had been a couple of police cars parked up in the drop off zone when he had first rounded the corner from the High Street, but they had since left together, hopefully on another call. He had bought another baseball cap in a different colour. Slowly but with that sense of purpose, he made his way into the station entrance without looking up. Feeling a little self-conscious, David tilted it so that the cameras would perhaps not pick up his features. *Just act natural,* he quietly said to himself. Amazingly, there didn't appear to be anyone at the barriers. They stood open and although also open, no one seemed to be manning the ticket office either. Well, this was not such a strange event really, as for the last few years the rail staff had been constantly griping about pay, conditions, contracts, pretty much everything really. With unemployment at such a high rate, David could not understand why they didn't just quit and let other less fussy people step in. But with not knowing the full details, who was he to say such things. *I'm a man with nothing* he thought drily, *not even my freedom it seems*. Staff shortages were now a regular occurrence on most networks and this was obviously one of those days. A small voice in the back of his mind wanted to offer another, more sinister explanation, such as staff and authorities waiting in the shadows to pounce on him the moment he got onto the platform, but David quickly quashed such thoughts before they took root. Panicking now was not the way to go.

Walking a tad quicker now, he went through the barrier and took a swift glance up at the information board. He had to wait 10 minutes for his train. There was another train that was already on the adjacent platform which didn't leave for another 20 minutes. *If I wait on this train, I can see anyone that may be following me or waiting for me as the London train comes in, then switch trains at the last minute*, he thought. Thanking his methodical reasoning, David slid onto the waiting train. It was going to Glasgow Central and was pretty empty. *Perfect!* He thought to himself as he sat by the window facing the station barriers. Keeping his hat on despite the stuffiness of the carriage, David silently waited, counting down the seconds on the digital platform display.

Again, he was amazed and yet so relieved that no one seemed bother him. A few people got on the train, passing him with no recognition of who he was, this fugitive from the law. No police had stormed down the platform in riot gear, being pulled along by angry dogs that wanted that pound of flesh. It really did seem like he would make it to London. Of course, once there, he would have to find his way to the safety of Xion's place, but hopefully she would be waiting and he would be able to relax knowing she would have a plan. It was a lot of "woulds", but his life was no longer as it was. From this moment forward, he had to reinvent himself; let fate take its course and just hope that it was on his side. Cold sweats suddenly overcame David and he ran for the disabled toilet, only just making it before vomiting bile and water into the sink. He felt dizzy and had to sit himself down on the floor, the smell of chemicals and other substances not making him feel any better. With slow and deliberate movements, David dragged himself to his feet and made his way to the nearest seat. There was a young lady, a student by the looks of her on the seat near the toilet and she glanced his way, a frown appearing on her attractive, elvish face. "You OK?" she asked,

looking straight into his eyes. "Sorry" he
instinctively apologised in that typically British way,
"I think I'm a little under the weather. Just need to
get back home." The lady smiled "Well, it's
apparently quite good weather in Glasgow today,
so that'll make a nice change eh?"
David just smiled and moved passed her to sit back
where he could see any danger.

This time last year he was minding his own
business by hacking into other people's, helping to
expose greedy corporate bastards that were
siphoning funds from employees to pay the rent on
their luxury villas or super yachts. Adam had taken
an interest too, as he hated power hungry fat cats
just as much as David. He had travelled to Croatia
on a lead and it was now his and Xi's job to cover
Adam's tracks. David was getting closer to Xi but
was worried that they had accidentally fallen into
that "friend" zone with. No, worse, he had become
like a brother to her.

There was a faint disturbance coming from the
station foyer. Hard to make out, it looked to David
as if some figures had been stopped as they tried
to get onto the platform. Strange how a couple of
guards were now present. They must have been on
a quick break or something when David had
arrived. Again, lady luck helping him out. He got up
and pressed the button to open the door. This
allowed him to hear the angry voices that

resounded through the air. "I'm sorry, but without tickets I can't let you through, it's policy sirs!" Shouted one of the guards, a large man with a long beard and immovable stature.

"We are looking for someone of great importance. He is a fugitive from the prison and we believe him to be here in this station. Now let us do our search and then we will be gone", came the reply. It was impossible to know from which figure the voice came. They were wearing long coats, three of them together and the voice seemed to create ice in the air. It made David shiver to the core. But this shiver was also the realisation that his luck had just run out. If they let these figures on the train he was screwed!

"I don't bloody care who you are looking for, you don't look like any kind of security or police to me and if you can't show me some identification I am going to have to ask you to leave. You are welcome to return with the police, but until then, you are unsettling the other passengers sirs". *Yes! Good for you mate!* thought David. These guards were totally standing their ground, despite the foreboding nature of the figures that towered slightly over them. There was nothing more the figures could do but to turn around and leave the station. But David knew if this train didn't pull in soon he would be caught out sooner or later. They would surely come back with the police, or worse, those dogs he had heard earlier whilst running for his life.

Just then, the metallic screeching sound of the London train pulling in made David almost weep with joy. It settled to a stop on the platform next to him, the doors opened and he waited quietly as passengers filed off. It was like just another normal day as the steady flow gave David his opportunity to debark, mingle with the throng and then climb aboard a now empty carriage. Due to leave in just 5 minutes, all he needed now was for that comforting beeping of the doors locking. The carriage filled up, which gave David some mixed emotions. He was positive his picture was not everywhere, but still, it would only take one to alert the authorities. Nothing he could do now. He just hoped that strange trio of gothic-looking characters did not manage to get through. With the feeling of slow movement out of the station, David slid himself into the old man's jacket, wrapped his arms around himself and closed his eyes, sighing deeply as he slipped into a well needed sleep.

No one chose to sit next to the man with strange, green-tinted eyes as he sat quietly. Everyone had got off in his carriage, the train now stationary at Stafford station as new passengers embarked for the return journey back to London. Having covered all possible avenues out of the city, He had been chosen by his employer to keep watch on trains to

London. This was his last train for the time being, an express with just a few stops. He had others waiting, watching at the London stations, whilst he would remain on the train for the whole journey. It was a longshot as to whether this David character would take this particular avenue, but it would be marvellous for Green Eyes if he could catch him personally. What an achievement! He would wait until the train was well on route and then start his search through the carriages, pretending to look for the toilet or a friend. Placing his hand in his pocket, he cradled the syringe laced with an antipsychotic. This should make him compliant enough for the journey, where his colleagues would be waiting to deal with him properly and deliver him to the Master. His phone vibrated silently in the left pocket and he took it out, reading the caller display. It was from Shayanne, who had been sent with a few others to pick up David's friend at her flat in London. Using her as bait would help to ensure this David character was compliant, not to mention if their more dangerous friend Adam should show up unexpectedly.

Twenty Three

Cradling her lukewarm mug of over-sweet latte, Xion pondered over why people couldn't just make a cup of coffee as to the simple specifications of the customer? *I mean, you go in and ask politely for a hot latte and it should come to you at a temperature that enables you to sit for a period of time in their establishment without having to quickly down the bloody drink before it is stone cold! You want to try something fricking difficult to achieve? Try working for a fricking vampire, erasing any trace or digital footprint and then deal with the possibility, no, probability that you will be killed for helping out a friend who himself is probably going to be killed!* She sighed, taking a large gulp and seriously contemplating going over to the so-called professional Barista and demanding a steaming new cup for free. But Xion then thought better of it. After all, the whole point of being here was to keep a low profile whilst waiting to see if her place, her private HQ, was blown.

Xion shivered slightly, realising that in her haste to get out of the apartment after hearing those tell-tale clicks on the other end of the phoneline, she had forgotten to grab a jacket. A blast of chilly air slithered over her bare arms with each customer entering or leaving, but she couldn't move from her spot. Just then, a black car pulled up, one of those BMW SUVs the city had no space for. It stopped directly opposite and Xion had a mind to duck down, but then thought better of it. Three men and a tall lady got out, all wearing pretty ordinary yet black trendy clothes, like some knock off from a goth band. To anyone else they would just blend in as weird but typical city folk, but Xion knew who these were. The car gave it away. Plus they had a self-assured sense of purpose that spoke volumes.

After trying the buzzer to her building a few times, two of the men came behind the woman, blocking any view of her by the door whilst the third man patiently looked up and down the street. He looked across the road, seemingly straight at Xion through the coffee house window and she froze. But then he glanced back up and down the street again and she knew he had not clocked her. *Maybe they don't know what I look like?* she thought, afraid to look away for fear of losing any detail of what was happening. The two men blocking the woman turned around as the front door of the building fell open, each figure then entering with a grace that seemed to imitate predators closing in on their prey. As the last of the men started through the door, Xion could have sworn she saw the glint of something metallic gripped in his right hand. *Was that a bloody gun?* she panicked as the door closed behind them.

After what seemed like an absolute age, the door opened again and one of the men, the one that had been the lookout, exited onto the street. He rolled a cigarette, lit it with a swish of a chrome Zippo before taking a long drag. He seemed pissed off at something, or from not finding someone. As he took a second intake of the cigarette, their eyes locked again through the coffee house window. This time, Xion was sure a glint of recognition hit his eyes. He casually dropped the cigarette, stamped it out and went back inside the building. *Shit!* thought Xion, *he knows who I am! No smoker who rolled their own would stamp it out after just two puffs.* There was nothing for it, she had to get out quickly, but onto the street would be suicide. Glancing back behind her, Xion saw the sign for the toilet which looked close to the kitchen. With luck, she would be able to go out the backdoor. Slowly climbing down off the uncomfortable stool, she edged back towards the counter, where the Barista asked how her drink was. "Tasty, but to be honest it could have been a little hotter". *Shit! Why did I have to say that?!* "Oh, so sorry. I'll happily make you another if you would like?

"No, honestly, it's fine. Please is the toilet just through there?" Xion pointed to the back.

"No it's upstairs. Just to the right there". The Barista pointed to the opposite end of the room. "I'll make you another whilst you are away", he added with a rather handsome smile. On any other day, Xion may actually have pursued this further, especially with his bottom lip piercing and red spiky hair that made his big brown eyes even more manga-like.

Sorry cutie, another time, if I'm still alive. "Sure, make it to go, thanks". She smiled back, quickly making her way to towards the stairs. As Manga Boy's back was turned, she ducked left through the back door and into the kitchen. There was only one other staff member in there, bustling around with her back to Xion as she busied about rinsing mugs and putting them in the pot wash. The rear door to the coffee house was open and Xion quietly moved towards it.

Just then, she heard the front door open and felt that chill of cold air reach all the way to the back. The door was clearly being left open as if a group had entered. She could only imagine who this group was and who there were after! Through the back door, Xion found herself in a small alleyway which ran the length of the line of buildings. There didn't appear to be another way out other than running as fast as she could to the end of the alleyway and so, taking a deep breath, Xion went for it. Halfway down, she heard a whistle followed by a series of footsteps running behind her. Afraid to look back, Xion just kept going until at last the end of the alleyway reared up in front of her and suddenly she found herself back on the main road. Cars screamed by, along with buses and a cyclist almost knocked her over as Xion desperately tried to slow herself down before falling into the road. A taxi pulled round the corner with its light on and at first, despite the frantic waving of her arms, she thought that it would just drive by. But to her relief it slowed with a screech of brakes and she got in.

"Please, just drive and I'll tell you where to go!" she almost screamed at the driver, who glanced angrily back at her through the rear mirror. But he said nothing and pulled off. The group, only able to run single file through the alleyway, came spilling out just in time to see the taxi turn a corner out of sight. The woman made a quick call and the BMW came hurtling round to pick them up, before doing a U-Turn into traffic, forcing a bike to mount the curb and then sped after the taxi.

PC Francis had been enjoying his bacon sandwich and decaf soya hazelnut latte as he sat on his break in the patrol car. Breaks were few and far between on this shift. There was always some kind of disturbance that ended up being nothing but a waste of time, but the main part of his job was community liaison and so he really didn't mind too much. But just as he put down the empty napkin which had contained the crispy bacon squeezed inside the sourdough bread, he was startled to see a black BMW SUV round the corner at break-neck speed, pick up a group of dodgy looking individuals before rounding into traffic and screech off! Normally this would not be his area but feeling that he had no time to call it in, Frank secured his latte in the drinks hole, switched on the lights and started after them. He then had a strange thought to switch the lights off. *Suspicious activity should not be met with brute force,* he thought to himself. *Follow and then call it in,* he reasoned with himself. And so, keeping a short distance behind the BMW, he followed.

Twenty Four

Before he knew it, daylight had taken all of the eerie shadows back to the underworld of night as Adam came to. Lack of blood had left him feeling weak again, a feeling he really wasn't all that used to in recent times. He had created for himself a perfect system whereby he could obtain bags of blood with a mere coded text, from wherever he was.

His team of geeks just had to see a simple asterisk as a message and then they simply triangulated his position, alerting the nearest blood bank. A member of staff there would then be ready to give him a bag when he arrived. It really had become that simple. No questions asked, no suspicion raised.

And then stupid David had got himself incarcerated and he was in danger of having his entire cover blown. And to make matters worse, he was now in the wrong bloody wing of the prison, with shady dealings going on and very little time to deal with anything! Adam took a deep breath, letting his heartbeat relax.

He knew if he let his hunger get the better of him, with the way he was feeling at this moment the predatory side of him would definitely take control. Part of him wanted this so bad, as he could easily overpower everyone, find David and be gone in a matter of minutes. But what would that solve? After all, the whole point of him being in here was to find his friend and stop whatever sinister was happening. 'Blood Bath in Northern Prison' wasn't exactly the headline legacy that would keep his own secrets intact now was it?!

He heard voices from somewhere in the corridor as doors starting being unlocked. His was last, despite being situated right in the middle of the floor. He did think it unusual, but before he could think too hard, his cell door opened and two officers filled the doorway, blocking his exit.

"Jones, it's your lucky day. You're being moved. Either you've seriously pissed off some of the wrong people or you've sweet talked someone up high, is all I can say about it!"

The other officer sniggered and made a hand gesture towards his mouth as if to insinuate Adam had given sexual favours. Without even thinking, rage bubbled up within him and he was across the cell in a split second, stopping a hair's breadth in front of the officer, looking him hard in the eyes. The colour seemed to drain from the officer's face, as if he had just seen a something utterly terrifying and he stepped back, tripping over his colleague's feet and banging into the railing. His momentum was such that he tumbled over even this, falling onto the safety mesh that covered the breadth of the wing. His left leg twisted underneath him, a crunching sound from a dislocated kneecap echoing all too loudly. As for his upper torso, this was saved by the officer's quick hands, but rather than cushion his fall, the mesh cut into the palms and fingers, making him squeal like a child. The noise made every inmate on the wing look up from their place in the food queue and as one the accumulative cheering and laughter filled the air.

This all happened in the blink of an eye and the other officer could do nothing but watch as his colleague tipped over the railing, only managing a "WHOAH!" Adam, however, took the opportunity to his advantage, pulling the officer towards him into the cell and sinking his teeth into his neck as soon as the flailing guard was out of sight. He drank quickly and heavily, a vice like hand clasped over the poor man's mouth, eyes bulging with utter shock as they tried to register what was happening. Adam was in heaven as he drank, feeling the exquisite metallic warmth flowing down into him, revitalising him.

He had only drunk a small amount from that first officer the previous day, nowhere near enough to get this forgotten feeling of bliss. It had been so long since he had fed like this he couldn't stop and the officer went limp in his arms. As he drew back, Adam quickly felt for a pulse. It was very weak, but he was glad that he at least hadn't killed him. Using a drop of his own blood, Adam smeared it over the puncture wounds, which healed and disappeared. He then gently lay the officer on the floor, just as inmates had started coming back up the stairs with their breakfast trays. The whole wing was a cacophony of banging and yelling and within minutes the emergency alarm had sounded.

Officers appeared from everywhere and Adam suddenly had an idea. He knelt down next to his unconscious victim and whispered into his ear "you fainted after seeing me push your colleague over the railings. I tried to grab him but he went over too quickly".

"Shit bruv!" shouted an inmate as he passed by Adam's open door, "what the fuck did you do? Nice one, but you is going down by the screws for this bruv!"

And with that, Adam was confronted by no less than 6 officers with batons and shields. And what a sight they saw! A sobbing officer laying sprawled on the safety netting, a graze to his face where he had made contact and with his left leg at a funny angle, his hands all cut up and bleeding onto the floor below. And then another officer unconscious on his cell floor, with Adam kneeling over him. Adam was forced onto his front with his hands behind his back. He was quickly man handled to his feet, much to the delight of the other prisoners, who were shouting things like "Yeah, way to go mate!"

"All you screws are next!"

"You'll see. He'll get all of you!"

It was a short walk out of the main wing and into the one containing all of the solitary cells. Adam was pretty much thrown into one and the door was slammed shut, plunging him into darkness.

He quietly sat down in the middle of the room, which was only around 10 feet square. The ceiling was fairly high, with a small window in the middle at the top, letting in the bare minimum of daylight through the heavily reinforced and aged glass. Adam then allowed himself a thin smile. Although not quite how he wanted this to go, it was not a bad way to get transferred. The officer would explain enough so as to not get him transferred out of the prison, but it would be enough to have him put here for a few days whilst they figured out what to do with him. Without onlookers, he could maybe open this cell door and look for David. He had close to four pints of blood flowing through him, more than he had been used to. It gave him a renewed sense of purpose. Adam could feel his dark mirror lurking just beneath the surface of consciousness. It was, in all honesty his true self, and he would use it to get out of this hell hole. And so he sat in silence and waited for his chance. He couldn't help but smile again as he heard the sirens of two ambulances making their way into the prison grounds. Misdirection was a wonderful thing.

Twenty Five

David kept nodding off despite the necessity to try and keep awake. The adrenalin that had been keeping him alert and on the move was now all but depleted, leaving an overwhelming lethargy that wracked his body, both mentally and physically. All he wished for at the moment was that he was able to bloody open a window! These new commuter trains had air con that never seemed to reach the sweat glands, but instead pumped out reused air. David remembered with fondness his travelling days, well, a gap year to be exact, when he travelled to Eastern Europe. The rickety carriages that took him both through and around the mountains with windows fully open, allowing the freshest air to heighten senses and make you feel you were flying. He had particularly liked his stay in Romania for he had a fascination with gothic horror and of course Romania, in his mind, was arguably the king of birthplaces for such stories and folklore.

Just walking the many hundreds of steep steps up to Vlad the Impaler's ancestral fortress, Poenari Castle, high up near the Făgăras Mountains was a massive tick off of his bucket list. Although not much to see now as it lay in ruins after a series of earthquakes and decay, it was still one of the first places David had asked Adam about shortly after they had first met. Vlad Dracul the Third lived in the 15th Century and yet, Adam lived and was then made a vampire some 300 years before! Vlad's horrific acts of cruelty, although not particularly uncommon during this dark age, still travelled far and wide, especially supposedly impaling mothers on the same spikes as their new-born babies. Adam had been reluctant to talk too much about that time, for he was willing to admit they were dark times for him too.

He had been part of a coven or nest then, a gang of vampires if you will, working their way through Europe doing pretty much what the hell they wanted; feared, revered and totally unchecked. But that was all he would say about the matter, apart from that he had indeed met Vlad the Third, whilst looking for his maker Leofric who he believed to have been an advisor to Vlad's court. Adam never liked talking about Leofric. David could always see that it made him either incredibly sad, or angry. Not a great person to be around in either case.

David woke with a start as the train rolled suddenly round a sharp corner. How long had he been asleep? However long it had been, a man now sat in the seat opposite him, reading a newspaper. He was moderately tall, with dark hair cropped short on the top and shaved at the sides. Even as he looked intently at the paper he was reading, David had a slightly foreboding feeling in the pit of his stomach about this guy. After all, he could have sat pretty much anywhere else in this practically empty carriage, but he had chosen this particular seat opposite him. After everything he had been through these past few months, David just wanted a moment to himself before getting into London and starting running again, hopefully with Xi at his back this time.

He took a deep breath and stood up, meaning to move to another part of the carriage, but as he made to turn, the man shot out a leg blocking him. In a voice that was both low and commanding he simply said, "sit down David". All of the colour instantly drained from David's face yet again and he thought he was going to vomit, even with nothing left in his stomach to expel. He slowly sat back down and the man withdrew the leg. Folding the newspaper up meticulously, the man placed it gently on the seat next to him and gave David a hard look, clenching his strong jaw. His eyes were a strange shade of green, not the usual emerald but more of a yellow green. They gave off a weird glow, which David figured must be his imagination through lack of actual restful sleep these last few days. The man relaxed the jaw a little to allow a thin smile to reluctantly leave his lips. The intent in his eyes, however, remained unchanged.

"Where are we heading David? All the way to London I'm guessing, to your bit of stuff. What's her name again? Oh yes, Xion isn't it? Peculiar name, like her parents watched too much of the Matrix or something I'm guessing?"

Each question had only rhetoric intentions attached to them. He was not really asking for he clearly knew everything about David. *Had he boarded this train to kill me?* David thought, *Or take me back to the prison dungeon and finish the job?* He was a dangerous witness after all. But then this stranger could have easily killed him while he slept and then have been on his way to another carriage without drawing any attention. Well, as long as didn't look at anyone that is with those eyes.

"You seem to know so much about me. I take it you're here to take me back?" David managed with effort, his voice sounded a bit like a strangled parrot through lack of saliva. "I've done nothing wrong except run for my life! I was happy, well, of sorts, in prison, serving my sentence and minding my own business. I didn't ask to be snatched you know, having to watch my cellmate being hung up and slaughtered like bloody halal meat! If you've been sent to finish me off, I'll tell you now I will not go without a fight!"

The man regarded David for a few moments before taking a deep breath and smiling even broader than before. Again, his eyes remained hard and suddenly David saw an expression not unlike a cat ready to pounce on his prey. "Well, you're right about one thing I suppose. I have been sent here to collect you. But you see, I'm now thinking that it might just be easier to dispose of you in the disabled toilet. You are after all totally out of your depth here, aren't you David? I mean, It's not exactly in your character profile now is it? Quite the possibility that you would take your own life instead of having to deal with the consequences of getting caught once we reach London. Your face is everywhere young man. You know that right?"

David had hoped Xion would be able to sort that bit out for him long enough for him to get into hiding, but clearly this had not happened. Which then meant that she may well now be on their watchlist too. But he had nowhere else to go but forwards to London, if he could somehow get free of this particular hurdle sitting in front of him. He sighed, before saying somewhat more confidently, although not very convincingly, "Like I said, you'll not find me easy prey. I've been through too much to stop now. I have contacts, powerful contacts that are trying to find me as we speak. You do anything to me and they will hunt you down and tear you to pieces".

Green Eyes sniggered, his eyes softening and losing their glow for a second. "If you are referring to your vampire friend, I'm afraid he won't be able to help you. You see, he got himself sent to the same prison as yourself just a few days ago. I'm guessing his intention was to break you out, but my employers have plans for him. Can you imagine how much his blood is worth on the black market? Just the mere thought of being able to possess even one of his abilities, let alone to be immortal! Well, I'm pretty sure there is no price too high for that right?"

David let his guard drop as he gasped in disbelief. *Holy shit!* he panicked to himself, *Adam had gone in to get me just as I went on the run. And now I've put him in danger. Probably Xion too! All of it not even my fault!*

"Oh, don't get too worked up over things", Green Eyes soothed, "they were always going to work out this way. Well, at least, since you got yourself arrested anyway. This has certainly put some interesting and wonderful cogs in motion, as it were. Now, before the next stop, shall we get this business done?" He moved his right hand which somehow now held a long, wicked looking knife, slightly curved at the end. "I was going to use a tranquiliser on you, but I think it's far better to go with the blade. I think it would be best if you stood up now and made your way over to the toilet door, don't you? A scene made means more casualties, right?"

Slowly, as if by an outside force, he found himself getting up from his seat. Green Eyes stayed still as David moved past him and edged his way towards the other end of the carriage, where the toilet was situated. Behind him, he felt the man rise with a fluid motion, as if he too was being pulled by invisible strings. Glancing behind him, there was now no sign of the long knife, but David was pretty certain it would be produced in a flash soon enough. He would be left to bleed out in the toilet, with no one to find him until well into London. This assassin would make sure of that.

Halfway along the carriage David suddenly noticed the remains of a takeaway breakfast left on a fold-down table. Next to it was a plastic knife and fork. He pretended to trip, knocking into the table and quickly grabbing the cutlery before continuing on down the aisle. Reaching the toilet door, David knew he had to act quickly if he was going to survive this. With only a plastic knife and fork, he would have to jab as hard as he could into the man's neck, hoping to severe the jugular. Or stab at his eyes. But to do that, David would first have to get the man onto his knees.

Green Eyes approached him. Suddenly the knife was back in his hands, a wicked blade designed for maximum deathly effect with minimal effort. A single slice would most likely pass through his clothes like butter and open him up. David backed slowly into the open cubicle, his mind racing way too quickly to make any properly calculated judgements. He felt himself starting to hyperventilate, as if his body was prematurely entering into its final throes of death before the fatal blow had even been struck. Everything had slowed down, but as the killer moved towards him into the toilet, David tripped and fell heavily next to the basin. Thankfully he didn't drop the cutlery. The man was on him in a split second, as he banged the button to close the door, his other hand extended fully to show his intent.

Auto pilot wanted David to get up to face him, but then a voice in his head calmly whispered *stay where you are, keep your eyes on his neck.*

Green Eyes moved into a gradual crouching position and as he did, everything sped up and all hell broke loose. David darted forward with incredible speed, his cutlery stabbing into exposed neck flesh, where both the knife and fork sliced both open and in a good two inches. At the same time, Green Eyes, the glow back and wide in shock, swung his knife wielding arm wildly, the blade cutting through David's sleeve and deep into his forearm. Both men yelled with pain, but as David recoiled his arm, his fingers refused to let go of the plastic weapons. They were yanked out of Green Eyes' neck, an arterial spray covering the basin, walls and mirror like a crimson fountain. All attempts to stem the flow with his free hand were futile, for the wound was far too deep. As he fell forwards, Green Eyes tried once more to focus an attack, but David moved to one side, his own forearm stinging and wet. The cutlery moved up again instinctively, this time glancing off the man's jaw and lodging themselves in the left eye. He screamed a strange high pitched sound, dropping the knife and making a grab at his face.

David was covered in blood, his jacket now all but ruined. He was now behind the man, inching his way out of the cubicle on hands and knees as Green Eyes lay on the floor, blood pooling around him, his life force draining away in utter shock and bewilderment at what had just happened.

For what seemed like an eternity, both men simply remained in a terrible freeze frame. Then David's wits came back to him and he slowly stood up. There was blood absolutely everywhere. Thankfully most of it was in the toilet itself. He cautiously went to the cupboard under the basin, careful not to step in the sticky pool and was glad to find a roll of "out of order" tape. It was hard not to get blood on anything else as it had decorated pretty much the whole cubicle, but David managed to wash his hands. He removed his blood soaked jacket and washed his hands and face, trying not to gag at the metallic scent filling the air. There was also another smell, the smell of someone shitting themselves. He had heard that a person more often than not defecates themselves on the point of death, but David never thought he would live through such a thing first hand. *Fuck it, let's just add it to my ever-increasing list of fucked up shit,* he thought sarcastically to himself.

There really wasn't much he could do to stop this horrific scene from being discovered, but at least he could close the door and cover the button with the "out of order" tape. As long as this bastard didn't bleed out so much it started coming under the door. Remarkably there was very little blood on his jeans and the trainers could be wiped off pretty well. David thanked his lucky stars that he had kept his jacket zipped up. He threw it on top of the now dead assassin before closing the door. Shaking again, he made his way out of the carriage towards the front of the train, where he sat at another empty set of seats. Looking out the window, David couldn't stop the tears from rolling down his ashen cheeks. Not only was he an escaped fugitive, but he was now a murderer to boot. His life would never be the same again, if he lived that long.

Twenty Six

The traffic lights definitely weren't on her side as the taxi driver tried to navigate Xion through the throngs of the city. Even being out of the centre, what seemed like the entire population of a small country had decided this particular day to come and say hi to her! With frustration and anxiety growing like a monster inside her, Xion's breathing becoming quick and loud in her ears as the taxi was halted at another set of lights. *These bloody pedestrian crossings!* she screamed in her mind, *what is the problem with having to walk an extra 10 meters to the fricking next one!*

A small blessing seemed to be the lack of buses on the road, which would have added to everything. "Hey mate, I really have to get to Euston station. Is there any other way through all this?" She knew that most taxi drivers chose a slower route so that their clock would elevate the price of the fare as they meandered from A to B. This was bad enough for tourists, but for residents it just took the bloody piss. Just out of curiosity, Xion looked behind her out of the window and noticed a black SUV that seemed a little too close for comfort, following the same route. Maybe it was just her sense of paranoia, but was this the same car that was outside her flat?

"Love, I can only go as fast as these lights will allow. Once we get through this bit I can take a side street which should cut out a bit of the time".

"Okay, thanks. Mate, what do you make of this car behind us eh? Seems a bit close right?" It was worth getting the taxi driver's attention. Maybe he would start to get anxious too and bloody speed up a tad!

"Hmm", he pondered, "strange car that. Blackened-out windows too. Looks almost like one of those SUVs from an FBI film doesn't it?"

Don't say that! Thought Xion. Panic was setting in at a high enough level as it was. Suddenly, as by some divine power, the next few sets of lights stayed on green and there now appeared to be fewer people, the taxi making quicker progress to the next junction, where the driver did indeed turn sharp left down a narrow street. At the end he took a right and the buildings changed to more residential, albeit very posh and Victorian looking, maybe Edwardian. Xion could only have dreamed of living in one of these, as did most of the population. She wondered about the types of families still living in these, or whether they, like so many other buildings, had been chopped up to shit and converted into pokey flats and then rented out, netting the owners a cool £70k a year in profits. Either way, her upbringing had been a far cry from this. More like something out of bloody Oliver Twist, only with laptops instead of picking pockets.

The black car was still behind them, which angered the taxi driver a bit. "This is a bit weird love, this car following us like that. Are you a wanted girl or something?"
"Ha-ha, no of course·not!" lied Xion "They must be tourists thinking you are a master at short cuts or something. But they are creeping me out a bit. How much further to the station?"

"Just around this next junction love, not far" replied the driver, just as a whizzing sound flew past Xion's face. A second made the car veer wildly off to the right and straight into a lamp post with a thud that lurched Xion forward into the glass of the taxi partition. From a glance to her right, she saw the taxi driver slumped over the wheel, blood dripping from a hole which continued out the front of where his right eye had been, an awful mess now covering his face. Xion tried her door, but the child lock had been activated as they were travelling and had not disengaged. Hard as she tried it just wouldn't budge. She tried kicking at the windows, but they too wouldn't give. It was then that she noticed the two neat holes in the rear windscreen, her eyes catching the two men and a woman getting slowly out of their black car, handguns pointed straight at her!

"Shit! Shit! Shit!" Xion heard herself repeating over and over as she flung herself around the taxi, trying desperately to escape. Then it was the glass partition that finally gave, buckling out of the housing that kept it in place and with a last ditch attempt, Xion managed to pull it free just enough to climb over the top and into the passenger seat. Trying hard not to look at the horrible scene next to her, she opened the passenger door and fell out onto the pavement. This all seemed to happen in slow motion, when in fact it took only few moments. The black car was further away than she had first thought, but her pursuers were gaining ground quickly and Xion heard another whooshing sound as a bullet thudded into the open door of the taxi.

 She scrambled around the other side of the door and without thinking or looking back, made a run for it, turning a corner to her right and then sprinting as fast as she could to the steady throng of people on the main street.

Once amongst a crowd of people again, Xion slowed down slightly and looked up, trying to get her bearings. She was very close to the station, but with people following her, Xion could not lead them to David, nor could she take a chance that more wouldn't be waiting for her at the station. Cursing again, the only thing to do now was to find a place to lay low and keep trying David's phone. So with that thought cemented in her brain, Xion ducked down another alleyway, twisting and turning through different streets until she was sure she had lost these attackers, then took a deep breath and went into another small coffee house. Sitting at the far end with her back to the wall and her eyes fixed on the front window, she waited, wondering which would come first; the ringing of her phone to tell her David had made it here, or the whooshing sound of a bullet sending her into a black abyss.

PC Francis had been quietly tailing the black car for around 5 minutes, before watching as it duked down a narrow street. *Strange* he thought to himself, *now where are you going I wonder?* He decided not to follow, but instead sped up slightly so as to meet the car as it had no choice but to connect with the main road a little further along. But as he turned left to intercept, PC Francis suddenly heard an almighty crash. It was as if a car had veered off the road somehow and without thinking, he slid the patrol car up onto the curb and got out, knowing that he would not be able to park anywhere close to the entrance to the narrow street from where he was.

Jogging slightly and feeling out of breath in a matter of seconds, he reached for his radio. "PC Francis to dispatch, PC Francis to dispatch, come in".
"This is dispatch, go ahead".

"Yeah, I'm just making my way down Mullfryer's Street on my way to a possible road traffic accident. Crashing sound heard of at least one vehicle and on route, on foot to investigate. Possible back up need as well as paramedics. Standby".

"Roger that PC Francis, standing by" came the response. He knew he should have waited until he knew exactly what he was facing before radioing it in, but PC Francis was in a bit of a panic, his brain working overtime along with his lungs as he got to the entrance to the Franklin Avenue. It was then that a small girl ran passed him, almost knocking him over. "Hey love, stop where you are! I need to talk to you!" He shouted after her, but she rounded a corner and was gone.

On approach, he immediately came face to face with a black taxicab that had smashed headlong into a lamp post. The driver was slumped over his steering wheel, but it was the sheer horror that used to be his face that took PC Francis back. Unfortunately he didn't have time to react anymore as a bullet whizzed first passed him, before a second landed square in his chest. It was like all of the air leaving him at once as PC Francis fell backwards, landed on the pavement. He felt paralysed, blinking wildly amongst an expression of utter shock and a searing unbearable pain engulfing him, like a molten liquid was pouring over his torso. A woman then stood over him, anger in her eyes as she pointed a gun towards his face.

There was a click and PC Francis saw blackness for a split second, then nothing.

Shayanne quickly holstered he gun inside her long black coat before motioning for the others to follow her as she sped after the target. *This is already going to utter shit and I will not lose you again!* she screamed into her own mind.

Twenty Seven

Charles McNeil was, for the most part, a very patient man. It was a trait he had acquired through years of not quite reaching the goals he had set himself, going all the way back to his childhood. He had never come from money like so many of his peers and this had meant actually working hard to impress everyone he came into contact with, rather than merely relying on a good name or legacy. On the plus side, Charles had something that most of these stuck up, slimy politicians could only dream of having, a real sense of the world below that of privilege. He knew how the working classes thought, the struggles they went through on a daily basis. And most importantly, what was really needed to get them on the side of the government. Well, Charles was not stupid. He knew also that this building, with its ornate, over exuberant furnishings that, if pawned would probably help to finance the NHS for a hundred years, was nothing more than a theatrical façade. The real work went on unseen, by those of far greater importance and influence. True power could not be gained here. And so he had made some morally questionable decisions of late.

To ease his conscience slightly, Charles had been telling himself over and over that what he was doing was for the greater good, but recently he could feel the cracks of reality seeping through to his soul. He always wanted to be a good man, a kind man who, although put his career first could always be counted on to do the right thing at the right time. But he had laid in bed with the most terrible of people to feed his ego and what soul he had left was now beyond redemption. He knew that.

His office phone rang, making him jump. He was getting more and more anxious of the tone it made, a high pitched shrill that seemed to challenge him to answer, baiting him. "Charles McNeil".

"McNeil, it has been a while since you last gave us an update. We have been waiting for news on the nationwide rollout of our operation. Has there been a problem?" *These voices!* He shuddered to himself *Why were they always harsh and high pitched, as if coming from a nest of vipers that had evolved the use of speech?* "Parliament will be back in session in a few hours and it is then I will announce my decision to visit as many of the prisons as possible within the next few weeks. Whilst I am making my inspections, as I have already stated, your "subjects" will be granted access to find appropriate venues to set up in secret. I cannot work any faster so as not to arouse suspicion".

The voice on the other end took an intake of breath, that familiar clawing sound as though nails were tearing at a blackboard "McNeil, do not forget your place. Do not forget how you came to be in the position you are in now, as you sit there in your cheap charcoal grey suit, drinking that cup of Earl Grey out of your favourite mug with the words "Greatest Dad in the World" imprinted on the side. That maroon tie your wife picked out for you this morning could well be the weapon of your demise, should it wrap too tightly around that spindly neck of yours. And what of your dear boy, Alex. As he sits at this very moment on his favourite bench outside the classroom tucking into that packet of smoky bacon crisps. So nice that his mother Julie packed his favourite today. Could this be his last day?"

"Don't you even think of…"
"NO CHARLES!" The voice suddenly went deep and loud, no longer the frail rasping, but more like a tiger ready to devour its meal, prey already caught and'flailing helplessly. "Understand this. If things are not in place and you are not on the road towards the next prison, we will begin harvesting from everyone you care about. Then we will harvest product from your wider circle. You see, we don't care who is in control down there, because no one is in control down there! You are all sacks of sacred blood. Your lives are nothing to us other than a vessel containing our product. We own you McNeil, and everyone around you, everyone you hold dear. We want results, we want to harvest every last one of the scum incarcerated behind walls. And you will ensure that it is done. You will direct our servants

as they set up practices throughout the nation and we will not see the same mishaps that have occurred in these last few days. Do you understand now Charles McNeil MP?"

If he hadn't been scared before, the sheer tone in this voice had absolutely terrified Charles. It felt so cold in the office he couldn't stop shaking. And his poor Julie and dear Alex? It seemed everyone was being watched, held to ransom. What had he got himself into? He took a deep breath. *Pull yourself together!* he chastised himself, *you knew all too well when you got Charlotte sacked and yourself promoted you had stepped into a pit of vipers.* "I understand. It will be done".

The phone went dead, a simple click on the other end. Suddenly the room seemed warm again, although the blood in his veins still ran cold. Then an anger engulfed Charles as he shouted out "Farling! Get in here now!" The slight, weasel like figure of his assistant slid seamlessly into the room and stood next to Charles, papers in hand as if he was about to give him the miraculous answer to everything that was wrong with the world. "Farling, we have to make sure that this tour of the prisons goes without a hitch. And this can only happen once we have apprehended this escaped criminal. Where are we with this?"

"Well, Sir, his face has been circulating across all news channels with the backstory of a drug addict that has raped and murdered a young girl. I have had word that someone has been trying to shut the news and social media links down, a kind of hacker known to him as I understand it. But she has been largely unsuccessful and she is being located as we speak".

"Well this day just gets fucking better and better, doesn't it?" yelled Charles, spitting slightly as his rage was unleashed. "So not only are we looking for someone with direct knowledge of what is probably the biggest and most dangerous underground operation in recent history, but we now have another criminal hacker on the run with probably just as much dangerous information on the cover-up. Anything else? Or is that it for now? I mean, please don't hold back there. I tell you what, why don't I just offer *you* up , drain you and sell your fucking "sacred product" as they call it? Hmm?"

Farling took a couple of steps back from this man who was clearly losing it. He spoke in a deliberately soft voice so as to indicate the need for discretion.

"Sir, we have professionals out looking for this girl. The last I heard they are closing in on her as we speak and will have apprehended her within the hour. As for this David character, I personally sent a specialist to take care of him. It looks at this stage as if these two were meant to meet each other in London. This will not happen. And if everything goes to plan there will be no more news coverage of this and we can spin whatever story we like as to what has happened. I know for a fact that the girl will not be missed. She can simply disappear".

Charles chuckled "If everything goes to plan eh? I won't hold my breath. Now, give me that speech and go deal with all this. I expect a rather more positive update when I next speak to you".

Farling could not get out of the office fast enough, almost tripping on the large floor rug as he reached for the door handle. As soon as he closed the door behind him, however, he straightened up and brushed down his suit. Looking back at the closed door, Farling grimaced. *Oh Charlie boy, if only you knew what was really happening you pathetic puppet!* He chuckled to himself as he turned and casually walked away down the corridor.

Charles realised suddenly that he was standing, his hands tightly gripping the edge of his desk almost painfully. He reached for his empty glass and filled it two fingers' full of brandy, downing it in one gulp. Then, with a few deep breaths and a small cough, he sat back down and slowly looked over this speech to the House. This had to go without a hitch. Whatever was happening under the surface, the marzipan had to look impeccable.

Twenty Eight

"Ladies and gentlemen, I'm sorry to inform you that, due to unforeseen circumstances, we will be making an unscheduled stop at High Wycombe. We will try and make this as quick as possible and the driver has informed me that as we are currently slightly ahead of schedule, so this should not greatly impact are planned arrival time into London Euston of approximately 1:35pm. We thank you for your patience and understanding. Oh, and the food carriage is now open, serving hot and cold snacks and beverages, situated in carriage E. Thank you again".

David was still shaking uncontrollably, now made worse by the announcement they were stopping at High Wycombe. That had to be soon, and it had to be about him. Officers would be swarming the platform, waiting to apprehend him. By his calculations, Taking a deep breath and calculating, David reckoned he had less than 20 minutes before they reached the station. He had to get off the train somehow. But how exactly? This wasn't one of those old trains from back in the 1990s with those windows that slid down and doors that opened manually from the outside. The only way he could open these doors would be to pull the emergency chord. That would be utterly ludicrous considering what he had just done, with what was now bleeding out in the disabled toilet a few carriages down from where he was now sitting.

Perhaps there was a way out at the back of the train? He thought, and got up slowly, his brain only just communicating with his legs. Blood pumped loud in his ears as adrenaline kept him alert. David just wanted to pass out every time he thought of both the sound and feeling as he drove that plastic cutlery into the man's eye. It was all he could do not to vomit and he swallowed down the bile creeping up, burning his throat. He checked his clothes, happy that any blood stains were now mostly covered up as he walked along the carriages towards the back of the train.

As he entered the final carriage, David couldn't believe his luck. Instead of the usual engine that would normally be attached to the back, omitting the need to turn the train round as it came back on its return journey, there was instead a standard carriage. Although highly unusual, he could only guess that staff shortages had led to such an error happening. *That must be why they were stopping at High Wycombe!* He sighed with relief. *Not to pick me up, but to attach the engine so the train could make its way back from London.* Then his heart fell again. *Don't be stupid! They can easily attach another train at Euston. No, they are after you mate.* Either way, David knew he was royally screwed unless he got off the train.

Thankfully he was alone in this carriage, as most people would not want to alight from the back of a long train. He tried the door at the end. Nothing. But at the top was a quick release mechanism. David thought for a moment, weighing up his chances of getting caught. If he activated this quick release, he could slide the door open, but at this speed he would fall to his death. With the train rolling along the tracks at a good 4 feet above ground level and travelling at a speed of up to 70mph, the odds of him surviving were minimal. He would also surely set off some kind of alarm, maybe even the emergency braking system. However, if he waited until the train was already slowing down as it came into High Wycombe, then he could potentially jump out and make his escape.

This is such a bloody nightmare! No one should have to think like this! David blubbered, letting desperation take hold as he sank to his knees. He let tears flow down his cheeks, all of the tension he had been holding onto for so long releasing in waves. He couldn't stop, and he felt the train starting to slow before he knew it. Looking out of the window, David saw that he was not at the station. Instead, there must have been a signal up ahead. He took a deep breath, knowing this was the perfect opportunity and pulled the release. Nothing sounded in the carriage, which meant a light would most likely be flashing in the driver's cabin. There were over 10 carriages between the driver and him and he didn't know where the conductor would be. David quickly pulled at the door, which after a bit of persuasion slid slightly open revealing fields beyond.

There was just enough space to get through and he fell heavily onto the space between the tracks. He felt the heat from the electricity pulsated from the rails and felt relief that he had at least not landed on those. His left arm seemed to have taken the brunt of the fall and hurt, sharp pains running up and down it. But there was no time to check. He got himself up clumsily and ran left towards some trees, not knowing if anyone had seen him, not caring that commuters would now be late to work.

The lives of everyday nine to fivers had always up until now really frustrated David. He couldn't think of anything worse than the monotony of getting up at the same time every day, to do the same job for what was probably a power hungry pleb who treated everyone like absolute shit. And for what? Just enough money to ensure that you didn't die on them whilst you continued the cycle again and again until you dropped down dead or got put in a home by family that didn't want the responsibility of changing your adult nappy; left to see out what remained of your dementia? Of course by then you wouldn't care or more likely know that you were shitting into a bag of some kind and not of your own free will either. No, David had chosen another, more lucrative path; a path that would have seen him rich, or more if had had the opportunity to ask Adam for it. He wanted to be made a vampire, had dreamt of it since he was a child. It was the most wonderful feeling to know that they actually existed, that there was a slim chance of being turned.

He laughed out loud as he thought of such stupid, inconsequential things. Everything had changed, nothing was now certain and he would actually give all of his savings to be where these commuters were now, stuck on a train with nothing to worry about other than being late for work. Instead here he was, traipsing through undergrowth to god only knows where.

At the other end of the clearing, David could see what looked like an industrial estate with the clear orange glow of a supermarket next to it. He was so hungry and desperately needed to change his clothes and wash himself, perhaps even have a shave if there was a disabled toilet. Then he stopped. *Shit!* He thought, *what if my face is all over the news? How am I supposed to show myself?* He made his way closer to the estate, having to climb over a fence and through more bushes and hedgerows before he could make out the car park of the supermarket. It was pretty full and he checked himself over, feeling the phone in his pocket. He was glad for the zip that had kept it from disappearing in his struggle with the Green-eyed man. No doubt the body would be found at any moment and he couldn't simply wait. David had to take the chance and so slowly made his way out into plain sight. Pulling his hood up, he must have looked like some sort of druggy, which probably meant he would be followed around the supermarket by security. He just had to keep his wits about him and act casually and deliberately. Even if that was what thieves did.

Although seemingly busy, there were not very many people walking around the car park as David approached the entrance to the supermarket. He grabbed a basket, took a deep breath and walked in. Thankfully, most of this chain seemed to arrange the aisles in a similar order to each other and he knew to turn direct left and head to the end of the store to where the clothes were. Picking a pair of jeans, a T Shirt and a sweater off the rails, David then grabbed a puffer jacket and a pair of trainers, only hoping that Xi had put enough on the app for him. Looking at the prices, it all came to under 60 quid which surprised him. David would never have shopped here normally, nor would he have chosen such items to wear. But he needed to blend in. As he made his way across to the main part of the store, he noticed a black baseball cap which he also picked up. With a bit, no, a lot of luck, no one would bat an eyelid.

Grabbing a pack of disposable razors and moving to the self service area, David noticed a few people glance his way, looking him up and down but with no real recognition. A security guard was also staring in his direction. He put everything through the scanner and could have screamed with joy as the payment went through. Taking everything into the toilets, David was also overwhelmed at finding the disabled toilet unlocked. He quickly got in and closed the door. Whatever happened now, at least he could face it clean.

Filling the basin with hot water, he stripped off the mud and blood stained clothes. His right arm was badly grazed from the half jump, half fall out of the train. Plus there were bruises down his left side from the struggle with Mr Green Eyes. As he gently patted the hot water over his torso, not caring that the water splashed onto the floor, David winced slightly. He was tired and achy over most of his body, his nerve endings now working overtime as the adrenaline once again subsided throughout his system. Splashing water over his face and hair, he removed the razor and, with a shaky hand began removing all the stress and trauma of what felt like an eternity from his face, then patted himself dry with a handful of paper towels. They felt rough to skin, but just to see a familiar face staring back at him made David smile thinly. If only the look he had in his eyes could be the soft stare he was used to. *I will never look at myself the same again*, he thought solemnly to himself as he pulled on the fresh clothes and trainers.

The bin wasn't quite big enough to stuff his old ones into, but he did his best, wiping the floor as much as he could before leaving the toilet. Again, no one was waiting for him and the security guard didn't even look his way as David left the supermarket. *Now where do I go?* He thought as he surveyed his surroundings. *How can I get to London now?* He decided to go back inside and grab a hot coffee. He had a bit of time at least and he desperately needed caffeine to formulate some kind of new plan. How much time, however, was very much in the hands of the Gods.

Twenty Nine

As he sat in the isolation cell, Adam really couldn't help but ask himself if David was really worth all this trouble? Maybe it would be better to simply leave him in here. There was no real danger of his secret coming out to anyone anyway. After all, the young man idolised him and Adam was also sure David dreamed of being turned into a vampire by him. He didn't have the heart to tell the fool that it just didn't work that way, not that Adam would want to do it even if he had the ability to do so. With everything in life there is always a hierarchy, and for his kind this was very much the case. Adam did not possess the power to make others and he was actually glad of it. The responsibility that must come with having vampire children just did not bear thinking of. No, David was useful to him in so many other ways. And he was paid handsomely for it. If he had to admit it, Adam actually quite liked the young chap. Even thought of him as a friend. Being stuck in a prison was not something he relished, but Adam had been in far worse scrapes. The question now was, should he unleash his full powers upon this institution or merely continue the charade that was John Jones?

Just as he was about to make a decision, the key sounded in the cell door and it swung outwards, revealing a tall figure dressed in a black cape with a hood that created a full shadow over its face. "Why are you here?" came a deep rasping of a sound from within the shadow, the faint glow of two yellowish orbs adding to the utter malice and sinister intent barely contained.

"Sorry what? I don't understand your question Sir" Adam answered in the Northern tones of his character, John. "There seems to be some kind of misunderstanding I think. The two officers tripped over each other when they opened my cell door to let me out for breakfast, and then before I knew it, I was dragged down here".

The figure sniggered slightly, a sound almost a growling rumble, but the amusement was evident, nonetheless. "I know what you are Mr Jones, if that is indeed your real name. I've been watching you in your cell you see. I have a vested interest in all of my…property here. And as for that incident earlier today, well, it merely confirmed my suspicions. So I'll ask you again, why are you here?"

Adam stood up slowly from the crouching position he had been in. It appeared that his disguise was useless against this obvious figure of authority and so there was no need to try and fool anymore. Even at his full height, Adam was still a good foot shorter than this figure and he felt his own eyes start to give off their orange hue as he stared into the hooded abyss that was its face. "It seems you have me at a disadvantage then, doesn't it? What is it that you think I am? Apart from someone who is clearly in the wrong place that is."

"Oh my ancient child, I must disagree. I think you are in exactly the right place. The sheer value of blood such as yours is uncountable, unfathomable. And I am betting that, unlike all of these other products here, we can make you last for a very long time. Am I right?" With bony, pearlescent fingers the figure drew back his hood, revealing a pale, almost male face with long, slick black hair. His eyes were not, however the same as Adam's, with a glow of yellow instead of orange to them. His jaw was elongated, the bones rising high up the skull giving what appeared to be a permanent smile to his features. To Adam, he almost gave off an impression of a serpent.

Adam had heard of this race of people, living deep in the shadows of the world for centuries, if not millennia. He had come across one in Budapest and hoped never to meet one again. They were a very nasty breed, only interested in control and power at whatever the cost. Not vampires, but something just as fierce to humans, if left unchecked.

"I see recognition in your eyes, vampire. You have seen my kind before, haven't you?"

"Once, long ago. I had hoped you had all died out to be honest. The last meeting I had with an Afeaa Shaytan did not exactly end with a friendly hug. And you know of me. So let's at least be civil shall we?"

"My name is Hashaan. I run this little operation here on this pathetic island. And in all these many years I have yet to come across one of you, until now". He gave a wide smile, the jaw bones stretching in a particularly unnatural way which made Adam shudder slightly before he could contain himself. These were dangerous predators, almost as much as the more feral vampires stalking the population out there in the world. But Adam was curious "Back to your question, I'm here for someone. I don't want nor do I need trouble. I'm guessing that only you know my secret in here. I have come to collect a friend. His name is David Jennings and he was put in the Vulnerable Prisoners wing. Let me take him out and this does not need to escalate any further".

Hashaan laughed a booming sound that echoed off the walls of the small cell. He stepped in closer, bending down slightly as if he was worried he might hit his head on the ceiling. There was a good foot or two above him, but Adam guessed this was just an automatic response. Most places would be too small for this creature, especially underground in dank tunnels and chambers. "Oh my fanged friend, you are in for a terrible awakening. This young man you speak of, how can I say this, he is no longer with us. My servants took him from his cell a few days ago to be part of the operation here". The serpent Demon smiled again, that smile that refused to meet his hungry eyes. "As I said, he is now no longer with us. In fact, there is no trace of him left here in this prison at all". His evil smile almost split his face in two.

Adam's mind was racing suddenly. Was David dead? Had he been killed by these retches? And what was this operation Hashaan kept speaking of?

"Your mind is going so fast to try and catch up. But enough of this chit chat. I am going to have to leave you, John Jones. You are no longer of use to anyone. I will leave you here for a while before my servants come to take you to our special processing room. I can't wait to see this exquisite blood of yours. I may even have a taste myself". As Hashaan turned to leave, Adam felt a surge of rage and lunged for him, lifting this cloaked figure straight off the ground and ramming his head against the ceiling, before throwing him into the wall of the corridor outside the cell. He hit hard, crumpling to the ground, a mass of white flesh and bone underneath a heap of black cloak material. Hashaan wasn't moving as Adam stepped out of the cell, nor did he make a sound. But Adam knew better than to think he had killed him. These creatures were exceptionally hard to dispose of, which is why they had survived for so many years.

Their bones had evolved to compress like those of a rodent. They were only barely human.

There were a few guards lying at different positions along the corridor, giving off the scent of death, fairly fresh but still deadly should Adam drink the already congealing blood from them. Heads poised at unnatural angles, no other marks were visible to Adam as he slowly made his way to the entrance of the segregation wing. All of the other cell doors were closed, but there were no sounds to be heard anywhere. *It's far too quiet in here!* Thought Adam. He opened one of the other cell hatches and peered in, curious as to why the other prisoners weren't making any sounds. As soon as he had started lowering the hatch, the smell emanating from inside the cell told him everything. In the centre of the room lay a man, although "lay" was perhaps not the correct word to use as to the state of him. He had clearly been dead for a day or two, his body lying in an entirely unnatural position. Legs bent at an angle underneath him and an arm up across his chest, his hand resting on the floor by his right ear, it was clear that he had been almost thrown into the cell post-mortem. The stench of death was ripe, but what surprised Adam most was the lack of any scent of blood. It was as if this poor bastard had somehow been drained of every drop of blood before being brought here to rot.

Closing the hatch, Adam moved to the next cell, and then the next, each one revealing the same gruesome scene. It was as if this segregation wing was in fact nothing more than a dumping ground for the remains of prisoners slaughtered.

How has this been allowed to happen?! Why hasn't there been a national uproar over the systematic killing of prisoners? And how the hell did I not know about this?"

Panic suddenly engulfed Adam as realisation set in about the fate of David. With an urgency and speed he opened the rest of the hatches, but David's corpse was not there. But if the Afeaa Shaytan was telling the truth, David was now dead and it was up to Adam to retrieve his body and get to bottom of all of this.

His eyes were a bright orange now, his teeth sharp and nails extended slightly beyond the fingers as Adam Vaziri no longer cared who knew his identity. If his friend had indeed been drained of blood for some kind of profit or meal, he would tear this place to pieces to get to the bottom of it.

Thirty

Xion jumped as her phone rang. Her nerves were pretty much shot as she had no idea what her next move would be. These people were probably still looking for her and all she could do for now was to stay put in the coffee shop for as long as possible. Of course the downside of this plan was that she had become pretty much a sitting duck. Fear had started to take hold, rooting her to the chair in which she now cowered at the back in the corner, as far away as possible from the door but with a full view all around her peripheral vision. As she took the phone out of her pocket, Xion sighed a massive relief as she saw it was David's burner calling. But was it him? Or had someone else got the phone? If so they could trace the call. *Shit, shit, shit!* She screamed in her head once more. What other option was there but to answer? I mean, she had to know if he was still alive. And she could really do with a friendly voice right now. Pressing the green answer button, Xion waited for a response, or some form of clicking sound to indicate a trace being activated.

"Hello? Xi? Is that you?" the voice sounded strangled and high pitched, only vaguely that of David. Could someone be trying to impersonate him? "Give me the name of that bar we went to just after we first met? The one where you got absolutely hammered on Guinness and ended up doing a fish impression in the middle of the street". Something random was perfect she thought. There was a pause before the answer came back "The Myton and Mermaid, Elephant and Castle. Xi, it's me Dee for fuck's sake!"

"Oh Dee thank God. Are you ok? Where are you? I'm having the worst fricking morning imaginable!"

"Well at least you haven't just had to do what I've just done Xi. I'm stuck somewhere close to High Wycombe. Everyone and his bloody dog is looking for me. Nowhere is safe. I don't know what to do!" Xi almost wanted to tell him straight the shit she was now in because of him but thought better of it. She was a survivor of the system and could get through this. Unlike Dee, who was the softer, more sensitive product of a pretty decent upbringing. *But then, how well did we really know anyone?* Xion thought to herself. *People are brought into your life just to let you down, right? That's why you trust no one. Look what Dee's now done to your life?*

"Just try and relax Dee. We need to come up with another plan. London is out. I have people after me".

"What?? Shit, I'm so sorry Xi. I…"

"It's fine, I'm fine, for now. But we need to regroup somewhere. Do you think you could hitch a ride South? As far South as you can?"
"Xi, my face is on the news everywhere! If I try and hitch a ride and they spot me, I'm totally screwed mate!" Xi could hear his voice gathering that pace that meant he was about to break down into tears.

"Ok, OK, get it together. What about the coach station. High Wycombe has a pretty big one from what I remember. You can purchase a ticket online with your phone. But Dee, you're gonna have to ditch that phone I'm afraid. Once you are on the coach I mean. Take out the SIM card and snap it in two. Then switch the phone off. They could well be tracking you. I'm pretty sure I got hacked. I had to leave my flat".
Xion thought for a moment, realising the danger they would be in if someone was listening to their conversation right now.

"Xi, where am I heading to?"

"Right, go to the place your mate Pav loves but never lived there. He's always a right royal dick about it too".

"What? Xi what are you on about?"

"Ok Dee, I'll see you soon yeah?" And she hung up before he could say anymore. Xion could only hope his nerd brain would figure out where she meant.

David started at the phone in disbelief. *What the is she on about? I don't know anyone called Pav!* He thought, and then the penny dropped. *It was a clue! Clever Xi!* Thinking quickly, he knew she wanted him to go as far South as possible. That would take him to the coast of course. *But Pav? Royal dick. Ah! Royal Pavilion in Brighton!* He chuckled to himself as he went online on the phone and booked a coach ticket to Brighton. There was one leaving within the hour. All he had to do was make his way into town. Looking down at his clothes, David hoped that he could still go unnoticed with everything he was wearing.

The town centre was close by and David marched with a sense of purpose, feeling confident after having talked with his friend. He felt really bad that she was now in trouble too, but then, she was always getting herself in and out of trouble and knew how to take care of herself. David on the other hand could do nothing more than put one foot in front of the other and pray.

Thirty One

Hashaan first moved one of his bony hands which had hit the wall first, twisting and breaking on impact. Concentrating on each joint, he slowly clicked each one back into place under the white smooth skin. The hideous popping sound they made reverberated along the corridor. He then continued the process throughout his body, turning and jerking until after just a few minutes he was sitting upright just below the point at which he had been flung as if a ragdoll being discarded in rage. Once his breathing had slowed and the initial stabbing sensations had subsided, Hashaan's face was once again split in two with a wide, feral-like grin. *This vampire is a strong one, clearly high up the chain. No other being has been able to move with enough strength and speed to do that to me. Not in a thousand years. His blood will be the most sacred. I will become truly a God with his powers inside me!*

He stood, the last of his snake-like bones clicking back into place in his legs, the cape falling smoothly down his tall and lean body. Had the vampire known more than just a little about his kind, Hashaan was sure this magnificent creature would have had the strength to crush his skull to dust with no hesitation. But he was ignorant to the physiology of the Afeaa Shaytan, the Serpent

Demons, and Hashaan was confident this vampire would never get the opportunity again.

Sliding along the corridor, Hashaan stopped at one of the guards lying on the floor in a corner. Lifting the body up easily, he ripped off the clothes first, before extending long talons and slicing at the scalp, removing the top layers of skin that held the poor man's hair in place. He then tilted his own head back, his lower jaw extending out so far he was able to lift the dead guard above his head upside down and then with horrific crunching sounds, began devouring the body. Blood trickled down from muscle and sinew being exposed and chewed, not to mention other juices from the brain and organs which dribbled onto his cloak. But Hashaan paid no heed to the mess he was creating. There was no one left living in here and he would get one of his subordinates to clear up the mess when they disposed of the other bodies in the cells. He need nourishment to fully recover from the crushing trauma done to his limbs. Within moments, the guard had been totally devoured, leaving just a pile of torn clothes, bloodied hair and a pool of blood.

As he retracted his jaw and gave his own neck a loud crack, Hashaan sighed contentedly. He was already starting to absorb not only the physical parts of this guard, but also his memories. It always gave him a slight euphoric feeling as he languished over the memories of friends, families, lives both lived and lost, of all he feasted on. It was the only way he could feel what it would be like to have a family of his own. Sometimes, Hashaan would have brief flashbacks of a life before he was elevated to this glorious form, a life that saw him with a wife and children of his own. It did not end well. In fact, they were his first meal, followed by most of the small village which he then shared with his new family. But this was such a long time ago, in a land that was entirely destroyed by its own greed and ancient expansive desires. They were worshipped then as Gods of the underworld, feared and revered. Now humans had become dangerous, with weapons and ways that could easily put a stop to their existence if they were not careful. But with this vampire's blood, Hashaan could rise up again, and all of them could be at the top of the food chain once more.

Turning, Hashaan glided along to the entrance of the segregation wing. The door was not only opened, but with such force that it hung at a slight angle as one of the hinges had come loose. As he passed through, he could hear faint jeering and odd shouting coming from somewhere in the distant part of the prison. His composure waned slightly as he thought of the vampire tearing his way through the wings. If any prisoner got out, all hell would break loose.

He sped up his pace through corridor after corridor until he came to the first mass wing, known as A Block. It was here that they housed some of the nastiest scum, the gangsters and murderers. But a few of the sounds that suddenly became evident were not those of malice, but rather of joy. For this bastard creature had released all the prisoners to roam freely in the open wing! Hashaan couldn't risk being seen, and so slinked back quickly into the shadow of the doorway, hoping none of the inmates saw him. Guards were desperately trying to gain some sort of control to the situation. Mattresses were being thrown from the upper floors onto the mesh netting, toilet rolls strewn everywhere and worse. Fights had started breaking out between what were obviously rival groups.

If Hashaan had his way, he would simply glide into the main part of the wing and rip a few of the inmates limb from limb. The rest would then cower before him and go back into their cells like the cowardly insignificant blood sacks they were. As his anger grew, officers in riot gear flooded into the space, rolling tear gas along the floor into the corners which quickly rose up to the upper levels. The noise dissipated just as soon as it had begun, with the inmates rushing back into their cells and closing the doors to stop the gas from causing anymore irritation. An unlucky few were lying motionless, dotted around the wing where they had fallen from blows inflicted by other inmates. Once all of the doors were closed, he put a hand to his face, his cowl covering up his head as he started walking purposefully into the main area of the wing. The officers immediately stopped what they were doing and stood to attention, well most. A few of the newer officers had yet to see who was really running the prison and looked a little confused, angry almost at this apparent intruder storming into their business.

"All back under control, Sir. No problems here" stammered the leader officer, a short plump guy in his late 50s with an over red face indicated years of drinking heavily. Hashaan looked around at the mess. "Get a few of the ring leaders to clear up the mess made here. If they refuse then you know what to do. Simply mark their cell doors and my...subordinates will collect them later. As for these souls lying here. Take them out into the yard and leave them there. Once done, I need everyone to do a clean sweep of the prison. We have another escapee, but this one is dangerous, and incredibly precious. He will not go down easily and if all you can do is let me know where he is, that is enough. Do not engage with him directly as he will surely kill every last one of you without even breaking a sweat. Do you understand?"

"Yes Sir, of course. But these inmates here..." He pointed at the poor men still out cold, "Will they be OK out in the cold?"

"You do not need to worry about these. We will take care of them".

And with that, Hashaan glided past them and out the other end. The best thing he could now was to get back to the cameras and try to spot where this vampire had gone, and what exactly he was up to. Just as he was about to exit the wing, Hashaan noticed another body lying motionless just off to his right. As he got closer, he spotted a piece of metal sticking out of the inmate's neck. This one was clearly dead. He smiled that wickedly snake-like grin. *Oh good* he thought to himself, *the perfect snack*. And with that, he picked up the body with ease, carrying it away with him to the control room.

Thirty Two

As Xion ended the call with David, she was wondering if she would ever get the chance to meet up with him in Brighton. It was all well and good trying to think in baby steps as people said, but for her that would mean plucking up the courage to get up out of the seat and venture out into the street. She would then have to somehow get to the station without being seen, climb aboard a bus or train – again without being seen - before praying that she made it all of the way there.

The problem at the top of her list, however, was her hair. She loved the shocking pink but Xion needed to cover up the standout hairstyle if she was to make it safely through the station, let alone to Brighton. They knew what she looked like, but Xion had no idea who to look out for. These were obvious professionals who had just shot an innocent taxi driver in cold blood, causing a road accident right in the heart of a busy city which was now very likely sealed off and surrounded by emergency vehicles. It would be full of paparazzi by now too and either one of those was not something Xion could afford to bump into. In any other scenario police would be a warm welcome and may well be able to offer some kind of safety for her. These killers would not dare come close to such a scene after all. But for Xion and her shady past, the more underground she could go right now the better.

Taking a deep breath, she rose slowly from the table that been her refuge for the last hour and looked for the toilets, hoping for another backdoor she could slip out of. As with the previous coffee house opposite her flat, this one too had toilets out by the kitchen. She made her way confidently over to them just as a guy came in through the front door. wearing all black and with a searching glance. Forcing her gaze out of the main window, she could see two other guys and a woman, also in black. *Shit!* she thought, *these are the bastards looking for me!* and she darted into the girl's toilet.

It seemed an eternity for her, waiting in the cubicle. She had started shivering uncontrollably, waiting for the woman to come in and put a bullet into her chest as she sat on the toilet. But no one came in. Five minutes passed, then ten and still nothing. Were they waiting for her to come out? Whatever the outcome, David needed her and if truth be told, she also needed him, if only to keep her from going insane. Gently, Xion pulled back the latch on the cubicle door and inched it open. It was a small toilet, with very little space and there was no one on the other side. She washed her hands out of habit, before opening the door into the main seating area. Again no one was waiting and staff and customers were just going about their lives. Peering around a corner, Xion had a good view of the outside through the main window. The killers had gone. But they couldn't have been far away. The only chance she had was to try and exit through the back as before, then double back on herself. She could then try and get to the back of the station which was only a few blocks away.

She then froze. Her hair was still a right giveaway! *Shit Xi, get it together!* she scolded herself. As she glanced to her right, she noticed the staff coats and bags hanging up just in the entrance to the kitchen. Most looked like men's jackets and far too big for her, but there was a small yellow bomber jacket hanging there with a green beanie draped over it. Trying not to get caught up in the guilty feelings of stealing from someone that was barely getting paid enough to live as it was, let alone having a nice jacket, Xion grabbed both items and made for the back door visible at the back of the kitchen. Luckily, it was empty and the door was wide open. She quickly donned the beanie and zipped the jacket up to the neck before rushing out into an alleyway. A young, tall skinny guy was putting some black bags into a large blue bin and he turned, briefly glancing at her. Xion was positive that she had been caught out and stopped dead fast, but the man simply turned away, saying casually "Hey Katie, off your break are you? See you in thirty, okay?"

"Uh huh" mumbled Xion as she passed him, hoping that her voice came out a neutral as possible. He didn't respond and she was back out onto the street again, feeling slightly better camouflaged.

With her head down and hands stuffed tightly in the jacket pockets, Xion walked first right, before taking a left and seeing the station entrance loom up in front. Again, there seemed no sign of her pursuers, but Xion did not want to take any unnecessary chances. She crossed the street and ducked into a small side lane, hoping it would give her access to the side of the station. Thankfully, there was a sign for deliveries which took her into a large open space. The sounds of people chattering as they rushed to get on the platforms was comfortingly audible to Xion as she followed the bustling noise through a set of large doors. She then found herself in the main forecourt. *If anyone knows exactly where to look, I'll be a sitting duck!* She thought fearfully, not wanting to take another step into the throng of travellers. But she had no choice.

Thirty Three

If there was ever a place where one could really feel important, it had to be the Commons Chamber in Westminster. The luxurious aroma of old oak polished to perfection; the smell of leather that added an extra feeling of style and grace to the slight crackle sound as you sat on the racing green benches; the slightly cool air bringing all the senses together in a cacophony of knowledge that something great was going to be discussed and decided, something that could very well shape society for years to come. Of course every politician hoped for a positive legacy left behind within these walls, but very few got their way.

But Charles was different. If there was one thing he possessed in far greater quantity compared to the other snots, it was drive. And when he spoke, people listened. Unfortunately for him, this had ruffled the jealous feathers of too many above him and had meant there being very little chance of Charles McNeil going any further in his political career. But he had something else in mind, something far greater. And today's session was all about planting the first of many seeds in these snots' trumped up and over fed brains.

The phone call of earlier that morning had really shaken him up. He had never been directly threatened like that before, because he had always done a good job. Or so Charles had thought. The problem was he had to rely on other less competent people to carry things out for him. He couldn't be expected to do everything himself, he was far too important for that. But this tour of the prisons had to be undertaken by himself. Charles McNeil MP had to show his true superiors that he was not afraid to roll his sleeves up and get stuck in for the sake of the future, for his stake in this operation. After all, they were paying him handsomely for it.

Farling had been an absolute expert in sorting out offshore accounts for them both so that their finances, which were scrutinised by the bloody media and watchdogs, looked modest enough for politicians and their assistants. But Charles was gradually starting to trust his assistant Farling less and less of late. He was most splendid at his job, but Charles had a knowing feeling in his gut that Farling was keeping secrets from him, secrets that involved The Society. It was almost as if two lines of communication were being drawn.

The first was to him from the Master and other scary, shadowy figures, which were more often than not relayed second-hand by Farling. The second lines of communication, Charles felt, were being drawn between Farling and The Master directly. But he had zero evidence. *Now if Farling should have an unfortunate accident whilst they were touring one of the prisons, now that could work*, Charles thought to himself as he sat in the one of the benches second row in, waiting for session to start. *Some dreadful fall perhaps from one of those balconies surrounding the central area inside a prison wing. If he was indisposed and no longer of any real use, he would most likely be taken away and drained as another product. His superiors wouldn't want what he knew getting out after all.* Charles smiled, suddenly realising that the chamber had filled up and a familiar politician was smiling back at him.

"Looking to spend more of the taxpayers' hard earned cash today are we McNeil?"
Randolph, MP for Sutton shouted a bit too loud as he tried to communicate across the bench through the low hum of voices.

"Well you would know all about that, wouldn't you Randolph. How is that lovely brand new Aston Martin DBX toilet seat treating you that you claimed on your party expenses last month? Keeps your posterior very comfortable I bet". Charles was shocked that Randolph thought he could get away with such things. As such, he was now under investigation, as were so many by the Parliamentary Watchdog at the moment. But nothing would come of it. They all felt they needed such vehicles to stand out as important representatives of their constituencies. After all, could anyone expect to turn up in anything other than a top of the range electric vehicle? I think not.

Randolph chuckled a little too nervously as the chamber started to quieten with the entrance of the party leaders. Then everyone stood as the Speaker entered, taking her high seat at the near end. She motioned for everyone to be seated, before announcing the start of proceedings.

Charles had earlier given Farling his proposal to give to Dennis Leary MP, his party leader. He hoped he would be first up, as he needed to get things going and head out to the first of many prisons. He was eager to show The Society that he could be relied on.

"Madam Speaker," started Dennis, "if I may, I would like to put forward a proposal by Charles McNeil MP, Minster of State for Prisons".

"You may proceed, Mr Leary" came the curt response. It was all of this pomp and ceremony that Charles loved. Nowhere else would he ever feel this important in life. Well, not yet anyhow.

"Thank you Madam Speaker. If I may be so bold, it may be better and more succinct coming from Mr McNeil himself?"

"If you so wish. Mr McNeil, state your business for the people of the Chambers".

Charles was slightly taken aback by the sudden invite to speak directly to his peers. Slowly he stood, clearing his throat which had suddenly gone rather dry. "Madam Speaker, Mr Leary, Ministers of the House of Commons, may I put it to you in nothing but the gravity of tones the shock I feel we are facing within our prison walls".

This is my moment! he chuckled to himself. "For too long now, we have been under resourced, underfunded and as a result prisons have for the last decade been given poor audits, whilst crime is going up and these same establishments are thus becoming barely manageable. They are volcanoes ready to explode, with riots constantly breaking out and with neither the resources nor the ideas readily available to quell them effectively".

He paused for effect as there was a rumble from across the benches. Everyone in this chamber knew of what he was saying and he was successfully building up the anger and frustration. "With the cost of living at a record high, focus is being shone upon what the public is calling a waste of money being spent sending offenders behind bars to serve sentences, for offences everyone knows they will only continue to commit once they are freed. We need to come up with radical strategies that will deter these criminals from offending again".

At this last sentence the noise from the chambers rose a bit more; unrecognisable grumblings that didn't appear to be on his side. Then an opposing MP stood up from his bench and the room went quiet. "It is fine telling us here what we already know, Madam Speaker, but maybe Mr McNeil can kindly get to the point and impart us with a little wisdom of his marvellous plan for prison reform. Along with a bit of money-conjuring magic perhaps? Or does he want us to use some of the school budgets? Or NHS money even?"

Now the chamber was alit with noise, a cacophony of muttering showing apparent support of Charles mixed with an agreement of Henry Standish's comments. He was, after all the Shadow Finance Secretary.

After the Speaker had calmed everyone down, Charles continued. "Madam Speaker, may I make it plain that the funds are in fact available and as most of the prison system is financed by outside investors, our Shadow Finance Secretary need not bother himself with such information he is not actually party to, being Shadow Finance Secretary. Unless of course I awoke this morning to a new government leading the country".

Laughter from his side of the chamber. *Bold and risky, but they seem to like me.* Charles was happy about that vibe. Good theatre was what this was all about after all. "I propose a series of visits, to be made personally with my assistant and a small team of experts, to carefully chosen prisons across the country. I can see first-hand both the current state of things, as well as come up with actual solutions which I can then bring back to the table here, so to speak. I have the backing of my party members, but of course Madam Speaker, I am fully aware that I also need the support of the House".

Before the Chamber could erupt once more, the Speaker banged her gavel down hard. "So that we can move on swiftly to the next matter at hand, may I please ask for a raise of hands in favour of Mr McNeil making such a series of visits to prisons and thus drawing up proposals for reform?"

He needed a two thirds majority and it didn't look like it was happening! Not even some of his own party were raising their hands at first. The blood started draining from his face. But then, one by one, as if in some kind of trance they all slowly raised an arm in agreement. It was odd for Charles felt sure at first that he had lost. Some of the MPs appeared to be looking up into the gallery seating, their expressions deadly serious before raising their hands. As Charles glanced up, he thought he could just make out a few black shadows of figures standing at the back of the public gallery. Or maybe it was his imagination playing tricks on him.

Then the Speaker concluded by saying "As there appears to be more than two thirds majority to the agreement of this, I pass the proposal as carried and can proceed immediately, with Mr McNeil to return to session within the next four weeks with his recommendations for reform. Thank you Mr McNeil you may be seated".

Charles sat nervously down, also overwhelmingly relieved that his plan could take effect. The Master would be pleased and would hopefully cease to threaten him and his family further. The rest of the session became just a blur of garbled and inconsequential drivel to Charles. He could not wait for the end and was one of the first to file out into the lobby, across the hall and through into his office. He closed the doors behind him and made for his desk and the expensive Brandy. But just as he was about to sit down, a deep, rasping voice from behind him made him almost jump out of his skin, turning the air cold.

"Well done. Of course, it needed a little persuasion from the gallery, but well done, nonetheless. I expect you to be making your way to the first prison in the morning. You will go to the North first. There are a few things that need clearing up as there has been some commotion of late. I want you to smooth things over there and report back to me".

After what seemed like an eternity, Charles seemed to gain use of his limbs again and turned around to face the door, but there was no one there. He poured himself a very large drink, downing it in one before calling Farling in to plan their departure first thing in the morning.

Thirty Four

Shyanne was positively livid. They had been traipsing around random streets for almost an hour now. *How could we have lost the stupid girl!* She thought as one of her team ducked inside yet another coffee shop and out again, shaking his head. They needed to rethink, that was for sure.

This Xion girl had the upper hand and there was no way she could double back to her flat, not now. Police had cordoned off most of the area around the streets leading to it anyway after the shooting. The team admitted that it had been a careless error of judgement shooting that taxi driver. And then there was the police officer. Shayanne actually enjoyed that particular kill. There was nothing more satisfying than watching the light vanish from the eyes of victims; of being present in that exact moment when they pass from this world. That was why she just loved using her beautiful knives. Guns were sloppy, lazy things wielded by careless and stupid thugs. *Present company* included she smiled to herself. As for the taxi driver, of course, they were aiming for the girl and using the mufflers meant no one heard anything up until when the taxi slammed into the lamp post. But now it was a crime scene, and this meant it was going to be hard for their target to do much else other than lay low. But where was she?

"We are running out of time. She has to be somewhere close by and that stupid pink mop of hair has to give her away. Unless she put on a hat. Shit! Come on guys, this is getting ridiculous!" Shyanne took a deep breath and took out her phone, checking the time. She knew for sure that they were on borrowed time now. If they wanted to get paid and avoid a face-to-face meeting with their employers, they would have to act fast and come up with some kind of result.

Grant, the older of the group tried to placate the situation with some kind of reasoning. He was definitely the calm one of the group, but also the most unhinged when it came to the 'wet' work. "We know she was trying to contact or had contacted by this David character", he surmised. "They were planning some kind of meet, which means she has to get to Euston station to catch his train coming in. He did get on that train, right? And Green Eyes was waiting for him…right?"

"I'm sorry Grant, I must have left my crystal ball at home, because I only appear to know everything you mere mortals do!" Shayanne practically screamed at him. "She may not have taken her laptop, but she would have taken one of her smartphones, that's for sure. And she's helping him somehow, we also know that. Clever girl this one. But she has to find her way out of the city somehow. Yes, let's get to the station. We can cover the exits there".

With that, Shyanne didn't wait for any kind of response or agreement from the others, she simply turned on her heels and marched off with some invisible compass leading her towards Euston Station. Nothing the rest of the killers could do but to follow her.

They were much closer than they first thought, for after a few turns the station entrance loomed up at them from across the road. It was here that Shyanne split them up to cover more ground and for better surveillance. Grant and Freddie went round to the left of the station towards the coach park. If Xion was to try and catch a bus out, they could apprehend her before she made an escape. Shyanne and Henryk went to the right, looking for a less conspicuous way onto the platforms and a high spot with which to gain optimum viewing. With luck, they could hook up with Green Eyes as he got off the train.

He was immaculate at disposing of bodies. There would be no trace of this David character, at least not on the train anyhow. It would be days, perhaps weeks before his body would be found, lying broken and half eaten by foxes somewhere trackside between here and the North. This gave Shyanne a little amusement, thinking how this little

weed had caused so much grief in so short a space
of time. It was unfortunate that Green Eyes alone
would reap the rewards of that kill. She hoped to be
able to deliver the girl to their employers alive. All
the secrets in that candyfloss-covered head of hers
would fetch a pretty price. If not, she would take
great pleasure in making her watch her own
intestines slowly slipping out of her belly onto the
ground, unable to scream for the small incision
made to her throat, disabling her voice box. That
was Shyanne's particular signature. That and
burning. She liked to burn too, like to hear the
sizzle and smell the flesh cooking, the writhing of
the bodies before their hearts gave out and that all
important light of life leaving the eyes.

"Boss?" came Henryk's gruff pitch, bringing her
back. "We need to be getting into positions, yes?"
Coming from Belarus, Henryk had spent the first
few years here in England setting up a successful
trafficking business, using his contacts both in
Lithuania and Denmark to ship young girls by boat
over to sell both as sex workers and factory
operatives. It was one of the biggest lines of
business and one he was always proud of boasting
about. Shyanne could always hear him saying the
same sentence, "Why do drugs? Human beings
much better, much more money in a product you
can use more than once, right?" He would always
finish with a laugh and then a toast of shitty
homemade vodka from his hipflask, showing the

few teeth he had left from all of the fights he had been in, defending his "merchandise". But, as with any business that is doing well, it is all too easy to get bored and in need of a challenge. And so Henryk decided to become a gun for hire. With very little, if any, morals to speak of, he fitted right in.

Grant and Freddie were a different ball game. They had come into the fold as a pair, although Shyanne knew very little about Freddie. He came only on the trust of Grant, and Grant had almost as bad a thirst for sadistic torture and killing as Shyanne. They had both apparently been dishonourably discharged as ground Troops from the Army, after reports of rape and torture in Iran. Tales of mass graves and the burning of schools were seen to most as mere urban myths, but Shyanne knew these arseholes were right there in the middle of it all. Grant at least made no bones about denying it. He relished in the stories of his atrocities. But Shyanne had just as many demons.

Originally from Sudan, she had witnessed her entire family slaughtered when she was just six years old. She had hidden in a cupboard for days, before living on the streets for the next eight years of her life. She had sold her body for food, stolen every day to survive and clothe herself, before finally falling into a gang of mercenaries that trained her to kill. Being small, she could squeeze into the tightest of gaps, open windows and she was so quiet, no target would hear her coming up behind them. But no one had expected her to get such enjoyment out of torturing her victims before disposing of them. She developed horrible ways of killing for one so young. And now, at just 28 years old, Shyanne was both feared and revered on the dark scene here in England. She practically named her price and was never short of work. That was when her current employers asked for her services, and to gather a small team to help find these two criminals. Just remembering that deep rasping husk of a tone as he laid out his instructions made Shyanne shiver. She, no they need to get this done so she never had to hear that voice again.

Finding an open door to the side of the main station building, hidden within a small side street, Shyanne led the way through and into a large room strewn with tables and chairs. It looked like some kind of recreation area for staff, with a steel sink at one end of a worktop and a fridge in the far corner. A couple of jackets lay over the backs of chairs and Shyanne pointed them out to Henryk. He went over quickly and gathered them up. High visibility orange, with "Rail Network" printed in black on the back, they would be a perfect disguise for getting into the station proper. The killers donned the jackets - both a little big but perfect for concealing their clothes and weapons belts within - and made their way out the other end and into the station. As they opened the door and walked out it was clear just how difficult this task could be, for there were people everywhere!

Looking up, Shyanne saw what seemed to be dozens of CCTV cameras pointing in every conceivable direction. "Right," she said to Henryk, "I want you to go find the control room for these cameras. And hang on…" she ducked back into the canteen and came out with a couple of walkie talkies. "These have been set to channel 1. We'll be able to hear chatter, so this should help us". They all had earpieces for communicating with each other. Shyanne instinctively touched hers as she spoke to Grant and Freddie "Grant, Freddie, have you found your sweet spot yet?"

Grant came back almost immediately "Yep. Got eyes on everyone here. Not that busy actually. Freddie's taken one end and I'm at other. You ready over there?"

"Almost. The main priority is this Xion. But if for some remarkable reason the runaway shows up instead of Green Eyes, then things will get, well, more exciting for us. Just hold your positions. Henryk is going to the control room to cover the CCTV".

It was then, as Henryk made his way smoothly across the main concourse that Shyanne glanced up to see the arrivals. Everything seemed normal except for one train, showing delayed but with no arrival time next to it. Frowning, she took a deep breath and went over to a bored looking guard at one of the barriers before stopping. Even in this vest she could have her cover blown as she just did not feel like train staff. Instead she backtracked, switching on the walkie talkie to a low level and putting it to her ear. "…as soon as we can, Simon. For now, just keep the board as it is so as not to cause panic. As soon as we get word from the police we can put out some kind of message, ok?"

"I'm sorry. I've just come on shift" Shyanne spoke softly into the walkie talkie. "Please can someone repeat what's happening, in case a passenger asks?"

"Hi, yes of course. As I just explained, there has been a fatality on the train, on the mainline from Glasgow. Now we don't have a lot to go on at the moment and we have been advised not to say anything at this stage, but it looks as if the fatality has happened in a carriage and not on the tracks, as we would expect. The train has stopped at High Wycombe. As soon we know more we'll let everyone know, but for now just keep your walkie talkie on. I don't want to have to keep bloody explaining myself, so I need everyone to help me out and pass the word around to any crew member without a radio".

Shit, this is not like Green Eyes, thought Shyanne. *He would not be this sloppy, unless something has upset his plans.* Trying to think, she touched her earpiece again, "Grant?"

"Yes boss?"

"I'm going to need you to contact Green Eyes. He'll talk to you better than he would me. I need an update on his situation. Then report back to me, ok?"
"Sure, I'll try his number now".

All Shyanne could do now was to focus on the business at hand. Hopefully this Xion had not thought to put on a hat!

Thirty Five

Adam had hoped that by opening the cell doors of the main wing, he would have bought himself some time. But as soon as they were out, the inmates instantly starting turning on each other as if feral beasts. Two went down immediately from blows to the head. They lay unconscious in the middle of the floor whilst others simply stepped over them. No one was interested in helping, only in causing maximum damage either to each other or the building itself. Within minutes, mattresses were being tossed over the railings and good old toilet paper streamed across from one side of the balcony to the other, some of it lit on fire. Adam simply stood for a moment, in utter amazement at the sheer lack of intelligence being demonstrated around him.

Then another inmate went down, blood gushing from his nose and, without even a thought, Adam was straight there, pulling the poor soul to one side as he sank his teeth into the neck. He quickly tried to gain some element of control, releasing his bite and letting the man sink fully to the ground. The taste was becoming too strong to overcome. Adam had fed too much these past 24 hours and so was becoming feral himself. If he didn't control his lust now, there would be absolute carnage. He checked for a pulse and found none.

Damn it! He screamed to himself, *now you've royally messed things up!* Acting fast, Adam snatched at a piece of metal, most likely a bit of bedframe that had been thrown over the balcony along with everything else. Silently apologising to this poor soul, he plunged the metal into the man's neck at the spot still showing signs of a vicious bite. As he laid the body down one last time and arranged the limbs into what he hoped what be considered a death pose, Adam glanced up to see a small and frail looking guy huddled up under the staircase, shivering and staring right at him.

This man was not wearing the standard prison gear, but instead was dressed in dark red tunic and trousers. There was something about the way he was looking at Adam. It was almost as if he was not shocked at all at either Adam's actions or the blood on this vampire's face. Adam wasted no time in rushing over to him amongst this chaos, grabbing his wrist and dragging him out through a side door. He ignored the man's protests, his struggles seemingly nothing in Adam's iron-gripped strength. Just as they cleared the corridor, turning left into the courtyard, Adam heard the voices of officers assembling from somewhere close by, the rattling of shields and equipment as they prepared for a breach. There really didn't sound like many. He hoped they would not be too injured in taking back control of the wing. But he had other things to think about.

Pulling the man into a small recess and behind some Biffa bins, Adam rounded on him, his face close so that this slight figure could get a full look at the oversized canines and glowing orange eyes. "Why are you not scared of me? You were shivering back there, but not because of me. Explain."

The man swallowed audibly before answering "You think I'd be scared of a mere vampire? I have seen so much, the likes of you are nothing more than a thistle or a nettle amongst a field of wildflowers. An annoyance yes, an irritant perhaps, but no more than that". He spoke with a strange accent, a man seemingly out of place in this century. Adam could not quite put a finger on it. He looked deeper into the man's eyes. As he did, he saw just a brief flash of yellow in them, before they went back to pale blue.

"Okay, now you've got my full attention, friend. So are you going to tell me who you are? You're not all human, the golden glint gave that away. You certainly don't talk like anyone from this century. You work here I take it? For this Serpent Demon?"

The man smiled "I'm not afraid. Not of you anyhow. I serve *them*. I have served for over two hundred years. I fear only their wrath for a job badly undertaken. You should fear them too…friend. They have eyes everywhere. They have been waiting for some…thing like you for a very long time! Let me show you, if you like?"

Adam did not like the way this was going. "Listen, I'm looking for someone. I'm not interested in whatever it is that is going on here. Well, mildly interested perhaps, but I have bigger fish to fry at present". The man looked confused. "What I mean is, I'm trying to find an inmate, a slight, insignificant looking young nerd of a guy called David Price. I was first told he had been sent to the VP Wing. Now I have heard from your boss that he is no longer in his cell, so to speak. Any of this ringing any bells at all?"

Adam found it hard to speak softly and calmly when the blood lust ran through his veins. It took most of his willpower just to stop himself from ripping everyone here limb from limb and bathing in the wonderfully warm, metallic richness. He had to try and focus on the matter at hand. The man thought for a second, before letting out a chortle. "Oh dear, I do remember this one. He was to become part of something great, but he somehow outsmarted us and disappeared into the night. No one has been able to find him for the last couple of days. But we are looking. And we will bring him back, preferably alive".

Adam couldn't believe what he was hearing. *Is this strange character lying to me?* Surely he knew the consequences of that. But if not, then David had apparently escaped and was on the run. He truly wasn't bloody here at all! How had this happened and how had Adam not known?

"Are you fucking kidding me?!" he yelled into the man's face, rage barely contained now.

"I can assure you that I am telling the truth. Now I can show you how he escaped if you like? It's just over here".

And the man stood, his frail form suddenly straightened and taller. His expression had also altered somewhat to one more confident and self-assured. Adam didn't like this. Things were changing fast and his hackles were definitely up.

This was supposed to have been a simple in and out plan. What the hell was going on in here?

"Ok" he simply said, his hackles definitely up now. "Lead the way".

Right in the centre of the courtyard was a round building. As far as Adam could tell from the front, it appeared to have no windows and only one door, a big oak affair that even he would find hard to break open. And yet David had managed to get out. The strange man, now walking almost as tall as Adam, seemed to have read his mind. "There is another smaller door to the side on the left. He escaped through there somehow unseen. But it is the room you'll want to see, trust me". Again, a weird feeling came over Adam as if his bestial side was trying to warn him of something unseen, something sinister laying inside that round wall.

On approaching the big oak door, the man produced a long iron key and turned the lock. The noise of the ensuing riot seemed far away from where he now stood, the walls thick and foreboding all around him. With a slight grunt, the man opened the door and ushered Adam inside. He was hesitant, every fibre of his being screaming at him to simply kill this evident butler of death and tear through the gates to the outside, where he now knew David to be. But then, was there something he needed to see in this chamber of a room?

Slowly, Adam moved inside and into the darkness. Even with his superb eyesight, he was failing to make anything out in the gloom, his hearing failing him just as much.

Then suddenly it was as if hands came from everywhere at once, pulling him to the ground despite his own unnatural strength and pinning him down. The oak door closed with a loud bang and Adam roared, a guttural sound that vibrated around the chamber. His hands were tied with a rope that burned his skin. And then a hood was placed over his head, also burning him and leaving him feeling totally incapacitated. The only thing that could have done this was not silver as everyone thought, but a wild herb called Mandrake. Before he could think any more on it, Adam felt the sharp prick of a needle and everything faded into blackness as he drifted off into what he could only think was a kind of sleep.

"Inform the Master at once that we have his prize. And string him up. Best we get on with draining him as soon as possible whilst he is weak". The man took the black cloak from one of the others and lay it around his shoulders, pulling the hood up. "It is wonderful to see the Old Ways at work still" he added, looking at Adam and lifting one of his arms to examine the burn mark on the wrist. "Be sure not to untie him. And cover the chains with Mandrake-soaked oil. If he comes to before his blood has been drained, we are all dead".

The hooded man opened the side door and silently left, leaving six other hooded figures to efficiently string Adam up by his ankles, using a small, curved knife to tear through his clothes. A needle was then inserted into his arm and deep into a vein, pumping more Mandrake tincture into his system, thus keeping him sedated. A smaller member of the group, what used to be the officer known as Janet, glided over to the side door and slipped through to the outside. As she closed the door behind her, a brief emotion passed her mind, one of sadness. It was gone just as quickly as it appeared, as if but a distant memory of another existence. She walked across the courtyard to another door which led to the control room. The Master would be pleased, she was sure of it.

Thirty Six

Shayanne sat patiently looking out of the window at the top of a kind of storeroom which gave her a wonderful viewpoint over the main concourse. She could also clamber quickly back down unnoticed, should she spot either target. Commuters appeared to be thinning slightly which was just as well. Touching her earpiece again, Shayanne checked in on the others. "Henryk, are you in the control room yet?"

"Yes boss. Had to incapacitate a couple of guards in here, but all good".

"Damn it Henryk! Not everyone who crosses paths with you needs to be dispatched you know. There are other ways".

"Boss, they're just sleeping. They'll wake with a headache, but no more. I'm not a total monster, not like Freddie".

"Oi!" came the response to that dig "careful matey. Remember, we all know what you did for a living before this". Grant also sniggered slightly at this.

"Cut it out children!" Shayanne shouted "Focus! I'm up to my tits with how this assignment is heading and I want this wrapped up tight before the day is out, do I make myself clear?" They all concurred.

"Right, Henryk, keep your eyes peeled for a small girl looking a bit shifty. She'll look as if she's lost, not sure which direction to go. Keep a particular eye on anyone staring at the arrivals board. Don't know if you all noticed, but it looks like Green Eyes is a tad delayed. Totally unlike him and it could mean our friend David has had the fucking luck of the Gods. We could be a man down".

"Boss, there are a few people looking up at the board, but one seems a bit edgy. Hard to see from here on the screen but looks like a girl wearing some sort of puffer jacket and a beanie. You see anything from where you are?"

Sure enough, the girl he was talking about came into view, although hard to make out as she was standing close to the storeroom building with her back to Shayanne. She then took a few steps forward, checking her phone as if expecting a call or text. Placing it back in her pocket, the figure started towards the far end of the concourse.
"Can you see her face?" Shayanne asked Henryk. "There are a few others also apparently staring up at the delayed train notice".

"Nah boss, I've got a feel about this one, but I'll keep peeling my eyes".

"Fuck me, I hope not. You'll not be able to see anything!" Grant joked at the bad English.

"What you mean tosser?" Henryk replied, a little riled up at Grant and Freddie's constantly jibes at his English. He had taught himself and was proud at the speed at which he had command of the language thus far. He loved the way the English felt the need to never quite say exactly what they meant, instead using strange riddles and puzzles.

"It's "keep my eyes peeled, as in peeled back, like wide open" Shayanne corrected, before adding "Grant and Freddie. If you can't focus on the job at hand then you are of no use. Being of no use makes you a liability and all liabilities will be dispatched swiftly. Am I making myself even the tiniest bit clear? Now let's work as a team and get this done!"

"Boss, do you want one of us to make our way over there and check this girl out?" came Freddie's gruff tone.

"No, you both stay there. If this is the target then she could just as likely try and catch a bus out than hop on a train. Henryk you keep watching the cameras and I'll tail this one. By the way Henryk, did you get through to Green Eyes?"

"No boss, he not picking up. This is very strange for him. We have to think about possibility of him no longer in the game, yes?"

Shayanne sighed deeply, "I think you may be right. There is something more to this David character it seems. He will not be making his way here. Let's concentrate on the girl and she can tell us where he is going. If it is this puffer jacket and beanie, then she keeps checking her phone as if waiting for him to call or text. Right I'm going down".

There was a quiet snigger from either Grant or Freddie. Shayanne swore under her breath. *Idiot children,* she thought to herself, *sooner I'm done with them, the better. They'll get us all killed.*

Making her way back out onto the main concourse, she glanced again at the arrivals board. Still no estimated time of arrival and there had been no recent chatter from the walkie talkies. Slowly, Shayanne made her way over to a barrier and pretended to straighten it whilst looking around. The girl with the beanie truly did seem a bit lost but was slowly making her way towards to the bus station. Shayanne followed at a distance but was stopped by an old lady with a yappy little dog just as the girl rounded a corner. "Excuse me, but will there be another train bringing the passengers here if that train is delayed? It's just I'm waiting for my granddaughter to arrive from Stockport".

"Sorry but I have no further information other than what my colleague has stated on the public Tannoy system. Please listen out for further announcements. Now if you would excuse me". Shyanne muttered without even looking at the elder woman.

"Oh, well I'm not sure I like your tone of voice young lady. You at least look at me when talking", huffed the old lady, the small dog yapping a little too close to Shyanne's ankles.

Without so much as a thought, Shayanne lent in close to the lady and spoke very quietly in her ear "I am going to walk away now. I want you to know just how close both you and your mutt have come to breathing your last breaths. Should you even so much as look at me again, I will end you both and your granddaughter will never find your bodies. Have a good day, you stupid old crow".

Smiling sadistically, Shayanne did not look back as she made her way towards the corner she had seen the girl take. She knew the effect her comments had made.
As she rounded the corner towards the bus station, Shayanne could hear a small commotion and someone screaming for medical attention. It appeared someone had suffered some sort of fit. And the sound of a small dog yapping even louder.

Thirty Seven

"Did you hear about D Block? Massive commotion, like some sort of riot gone on over there".

Sam stood over the Table Football chatting to his friends as they watched the game unfold. It was always the same people playing and no one had the guts to ask if they could have a game. Just one of the many unspoken rules of the wing. Sam had been here for just over 6 months now, making a bit of a name for himself but in a good way, which was rather rare in prison. It could also be seen as slightly dangerous and so he had also somewhat befriended a guard or two. His friends were all part of the same class he attended, Creative Writing. It was also a music class and a great way to escape from the constant "watch your back at all times" vibe that went on everywhere else.

Sam had a degree in Creative Art and had also been a musician on the outside, so for him this was a nice, easy and relaxing way to spend his time. Without some sort of routine that didn't involve having to mix with the low life plastic gangsters in here, Sam was surer he would go mad and probably suicidal to boot. It was bad enough that they had taken his anxiety and depression medication away from him when he arrived. He had been made to wait a good two weeks before getting anything, and even then it was a case of going down to the medical hatch every morning to get the pills, standing in line with all the other reprobates that tried to hide theirs under the tongue so they could trade them for tobacco, or Burn as they called it in here. But Sam had soon fallen in with the right crowd, listening to the right conversations which had now not only got him onto the Creative Writing Diploma, but also into the church band. To be fair, it had been nothing more than a duo at first, consisting of Aiden, the lead singer with a voice not dissimilar to Elvis and Gary on the acoustic guitar and backing vocals.

When Sam first went to the Sunday service, the first things he noticed were the two talented blokes singing contemporary songs, but also the other instruments laying untouched alongside them such as a full size keyboard, two electric guitars and a set of drums. So as soon as the service was over and everyone was making their way to the back of the chapel for a cup of tea or coffee and a biscuit, Sam approached Aiden and Gary. They enthusiastically took him under their wing and he was playing the keyboard with them at the following service, rehearsing every Wednesday afternoon. Since then, Sam had also found a drummer amongst his compatriots, not to mention a young lad who played some basic bass guitar chords. And so this was now his routine; it not only kept him busy and out of eyeshot with the lowlifes on the wing, but also enabled him to pass the time doing things he loved with people he genuinely deemed friends.

The small wooden ball rebounded off a blue peg player and Sam caught it in mid-air. "Nice catch bruv" said one of the guys as he beckoned Sam to drop it in the middle of the table, thus starting the match again. Richard and Paul carried on with the conversation. "Yeah, I heard from one of the lads on medical watch that it was pretty bad. Someone had somehow gone in, unlocked the cell doors and practically coerced them all into a frenzy. But then he said half of the inmates had the shit beaten out of them and four were killed. Bit farfetched if you ask me mate".

"Well" added Sam "whatever it was that went down there, I heard we're getting a few of them in here until they sort the wing out. So watch your backs guys. We are separated from them for a reason after all. Now I don't have a beef with anyone, but that doesn't mean we're not having targets painted on our backs for merely being here in the VP Ward".

"Oh don't we know it! N.O.N.C.Es the lot of us aren't we?" sighed Richard. "I'm staying out of here and keeping to my floor during the socials".

Sam had to agree. They were on the top floor with cells on the same side. Sam shared with an older guy, a disgraced priest called Patrick. All in all, he was a decent enough chap, apart from particular tastes that had got him in here. He was frequently on suicide watch due to having severe depression. Sam had no sympathy for him and was sure there was more to his story than he had told, but in here everyone had secrets. The biggest and most terrifying of secrets seemed to be the disappearances. More and more cells seemed to lay unoccupied, which was probably why they were getting the new visitors.

Sam had known both Billy and David. They were nice guys and David had even helped him to suss out the keyboard in the chapel. It was a Korg which needed an amp to work. David had helped to set it up and even showed Sam how to work the amp, plugging in a mic too and setting the levels. They had got talking and found that they were inside for very similar things. The only difference being that for Sam, it hadn't been an accident.

His little brother Mikey was having the shit kicked out of him one night outside a club in Rotherham and it was only sheer chance that Sam had been grabbing a kebab with a few friends just opposite. Without even thinking, he had run across the road and landed a flying kick at one of the assailants, who fell heavily. Another guy came at him, but Sam knew how to fight and rounded on him faster, knocking him out with a single well aimed punch. The fight was over, but as Sam picked up his brother, he noticed the unblinking stare of the first guy he had floored, blood pooling from under his head. And so here he was, serving a 2 year sentence for manslaughter. He was lucky that there had been a lot of witnesses to the event and he was also lucky to be put in here on the VP Wing. But the other guys he had publicly embarrassed that night had friends in very low and far reaching places. And this worried Sam, especially when he heard some of them might well pay him a visit soon.

"Alright, time's up! Make your way back to your cells" came the familiar shout from one of the guards. Sam, Richard and Paul made their way up to the top floor towards their cells. As they approached the middle floor, Sam noticed that Slippery George wasn't in his cell. In fact, Sam hadn't seen him at all. "Hey guys, have you seen George? He's normally skulking around somewhere right?"

Paul shrugged "no, not seen him around for at least a day or two. But he was in long-term, which can only mean he's been moved out like David and Billy".

"And the rest!" came the scared response of Richard. "This is getting out of control now. And no one is saying a bloody thing about it either!" His voice was a little loud for Sam's comfort. "Look, keep your voice down. There's nothing we can do about it now. But maybe we can talk to some of the others arriving from the other wing. Maybe they know more".

"Good point" agreed Paul.

With that, they said their goodbyes and Sam went into his cell. Patrick was laying on his bed on the bottom bunk, peaceful in rest with his arms crossed over his chest. Sam had noticed that he had been very anxious of late, chattering about shadows coming to get him. Sam had taken no notice and instead had engrossed himself in a good book he was reading or watching the usual shit on TV. Every cell had a small portable TV which had a fairly decent picture. Sam had ordered a small portable radio from Argos not long after he had arrived. He thought he would have been able to have his MP3 player, but apparently there was the possibility of sneaking dodgy stuff on it. Sam only hoped it would not be pawned off amongst the officers before he could get it back.

As he switched the kettle on and got their plastic mugs out, putting coffee powder in his and a teabag for Patrick, Sam spotted a note on the table. Written in shaky handwriting, not like the beautiful script Patrick normally wrote with, it read:

Sam,
They are coming for us all. We are just meat in a farm. I think I may be next.
Don't let them come for you too. You have been a good friend to me.
God bless you.

Patrick

Panicking, Sam rushed over to where he thought Patrick was sleeping. His chest was not rising and there appeared to be something not quite right about how his head was sitting on his shoulders. Carefully, Sam touched Patrick's shoulder and gave him the slightest of shakes. As he did, Patrick's head lopped off to the side towards him, before continuing to fall away from his body altogether and land on the floor with a terrible thud. There was no blood to be seen and the torn flesh around the base of the neck seemed almost cauterised. Then hysteria kicked in and Sam yelled and thumped at the cell door until it was finally opened by two guards who stood in shock at the scene in front of them.

Thirty Eight

David's trainers were pretty thick with mud by the time he had crossed the two fields that led him onto a main road heading into town. But then, this would hopefully mean any evidence of blood still lingering on the soles would have been rubbed away. Just thinking about the blood brought back memories of this strange but deadly killer slumped in the toilet cubicle, a knife and fork sticking out of his head like some sort of grotesque Halloween attraction. And all that blood! Pooling out around him and covering the floor. The whole town would soon be closed off and teeming with press and police. And he was already on the news as it was. The moment of calm assurance Xi had given him less than half an hour ago had all but vanished and he was starting to panic again. She had said that she was in trouble too, which also meant she was on the run out of London with people following her. And it was all his fault. Well, unless she was being chased because of one the numerous internet hacks from the past catching up with her finally. *Highly unlikely*, he thought to himself.

The main road seemed to be alive with emergency vehicles, mainly police cars streaming past him, sirens blaring. A few fire engines and ambulances passed too, along with some very scary looking black unmarked BMWs with blacked out windows, blue lights flashing through the front grills and on one side of each of the headlights. *Just keep to yourself, keep looking down,* David told himself as he kept at a pace he thought would show nothing out of the ordinary. He pulled the brim of his baseball cap down a little further and moved onto the grass verge, sliding his shoes in an attempt to scrape off any excess mud. Once all of the vehicles had gone by, turning right towards the rail tracks, David crossed the road and picked up the pace a bit.

The bus station would be 10 minutes away max, turning left and then right. There weren't many people around as he slowly made his way into the waiting area and his coach to Brighton, via London Gatwick, was already there waiting. In case the coaches were being monitored, David waited until the last 5 minutes before joining the small queue. The driver was busy trying to fit a suitcase the size of small elephant into the only remaining space in the hold, which unfortunately wasn't giving up its freedom so easily. This meant that a member of staff from the station was forced to check tickets and to David's luck, this member was a young, spotty kid with no real conviction in anything more than when his next break was.

And so, with his E-Ticket checked without much actual checking, David climbed aboard and found a seat at the back. He took out the phone and, using the small metal pick that had come with it in the box (the nerd in him had instinctively put it in his back pocket back in the alley before disposing of the packing in one of the Biffa bins in the alley), he opened the compartment that contained the SIM card. It sprung out of its housing and fell onto the floor by his feet and David cursed out loud, but no one had heard him. The coach was half empty and for once, the rhythmic beat of an unrecognisable tune leaking from behind a pair of ear pods to the right of him did not bother David at all. He scrabbled down between the seats picking it up and was about to do as instructed by snapping it in two, when he stopped. As long as he didn't insert the SIM, once in Brighton he might be able to use it to his advantage. After all, that was his job right? To hack and trace himself? Putting both the phone and the SIM in his pocket, David slouched back into his seat.

Once the coach was underway and joining the link road to the M6, he actually found the bass from the headphones opposite soothing enough to help him drift off. Thoughts and dreams of meeting up with Xi in Brighton filled him with hope that at last this nightmare could be over. He could meet up with Adam, who could then hopefully explain to them all what exactly had been going on in the prison. *A lot of hope with no substance* he thought drily as the coach slowly reversed out of the station.

David woke with a start, his heart beating way too fast due to the bad dream he had been having. It was one of those totally irrational dreams, full of monsters and zombies chasing him through some weird, apocalyptic version of familiar places with seemingly no escape. The coach had halted and he suddenly thought they had been stopped by the police. He glanced out of the window to his right, sighing with relief at the stationary traffic next to him, the same on the other side of the motorway. What had jolted him awake was actually the driver explaining that there had been some kind of accident right where essential roadworks were being done. They were on the M25, the road to hell apparently and it certainly didn't disappoint.

"Once again folks, all I can do is apologise for this delay and to assure you that the estimated arrival time into Gatwick has factored in the possibility of roadworks. Unfortunately, however, not stupid people that can't read road signs and instead come to the harsh reality all too late that they are not in fact Vin Diesel or Nigel Mansell".

This got a few sniggers from passengers, whilst one or two of the younger passengers looked slightly confused at the middle-aged reference to an old racing driver. David's dad was a huge fan back in the day and had taken both him and his brother to many race days at Silverstone when he was younger. David smiled as he remembered being right behind the mesh trackside watching an hors d'oeuvre of a race involving trucks screaming around the track at impossible speeds, only to have one careen off right towards them. The thrill was intense and it hit the mesh just yards away from where they were standing. As the years went by, however, it had grown increasingly difficult to filter out the good memories from those violent, bitter ones he would rather forget. And these past few days had just added to them exponentially.

"As a result of the inevitable delays, I will not be stopping at the main station at Gatwick Airport but will instead go only to the drop off point at South Terminal. There will no longer be the scheduled stop of 15 minutes. Sorry for any inconvenience this may cause, but there are free shuttle buses to take you on further".

This last comment brought a few murmurs which floated angrily along the coach. But for David this was perfect! The less time spent at the airport, the less chance of being recognised. As the coach edged forwards, he felt himself unable to control his eyes from closing once more. Thoughts went straight to formulating some kind of plan once he got to Brighton. After all, he had nowhere to go and couldn't think of anyone they knew there. As it had been almost two hours since the last call, David opened his eyes and took out the phone. Turning it around in his hands, he started weighing up the odds of it actually tracking him. *But I need to know if Xi's okay!* He told himself, before putting the card back in and switching it on. He tried her number, but it didn't even go to voicemail, just disconnected. This meant that either her phone had been destroyed, which would severely mess up every plan going forward and leave him alone in Bloody Brighton, or she had a good reason to disconnect herself. *Maybe she was still trying to evade her own pursuers?* He thought to himself. He so wanted to send her a text to let her know he was okay and on his way there but knew that this would be suicide for both of them should it be intercepted. He quickly switched off the phone again and removed the SIM card. All he could do was hope once again that things would work out. He needed the toilet badly, but didn't want to get out of his seat, tucked up at the back in the dark corner of the coach as he was.

True to his word, the driver pulled into the drop off point at South Terminal and the coach stayed there for a mere five minutes with strict instructions for everyone to remain in their seats unless disembarking. He once again wrestled with cumbersome luggage that should not have been allowed due to Health and Safety reasons, the poor driver massaging the small of his back as he clambered aboard, closing the door. He then announced on the Tannoy system "next stop, Brighton, where we will first be calling at Patcham, followed by Preston Park, London Road and finally

Poole Valley bus station". And with that, he pulled the coach out onto the slip road and David knew he was only an hour away from seeing Xi and figuring everything out. *Please be okay and on your way Xi!* He prayed to himself.

Thirty Nine

Xion felt like a fish in a barrel as she made her way round to the bus station. Although confident of her camouflage beanie and jacket, this place was just far too open plan for her. And there weren't enough people moving around for her to try and blend in properly. She had not even bought a ticket yet as there was no information on buses that she could see from the main station. Xion had not had time to look online from her phone and she had hoped that there would have been a bench or seat off to the side somewhere out of eyeshot, but no. Thanks to recent bomb scares everything had been placed right in the middle of the space in Euston, like something out of a commercial for a Feng Shui magazine. *Keep it together Xi, keep it together,* she kept telling herself as the bus station platforms came into sight. Here it was a lot busier, probably due to the delay of the train David had been on. She shuddered slightly at the thought of what exactly had happened there, but this was one of many conversations they could have once arriving safely in Brighton.

Seeing a queue forming around one of the ticket booths, Xion quickly glanced up at the display boards, seeing a bus going to both Gatwick and Brighton in the next 10 minutes. It was already almost half full and the queue was long for tickets.

Without another thought, she pulled out her phone and went onto the website. The Wi-Fi service was pretty fast here and with just a few clicks she was purchasing her own E-Ticket. Why people felt the need to herd together without thinking for themselves, Xion just couldn't get it. *I mean, everyone had access to a frickin' smartphone nowadays right?*

The thought had barely left her brain before there was a scream and a young girl similar age to Xion fell to the floor, clutching at her arm. Blood was seeping over her fingers, but instead of going to her aid, everyone started running in all directions like chickens trapped in a coop with a fox.

Then she heard it, a popping sound, or was it more of a whooshing as something flew passed her, hitting the plaster covering of a pillar behind her to the left. She ran to the Brighton bus just as the driver closed the door. Banging on the window, Xion pleaded and pleaded with the driver to let her on. He clearly had second thoughts, wanting to get the hell out of the station and commotion. Shaking his head, face white as a sheet, he started to pull away and Xion spotted that he had left the baggage compartment open slightly. As if driven by madness, she dove in, covering herself with bags. It must have been on some kind of automatic closing system as it slowly closed in on her, but not

before she noticed a woman running towards the
bus.

With an orange hi vis vest over the top of a black
combat-style jacket and gun in her hand, there was
no mistaking her as the female killer. Two thuds
reverberated in the dark space, tell-tale signs of
desperate gunshots hitting the bus as it pulled
away. She could hear the frantic yelling of the
woman trying to get the bus to stop, but thankfully it
was to no avail. The bus driver slammed his foot
down on the accelerator, driving the coach forwards
as he yanked the steering wheel round to the right.
Passengers were yelling and screaming as bags
dropped from the luggage compartments overhead,
but the driver paid no heed.

The screams became muffled as the bus left the
station to newer, sharper sounds of car horns all
around her. The driver had obviously just kept his
foot to the metal as he sped out of the station,
hoping all other traffic would stop to let him get out
and onto the main road. Then came the sounds of
sirens, three distinct sounds signalling all
emergency services. As she lay there, Xion started
sobbing, both out of fear and helplessness. She
was used to all kinds of danger, but mostly these
were virtual online dangers. Nothing like this! She
was always the one in control, not hiding in some
boot like some refugee fleeing a war torn country.
But this was exactly how it felt right now. And all

because of David. No, this couldn't all be because of him, this had to be something bigger, right? *What did you bloody well get caught up in?* she could only think.

Shayanne ran as fast as she could after the bus, but the recklessness of the driver seemed to have worked in his favour. For now at least. Pressing a finger to her earpiece, she screamed at the others. "For fuck sake! Who fucking fired that shot? She was right there! A bright fucking yellow target. And now we have more bloody witnesses. This is a total shit show. I'm at the bus entrance. Get the car and pick me up. I'm on foot in pursuit."

And with that, she sped up her pace. Shayanne had managed to get a couple of rounds off at the baggage compartment section of the bus and with luck had hit the little bitch as she hid. But there were no guarantees. Traffic was bad, but the sounds of sirens meant only trouble if she kept up this running after the bus. It would draw too much attention. She tucked the gun back behind her belt and took off the orange hi vis. Spotting a café with tables outside, she made her way over to where a group had left jackets whilst going inside to order. *Typical tourists thinking that the world was a safe place whilst on holiday,* she grinned, smoothly picking up one of the ladies jackets and pulling it over herself in one motion. A soft cream colour, it looked expensive, but the length hid her clothes nicely, changing her look.

Emergency vehicles were streaming past her as she ducked down onto a side street, pretending to speak into her phone. "I'm on Jameson Street. Where the fuck are you all?"

There was a pause before Henryk answered "We have problem, boss. Grant and Freddie are out. Police and security have them boxed. I knew trigger happy wanker would mess this up. I'm on route back to car boss. Be there in five".

Shit! she cursed to herself. *That's three men now down, with prey so much less dangerous than they had encountered before. What was going on here?* Wishing she had done a more rigorous check on this Xion character, and David thinking about it, Shayanne knew they were now playing a longer game. The city would now be in lockdown and they needed to get out and rethink. She knew where this little snot stain was heading and they couldn't risk Gatwick. She had to make her way to Brighton, of that Shayanne was sure. Which meant if this David character was still alive, he too would be heading there. With no word from Green Eyes, she had to assume he too was out of the game.

A blue Ford Focus suddenly screeched to a halt by the entrance to the street and the passenger door swung open. "Get in boss" came Henryk's voice form inside and Shayanne jumped in. As it sped off, she glanced over at him with a stern look "I loved my SUV. Have you just fucking left it in the car park?"

"It would have drawn too much heat retrieving it boss. Better to use something less conspicuous, no?"

"Good thinking, I guess. I swear, I'm going to kill those idiots when I next see them. In fact, better that they just disappear. But we may have another problem to deal with soon".

"What you mean boss?" Quizzed Henryk.

Shyanne paused before admitting "I have also been reckless, my comrade. I stupidly put a couple of shots in the baggage compartment of the bus. Which means not only will the driver freak out when he gets to Gatwick, but it also means he may well have to deal with a dead body too".

"What you want to do next, then?"

"I say we head to Gatwick as fast as this piece of shit can get us there and wait for the bus to arrive. We can park up and wait. But stake out only! We are in a longer game now".

"No probs boss" came Henryk's reply as he turned right, following signs for the motorway. "Nice jacket by the way, suits you".

"Fuck you".

Forty

Charles McNeil MP couldn't sleep. This had become an occupational hazard of late, but tonight was different. Shadows seemed to move across his study walls even though there were no shapes or light movements to make them do so. It was a quiet, still night outside and no traffic reached the house. They were a good one hundred metres from the small country lane, up a twisting driveway lined with beautiful silver birch trees, old and gnarled and full of character.

The house itself was true testament to Charles' success as an MP, a five bedroom detached country property with enough land to keep Alex and any future little McNeils occupied. The garden had a large pond and small wooded copse at the back. Charles, with the help of his friend and fellow MP Ranleigh, had even managed to put up a tree house for Alex. All these were things Charles had never even been able to conceptualise having as a child. He wanted the very best for his son. And for Julie too. She was a doctor but had not practised for a good six years now. This made her slightly bitter towards David, but their joint love for Alex kept them together, for now.

Deep down Charles loved Julie with all his heart, but the deeper he was getting into this dark, lucrative side-line, the more he was planning an exit strategy. Not for him, but for his family. Charles himself was too far in it now, he knew that. All he could do now was to make his mark as greatly as he could, bank as much money as possible and then get his family the hell of here!

His phone bleeped, indicating an incoming message. He put down the glass of Brandy - a drink he was becoming far too fond of as of late - and picked the phone up. It was a message from Ranleigh:

Got time to chat? I know you'll be wide awake and I'm worried about you. Ran.

Charles dialled his number, but the ringtone on the other end echoed from outside his study window. "What the...?" he mumbled as he got up and opened the door of the study that led out onto the garden. There was Ranleigh, smiling at him from the patio area.

"See? I know you too well matey. Bloody cold tonight eh? Got time to chat?"

"Sure, come in Ran. You've just saved me from drinking the whole bottle of Brandy".

Ranleigh stepped in from the cold, dark garden and Charles noticed dark lines under his otherwise youthful eyes. He was a few years older than Charles but had been served a more sheltered upbringing. His father had been a Colonel in the army for over 20 years before retiring with a very fat pension. He now helped to train officers and Ranleigh had never wanted for anything. But something was troubling him as he didn't usually turn up out of the blue like this, not this late when he risked waking up Julie and Alex.

"Got to say old chum, not a fan of you swanning off to these prisons. You never really wanted this position in the first place, remember? Surely you could get Farling to do it, or some other mug. We need you here in Office. Shit is really hitting the fan with this escapee on the run and all. And with the budget coming up too, the public will want to know where the dosh is coming from to fund this jolly jaunt of yours".

Ranleigh stopped there, not wanting to go too far. After all, he was as much a colleague as a friend, whether off the record or not.

Charles took a deep, shaky breath and put his glass down. He wanted to explain everything so badly, but whoever he told would be dead before the night was out. And he liked Ranleigh. He didn't have many friends, actual friends he could count on. But how could he even begin to explain that he had been asked to set up bloodletting rooms in prisons across the UK? That he was being commanded to do so by an ancient order of creatures so terrifying they would haunt your dreams and make you piss your bed like you were five all over again! *Ran can't be part of this* Charles thought as he struggled with an alternative lie.

"Ran, I appreciate your candour but please. I have been instructed from up high to get this done. It's been long overdue. The prison system is literally bleeding money and figures for re-offending, once released, are higher than ever. I need to see for myself what's going on. The budget will thank me for this, you'll see".

"You are like a puppy with a new toy aren't you? Just can't let it go. You believe you can really make a difference in a world that requires us to ensure that things don't change. People don't want upheaval, they want to be wrapped in cotton wool and told that everything will be alright, that we are taking care of things even if we are in fact messing everything up!"

Charles stepped closer to his friend, his expression bringing on a pleading look. "Ran, you have no idea the pressure I'm under here…"

"True my friend but listen to me. If you start ruffling feathers in the Commons you will be used as a scapegoat and ousted before you can blow your nose. You know this for God's sake!" Charles placed a hand on Ran's shoulder in an attempt to calm him down a bit "Please Ran, keep your voice down."

"Sorry Charles, but you have worked so hard to get here. You have to think of Julie and Alex and not your ego".

At this comment, Charles burst out laughing, despite himself. "Is that what you think? My bloody ego? And there was me thinking you knew me Ran! And as for my family, they're all I can think about. I lay awake every night thinking about them, about what I've got them into".

Ranleigh was taken aback by this sudden comment. *What do you mean by this?* he thought worryingly, *What aren't you telling me?* "Is there something I should know Charlie? Something you're keeping from me?"

"Don't call me that, I'm no child. You've always held that particular card". They both grinned and chinked glasses before taking another swig of warming, fiery liquid. Then, after another long, deep breath, Charles responded "You know how it is Ran. When we are given orders we have to obey. As you said, no reason to become another scapegoat. But this does have something to do with that escapee. What was his name, Daniel?"

"David. Apparently a complete nobody. No priors
either. Really odd how he is evading the authorities,
so the news says anyway. What more can you say
about him? You must know more, Charlie, sorry,
Charles?" Another cheeky smile spread across
Ranleigh's face.

Charles had to be very careful here. Something
seemed suddenly off and Ranleigh seemed to be
phishing. "I don't really know much more about it.
The police are keeping it very hush hush for now.
They've leaked a bit of information to the press, but
only to get the public tongues wagging and minds
slightly wary of strangers."

Ranleigh smiled again, but this one seemed a little
void of the warmth and didn't meet his eyes. He
downed the last of his drink and stood. "Well, my
friend. If I can't talk you out of this, then I let you go
with my blessing".

"Shut up Ran you infant!" Charles sniggered as he
too stood and embraced his friend tightly. They
stayed like that for a few moments, before Ranleigh
felt Charles shaking slightly in the embrace. He
pulled away, his hand on Charles' shoulders as he
looked into teary, bloodshot eyes.

"Hey! What's going on with you? I can't help if you
don't tell me. For months now you've been all too

secretive. Ever since you took this bloody post! And now you're sobbing into my bloody shoulder? I'm worried about you mate".

"I...I can't tell you Ran. For your safety and for the safety of my family. There's too much at stake". He leaned in close to Ranleigh as he whispered in his ear "Ears everywhere, can't trust anyone".

"Oh Charles. Listen to me. Whatever it is, whatever you're involved in, there is always a way out. When you get back from the visits, we'll approach the Commissioner together okay? Talk this through in private".

Just then, Charles phone rang. Colour drained from his face, as no one in their right mind would be calling him at this late hour. He started at the screen not wanting to answer. Ranleigh had other ideas. Snatching it out of Charles' hand, he answered, putting the phone to his ear. Then, almost as if he was having a seizure, he started shaking uncontrollably, unable to take his hand away. There was a faint sound emanating from the speaker, a strange shrill that seemed almost too high pitched. Blood started trickling out of Ranleigh's nostrils, his piercingly blue pupils rising up and back inside his head. He then slumped to the floor, convulsed a few times before lying still, dead.

The screen of Charles' phone was still glowing with **Unknown Caller**, but the sound had disappeared. It then went to speaker without him even touching it, a familiar voice on the other end. "Charles, that was close wasn't it?" It was Farling, his Assistant. "Ah Charles, you almost gave the game away. And to Ranleigh no less, a man well known as a gossiper in parliament. Such a shame though, I quite liked him. And he was like an uncle to poor Alex. Maybe a bit too friendly to Julie if you ask me, may have done you a favour there to be honest".

"Farling! What the hell have you done? How did you…?"

"Oh don't you love technology? A signal so high pitched it causes catastrophic haemorrhaging in the brain, a massive bleed like a million microscopic balloons popping all at once. You were going to tell him everything. Or he was about to find out enough to displease the Master. Now, wipe those eyes, there's a good boss. Better get some rest. You'll need it. We need to leave early tomorrow. People are on their way to collect Ranleigh MP deceased as we speak. Julie and Alex will not know a thing".

And with that, he hung up, leaving Charles standing there open-mouthed, his body rigid and unbelieving of what had just happened. *Farling you bastard. You are a sneaky son of a bitch aren't you? So, you're working for the Master directly eh?* Such a mix of emotions flowed through him. He grabbed the remains of the brandy bottle and went out onto the patio. Anywhere but seeing his friend bleeding out on the study floor. *I wasn't going to tell him! Was I?* Charles thought as he downed the brandy straight from the bottle.

Forty One

The wraith-like shape tried not to let it's sadness and despair show as it walked behind three more of its kin towards the entrance to A Block. There was something wrong, an overwhelming feeling that it was someone else, meant to be somewhere else. Traces of a female trying to claw to the surface of its mind from deep within. And a name kept whispering in its head, *Janet! Janet!* And another name that brought up feelings of rage, *George! You killed him! You let him down!*

Before realising that it had stopped walking, one of the other shadowy figures turned back and gave it a hard glare, yellow eyes boring into the soul. A bony, pale hand then beckoned impatiently to follow and keep up, before carrying on. Not wanting to anger them, it followed back in line as they approached a small pile of bodies crumpled up by the entrance to the block. There was a scent of decomposition emanating from the corpses. Well, all but one. For it was twitching ever so slightly as if trying to free itself from the rotting flesh. A hand jerking and a foot too from under the pile.

The cloaked figure at the front tutted audibly before dragging the body out. "This one can still be of use. You at the back, take it to the letting room and string it up. We will be there momentarily to help drain it". The wraith-like shape at the back slowly shuffled up and lifted the twitching body with ease, defying the difference in weight. It then threw the body over its shoulder before marching off towards the round building, the bloodletting room.

As soon as it was no longer in earshot of the others, it gave out a sigh, which sounded almost female and gave way to tears which flowed down its white cheeks beneath the black hood. They stung its yellow eyes as if trying to purify them, making it hard to see ahead. *Janet! Remember who you are! Let me out!* came that voice again from deep within its mind. But the figure simply shook its head rigorously and walked faster, almost trotting towards the big oak door of the round room.

Dropping the body, which had stopped twitching now, the cloaked form opened the heavy door before bending down to drag the near-corpse in. but something stopped it in its tracks. Recognition. Again the female's voice pierced its mind *Barry, his name is Barry, you know this man! Remember who you are!* And then a sudden burst of pain ricocheted its skull, forcing it to its knees in screaming agony in the doorway.

Adam jerked awake, totally disoriented as he swung upside down from chains that secured him by his ankles a few feet off the hard, blood soaked ground of the cold, dark room. Light seemed to be spilling in from the far end, forming the shape of a doorway, but everything was blurry and confusing. He felt faint, as if lacking in power somehow. *How could this be possible?* He thought. *This feeling is one not of a need to feed, but of something taken away.* And with it came another long-lost feeling, a feeling of fear. Slowly his eyes adjusted to the lack of light, much slower than they should have. He felt much more human, more vulnerable. Then he remembered the mandrake root. They had injected him with it, a large dose that made him lose consciousness. *That must be what is keeping me docile like this! It is still in my system!*

From what Adam could deduce, he was strung up in a kind of dungeon or medieval torture room, with round walls that spoke of age and evil purpose. Below him were two large vats filled with a dark treacle-like liquid that smell metallic. *Blood! My blood?* he panicked, shaking in his bonds as he tried to free himself. The chains seemed far too tight, again a feeling he was not used to, not for many centuries. His hands were bound behind his back and Adam knew that he could easily dislocate his shoulders to bring the arms over his head. Normally they would pop back immediately with little pain, but in this state he could not risk injuring himself more. The cold of the room was seeping into his joints, making them stiff and difficult to manoeuvre. And there was an awful stench that filled his senses, not one of blood, but one of tortuous death. People in here had been strung up screaming, their blood drained out of them as they swung helplessly. And Adam was next in line it seemed. But they had obviously failed to understand that he healed almost instantly, making any kind of incision impossible to keep open. And yet the mandrake root had weakened his system enough that they had managed to extract a reasonable amount from him.

Having possession of his blood was something Adam could not allow. It was probably one of the most valuable and dangerous things anyone could possess. To his knowledge it had never as yet been attempted with any success, but if properly synthesised, his powers could be passed on to others and there would be a whole new army. Suddenly what blood flowed through him turned icy cold. *The snake cult! If they ingested his blood, they would add to their arson of abilities and become pretty much unstoppable!*

A noise at the far end of the room by the open doorway drew his attention. There appeared to be a small black figure silhouetted there, crouched down and looking like a pile of shadowy rags. It appeared to be sobbing.

"Hey!" Adam croaked, the sound barely audible but rebounding off the walls. "Hey you! Get me down from here!" Louder this time, loud enough for the figure to slowly stand. It then dragged a still, lumpy form into the darkness, right up to where he was swinging. Adam could make out a body as it was dropped by the cloaked figure. It then looked up at Adam, yellow eyes strangely human, searching for something.

"What is your name?" Adam tried.

The figure seemed to struggle with a sound, before answering in a rasping, female tone "Janet, my name is, was, Janet". It then burst into tears once more and fell back down onto its knees.

"Janet, you have to let me down. It appears that neither of us belong here and surely others will be back soon, yes?"

Janet continued crying but looked over at the still form of Barry lying there on the dirty concrete "I can't do it. He was my friend. You understand? He was my friend!"

Adam was a little confused. This creature was obviously battling inside with its identity. "Janet, that's your name right?"

"Janet was her name, yes. she was good at her job, kind to the prisoners. She killed George and now they want her to kill Barry, but she won't do it!" There was a sudden flash of anger and her eyes seemed to glow suddenly in the dark, like a cat's against the brightness of headlights.

"Okay Janet, I can help you, but first you need to loosen the chains from over there on the wall. The pulley system, you see it?"

"If they come back, they will kill me. I need to obey". She said simply.

"But you don't want to obey, do you? You remember who you were, I mean who you are". Adam was struggling to keep composure.

He was in pain, not to mention angry and hungry. *How could I still be in pain?* he thought. "Janet, please. Do I have something attached to me? Something pumping a chemical into me?"

Slowly, Janet nodded and pointed to the other wall. As Adam twisted his body, he made out a tube making its way over to a table. "Yes Janet! That's what I need you to take out. I will do the rest and I promise not to hurt you. I can save you and Barry. But first you need to take out the tube. OK?"

Janet seemed to battle again with voices from somewhere inside her mind. *It must be horrible for her*, thought Adam, as he knew all too well the inner struggles that come from being two people, the struggles of trying to maintain control and not let the demon out to play.

Then, as if her mind struggle was over, Janet straightened up, walked over to Adam and yanked at the tube that he realised was dug into his thigh. Almost immediately, Adam felt a warm strength flow through him and the room became lighter and lighter, as if his eyes were now drawing in every molecule of available light and intensifying it a thousand percent. He was back to himself again and with that came an awful cracking sound as he moved his arms down and round over his head, snapping his shoulders back in place. Seeing that his hands were just bound with rope, a quick jerk broke the bonds. The rope burned into his skin from the mandrake oil that soaked them, but the marks healed almost instantly. All that was left now was to bend up and brake the chains holding his ankles. Snapping the metal, Adam imagined how it would feel to rip these beings limb from limb. *I have not been kept like this for at least a century. You will all die for this!* he thought to himself as he jumped easily and softly onto his feet.

Standing on the cold floor, Adam tried to soften his gaze as he looked at this small, cloaked form standing in front of him. It was hard to imagine this thing being a female called Janet, even if he had never met her when she was human. But he felt sorry for it, nonetheless. After all, being changed against her will was indeed like having a kindred spirit standing here with him. And he suddenly had the overwhelming urge to save her, as if doing so could save a bit of his own soul.

"Thank you Janet. We all have to get out of here OK? But first I need to know, was an inmate called David brought here? Think hard. Do you remember the name David Jennings?"

A weird smile crossed Janet's thin mouth as she answered "Nice, skinny lad David. Shared a cell with Billy Finnegan. But Billy saw too much. Talked too much. They took him and David here to be drained".

"What? NO!" screamed Adam, his other side emerging in a roar as he picked the cloaked form of Janet up with one hand, lifting her high in the air. Realising his actions, he quickly set out her down again, but his tone remained firm "Are you saying he was killed here? He was drained?"

"Billy was, yes. But David found a way out somehow. We were all so amazed. *How could it have happened?* we all thought. He still hasn't been found, after days of looking. But the Master is searching hard. Oh yes, they are all looking very hard for him, and his friend with the pink hair".

Shit! thought Adam, both relieved and now reeling in emotion *That means he's on the run somewhere and has been so for days. He could be anywhere! And now they're after Xi too!* "Right, thank you Janet. We have to get out of here now. We will take Barry with us. Is he conscious?" Adam could hear his heartbeat, but he did not look well.

Janet went over to him and knelt beside him. "He was my friend, but he is losing the fight". Then she looked at the vats of Adam's blood on the floor. "I need to drink the essence of life. It can change me back". She made for one of the vats and Adam, with the quickness of a bullet shot out an arm and threw her away against the wall.

"NO! You cannot drink my blood! What do you mean anyway? Why would you need blood?"

"They took mine from me, Made me ingest the Master's life force. I need to purge him out of me".

Time was running out and Adam knew others would be back any minute. In fact he was slightly curious as to why they had not been ambushed already. Maybe they were simply waiting for them to exit the room. He strained his hearing, but no other sounds were coming from outside, no other heartbeats or breathing, no shuffling of feet on gravel.

"I need to dispose of these vats of my blood. No one can have this, you understand?"

And with that, he picked up on of the vats and threw it against the far back wall, spilling the contents everywhere. He then did the same with the second vat before moving towards where a hosepipe was wound around a metal coil. There was a tap next to it which Adam turned on before unravelling the pipe and washing the blood down the long drain that ran the length of the room. It only took a few minutes before he was content that his blood was either washed away or contaminated enough so as to be unusable. As he turned to get Janet and Barry, Adam stopped in his tracks. Janet was leaning over her friend and colleague, drinking from a nasty gash in his neck. And then all hell broke loose as she tipped her head back and screamed, her body seemingly filling out and growing slightly. She turned to look at Adam and her eyes were no longer a glowing yellow, but the pale blue of a mere human. As her hood fell back, gone was the malformed skull and now a reasonably attractive woman faced him. She had no hair and it looked as if Janet would never again have flowing locks, if indeed she ever had.

Adam was now conscious of the fact he only had underwear on, but his modesty was short lived as the meagre light of the open door was suddenly blocked out by shadows moving outside, although still no noise could be heard, nor heartbeats. *These truly are wraiths,* he thought as he smoothly stepped across the room and out into the courtyard, Janet appearing behind him. The cloaked figures filled the space in front of them, parting slightly as a taller, thinner figure slid in. it was Hashaan. And he seemed different, his eyes not the glowing yellow of before, but more orange like those of Adam.

"I see you are more robust than I thought" Adam remarked darkly.

Hashaan grinned widely, showing a menace that chilled Adam to the core as recognition dawned on him. That smell, that aura surrounding him; Hashaan had ingested his blood!

Forty Two

It took a little longer than David had first thought to get to Brighton. Traffic jam after traffic jam seemed to impede them, but finally the coach pulled into Pool Valley and came to a stop.

"Well folks" came the voice of the driver through the Tannoy, "We have now arrived at Brighton Pool Valley, our final destination. Sorry again for any inconveniences caused by silly drivers and roadworks. I hope you all have a safe onward journey and thank you for travelling with Southern Coaches".

As if controlled by a single brain, the passengers rose at once, knocking against each other as they scrambled to get their bags and jackets from the overhead lockers. David merely stayed where he was until most of them had clambered down onto the coach park. Only then did he slowly stand, nervous of what may find him as he disembarked. To both his amazement and relief, no police nor strange, unmarked vehicles were wating for him as he set foot on the concrete and he quickly moved away through a side street and into the Lanes. Small, cobbled streets of what was once the old pirate town of Brighton seemed oddly apt to David, but he still had no idea where he was going or where Xi was. He couldn't or didn't wish to wait by the coach. Instead, he ducked into an old dingily lit pub, ordered a beer and then sat at a corner table and got out the phone.

Putting the SIM in again and switching it on, it immediately flashed up saying there were three messages, one of them a voice message. He looked at the two text messages first, seeing that they were both from Xi, saying that she was on her way to the bus station and the second saying she didn't think she was being followed anymore and that she was now wearing a green beanie and yellow puffer jacket. He then played the voice message and froze with fright,

"Dee, oh shit! They've found me. They bloody shot at me from the station, shot an innocent girl! I'm now hiding in the baggage compartment under the coach. It managed to get out of there before they could get on, but I'll have to get out at Gatwick, if I can. Otherwise it'll be Brighton. I'll call back as soon as I can. Just make sure you get to the…" And then the message cut off.

Get to the what?? Where the fuck does she want me to go? he thought with dread at the fact that he was now most likely on his own again. Poor Xi was right in it too. David drank deeply from his pint as he thought about what he knew of Brighton. Then it dawned on him.

Three years ago he and Xi had been sent here by Adam to check on a blood bank contact at the Brighton General Hospital. An old, creepy looking building that had once been some kind of workhouse for the poor, the hospital had a blood bank out of sight to ordinarily folk. But they had heard of a nurse that had got attacked whilst trying to sort out some O Negative for Adam. CCTV had captured the image of a woman seemingly being bitten on the neck by another, taller figure but the image was blurry. Adam said it wasn't him and whether or not he and Xi believed him, their job was to go to the hospital and erase all footage in person. Although the images could be hacked remotely by Xi, the hospital still kept DVDs in a storage room. And so off they went.

It turned out there was actually more than one image and the nurse in question was caught two days later trying to steal blood for herself. It appeared that she had been turned and subsequently disappeared after escaping the Brighton holding cell. David had always been slightly jealous of this woman, crazy as it sounded. *Maybe once all this was over Adam would still consider turning me after everything I've been through,* David thought longingly to himself. They never got a clear image of who it was that had turned the nurse, but the letter 'L' had been written on a wall in a nearby alley surrounded by a heart. It was one of those items on a long list of things to try and bring up with Adam, should the moment arise to do so.

So, whilst staying overnight at a bed and breakfast near to the hospital, they had got pally with a couple who were opening their own little corner shop. Could this be who Xi meant to go and see? It would make sense and David couldn't think of anyone else they would both know here. It was a longshot for sure, but he had no other options. He could call her from there, even perhaps use their internet and lie low. He just had to hope that they would believe him not to be an escaped loony and that his face wasn't still plastered all over the news.

The weather had turned slightly worse, a light drizzle making the seafront seem misty as David starting walking past the Palace Pier along towards Brighton Marina. There weren't too many people about as it was out of season for the tourists. A group of exchange students waited with him at the pedestrian lights, their matching yellow backpacks banging him as they all tried to squeeze onto the pavement at the other end. A few of their friends had dared each other to run across on the red light between the traffic and giggles followed by squeaky French dialect filled the air as he too crossed the road. David smiled. It had been what seemed like a very long time since he had heard any laughter, or anything positive to be honest. One of the young students, a boy of around 14 turned to him suddenly as he turned to walk away.

"Excuse me Sir, please can you help us?"

"Of course, with what?" he answered.

"We all 'ave some questions we 'av to write down about Brighton and this one 'ere is difficult. Can you 'elp us please?" He showed a crumpled piece of paper to David which had started to get all wet in the rain. There was a question about the Royal Pavilion, asking the name of the king that had it built.

"You know if you went to the Pavilion over there you will see a sign that I'm sure tells you about the king". God, he felt like a right grump saying that and the boy looked at him pleadingly. "Ok, it was built by King George, but he never actually lived there as he didn't like it once it was finished".

"Ah, that is also the next question too! Thank you so much!" And off he ran to tell his friends.

David carried on, crossing another street that took him right onto the seafront. *It must be so nice having those questions as the only thing to worry about*, he thought as he walked passed the Sealife Centre. He still had a bit of change on him and so, instead of heading straight into Kemptown up one of the many connecting side streets, David stopped off under the arches at a traditional fish and chip shop buying himself a cone of chips with a battered sausage placed gingerly on top. As he sat down on a bench to tuck in, his phone buzzed again. At first he cursed himself that he had left it switched on. He checked the display and saw that the message had come from yet another unknown caller.

"Christ! How many bloody phones has Xi got?" David said aloud as he opened it up. Before he could read the message, the display shimmered and a loud beeping started. He cursed his stupidity. His phone had been hacked and he had just activated some kind of malware!

Throwing the phone down, David stomped on it fiercely, almost dropping his food. A couple of passers-by stopped and asked if he was ok. "Yes, sorry. Just playing a prank on a friend, it's an old phone. Stag do actually, I'm waiting for others to arrive". They then carried on, but the expressions on their faces definitely showed scepticism.

They couldn't have had enough time to track the phone David thought. *And anyway, what can I do about it now anyway? If they find me, they find me. I'm beyond caring"*. He was tired and empty both physically and emotionally. Xi had not contacted him since that voice message. He took a deep breath and carried on eating the chips. It could be the last meal he would have in a while if his idea didn't pan out.

Forty Three

The black executive coach sped up the M6, topped and tailed by official black BMWs with blackened out windows. It was an official visit after all and there would be plenty of journalists waiting for Charles and his entourage once he arrived at their first port of call, Stafford prison. He sat quietly brooding in his armchair, watching the ice cubes rock gently in his brandy glass. Life had suddenly taken a very bad turn. His friend had been murdered in front of his eyes and although he had suspected Farling of being more than he appeared, it was still a bit of a shock to have him speak to Charles in the dark, evil tone of last night. And although he was privy, if not a direct accomplice himself in the killings of inmates, but it had felt a million miles away, not right there at his front door, so to speak. And now he wasn't being let out of anyone's sight, with a group of foreboding men in black suits attached to him.

Farling sat at the other end of the coach, busily typing something on his laptop and not giving Charles even a hint of any kind of recognition. It was as if Charles had suddenly become merely something to parade in front of the cameras whilst the real work, whatever that was, happened away from him. And that was what he had pretty much been instructed from an email he had received earlier this morning. With no forwarding address, it had simply said that he was to do whatever Farling said and keep the journalists and anyone else away whilst they conducted the search. He was not to interfere or comment on anything he saw and he had to merely deflect any suspicions raised during the visit. But Charles was not told exactly what was happening during these visits anyway, so that part wouldn't be too difficult to execute.

And so he just sat there, staring into his glass. And then his phone rang. Afraid of what might happen should he put it to his ear. Charles laid it on the table in front of him and pressed speaker.

"Charles McNeil MP" he said suspiciously.

"How's the journey?" came a rasping, metallic-like voice on the other end.

"Sir, it's very smooth, Sir. Should be there soon I think".

"Good. Listen McNeil, I wanted to apologise to you for last night. I appreciate the man Ranleigh was your friend. I also want you to know that I did not ask Farling to kill him, he made that decision on his own. I appreciate it may cause a bit of an incident in Parliament and if it does, I will give instructions for you to let him go, shall we say".

Charles felt suddenly emboldened by this change of tone from the Master, confiding in him like this. "Thank you Sir. He was indeed my friend and I can assure you I would never have said anything to him, I did not say anything to him".

Charles quickly looked up to see if Farling could hear any of the conversation, but he was right at the other end of the coach and was engrossed in something on the laptop.

"I need to be able to rely on you, McNeil. Your wife and son need to rely on you. When the time comes, if you do all that we say, you will be elevated. You understand?"

Charles didn't quite understand what this wraith-like voice was getting at. Could this be a promotion? "I will not let you down, I can assure you. I will keep the journalists at bay".

"Oh I'm sure you will, and don't worry about Farling. He has his own path, as do you". And with that, the phone went dead.

Too many bloody cryptic messages! Charles thought to himself as he gulped down the brandy and stood up, walking towards the drinks cabinet. As he took the first step forward, one of the black suited men got up with a lightning motion that made Charles almost fall back down into his seat. "Let

me, Mr McNeil" he said with a cold, toneless voice. He sounded almost like Lurch from The Addams Family.
"I can get my own bloody drink man!" Charles shouted at him, rather more angrily than he had intended. The man smiled at him before slowly moving aside. Behind him, Farling was standing there with a fresh glass of brandy on ice in his hand, holding it out to Charles.

"Here you are Charles" he said simply.

"Farling" Charles responded simply as he took the glass, taking a step back and falling back into his seat. *So*, he thought to himself, *you are listening, you slimy bastard. How much of that did you hear I wonder?*

Farling thanked the man and went back to his seat, opening his laptop once more. On it was a fresh email with no forwarding address. As he opened it, Farling read the few sentences:

Charles McNeil is reaching the end of his worth. You will take his place as MP after this visit, but first you must be elevated. Congratulations.

He couldn't keep the joy from reaching his face as his smiled widely. He had never liked Charles and hoped that he could be the one to make him disappear. He had done it to his predecessor after all. So fitting that her blood now joined the thousands of other bags distributed around the NHS. It certainly looked like Charles would not leave HMP Stafford. Maybe they would even let him be the one to slit his throat and smile down at him as he squirmed upside down, the light leaving his smarmy eyes as the useless bastard's Imposter Syndrome was finally realised. *But I need to let him know I'm taking his place before he dies,* Farling laughed to himself.

The coach slowed down as it turned off the motorway into Stafford. Then, after just a few more minutes the prison came into view and they slowly drove in through the big brown wooden doors into the courtyard. Interestingly, no journalists awaited them. Instead, a group of hood-cloaked figures seemed to be surrounding a half-naked man and behind him a strange looking woman, who also seemed to be wearing a robe. The man looked as if he was capable of killing everyone, apart from one figure who stood in the middle of the group. There was something not quite right about the whole situation and Charles wanted nothing more than to stay on the coach.

"What is this?" Farling shouted to the group of men "Go down and find out what is happening. We will stay on here with one of you as protection".

Four of the black-suited men got up and as the door of the coach opened, climbed down. Then all hell broke loose.

Forty Four

The commotion that was going on outside in the inner courtyard of the prison had not yet spilled into the Vulnerable Prisoners wing. But the screams and yells of both the guards and of Sam were more than enough. The two officers that had found him in his cell next to the decapitated body of his cellmate were holding him down on the balcony floor of the corridor as he thrashed and screamed "It wasn't me! It wasn't me! How could I have done that to him?"

"Alright McIntosh, just calm the down alright?" One of the guards said as calmly as he could "Let's get you downstairs, away from all this. Alright lad?"

Together, they managed to haul Sam to his feet, but couldn't stop his hysterics as they started to lead him along the corridor and down the central stairs that would take them to the ground floor.

"Killed him they did! Fucking killed him! And forged a suicide note to boot! Watch out everyone, you'll be next. They're gonna kill us all, you'll see!" he shouted, with inmates pounding in response on their cell doors. The guards ended up dragging him to a segregation cell opposite the medical hatch, before slamming shut the clear door and leaving Sam lying on the floor like a rabid animal, isolated so as not to attack the other animals. The banging slowly subsided around the wing and Sam stopped, left to lie there sobbing.

A nurse came over to where the guards were starting to walk away. "How are we going to handle this?" she asked in a stern, cold voice. "Do we need to let them know? How had Fitsimmons been left in the cell like that? Is it a message do you think?"

"For heaven's sake Brenda" interjected one of the guards "Easy there with the Spanish inquisition. You know as much as we do! I've locked the cell door and hatch. The body will have to stay in there for now or there'll be a bloody riot. Let's get back to the office and figure this out".

"I'll give him a sedative, make sure he stays quiet. That ok with you two?" Brenda asked, but her tone made it more of a statement.

"No arguments from me, love. As long as we get some too!" the other guard replied "I tell you, this bloody place! You know, Fitsimmons was pally with Slippery George. And he was speaking to Janet the other day too. Don't know what about, but a bit of a bloody coincidence George is gone, Janet didn't turn up for shift this morning and now Fitsimmons is found in his cell with his head neatly detached from his bloody body!"

"Sssh!" the first guard butted in "For Christ's sake Bill, don't go thinking in public! Let's wait till we're out of earshot ok? I totally get it, but please. Keep your thoughts to yourself".

Brenda simply nodded and went back to her medical cupboard to get the sedative for Sam, whilst the two officers proceeded to the wing office. Entering first, Bill went straight for the drawer by the desk and pulled out a bottle of whiskey. "Fancy a coffee Charlie?" he offered whilst shaking the bottle.

"Hell yeah, make mine a strong coffee alright?" replied Charlie, the colour only just returning to his face.

No sooner had they taken a long sip of the Irish coffee than an alarm sounded, pulsating high-pitched around the whole prison. Red lights were flashing alongside the corridors and the inmates started up again with their feral-like banging and screaming. All officers on duty knew that this meant total lockdown and thankfully no cell doors were open at this time. Bill and Charlie grabbed a vest each and helped each other fasten them. Both had to breath in slightly as the clips were down up and Bill couldn't help sucking in a bit of breath and commenting "Ooh, when's the riot fresher training again? I think I might bloody fail, no word of a lie there".

With their batons and pepper spray locked and loaded on their belts alongside a couple of pairs of handcuffs, both officers calmy walked out of the office, expecting all kinds of shit on the wing. But there was no one to be seen. "Where's the trouble?" asked Charlie. "Must be in another wing. What do we do? Can't leave these animals here alone. What if they get out?"

"They're all locked up Bill, nowhere to go. Let's take a peek outside and see if there's commotion across the courtyard. That way no one can say we've left our post, alright?"

Bill grunted begrudgingly and they made their way through the entrance corridor that led out into the courtyard. Charlie was the first out and was immediately hit by a bullet that, with the upmost bad luck pierced his neck, coming out the other end and spraying blood over Bill's visor from behind him. Falling backwards and clutching at his ruined throat, Charlie's vision started to blacken with shock even before he hit the ground. Bill was wiping the blood from his visor shouting "Christ! Bloody Christ!" before realising Charlie was down and out. He leapt to the right, his baton cracking a rib as he landed on his side. He screamed out in agony and rolled onto his back, before scrabbling to his knees so that he could drag Charlie back into the wing.

Brenda was staring ashen faced at the pair of them as Bill undid his vest before pulling off Charlie's helmet. Blood was pooling underneath him and he pressed down on the neck wound as hard as he could. Coming to life, Brenda took off her nurse's coat and pushed it onto Charlie's neck.

"What the fuck is going on out there?" She could only shout.

Bullets seemed to be pinging off the walls outside, followed by guttural sounds and roars only beasts would normally make. The alarm only seemed to exacerbate things further. Bill moved back against the inner corridor wall, sitting with his back against it and clutching at his side. His breaths were laboured, but all he could do was to stare at poor Charlie choking on his own blood in front of him. The nurse's coat was completely drenched in blood, with more still pooling around him. Then the gurgle sounds ceased. Charlie was dead.

"I can't take this!" cried Bill involuntarily. "I'm not a bloody soldier! I never signed up for this".

"Oh shut up Bill! You take a payment same as the rest of us to look the other way. You knew people were being killed. Don't act all coy about it now, just because things are going tits up. How did you think this was going to end? Eh? ANSWER ME!" Brenda was a little hysterical herself, but her anger had taken over now. She had known for the past week that they were all pretty much done for and that there was nothing they could do about it. She had met the cloaked figures. She had even met Hashaan.

"But it's Charlie! Low lives are one thing, I can live with them not getting back on the street to commit more crime. But Charlie? He was fucking innocent!"

Brenda simply took her hands away from where she was applying pressure to Charlie's neck and stood up, leering over Bill. He was shocked at the smile crossing her face, a smile that failed to reach her eyes.

"None of us are innocent here Bill. We are all dead already, surely you knew that?"

And with a swift motion Brenda took off one of her shoes before imbedding the heel into Bill's left eye. She then punched it further in, leaving Bill to twitch a few times before slumping to the ground next to Charlie. Brenda then quickly went back to her cupboard, pulling out a long tube with a 22-guage butterfly needle attached to one end and a bucket. She then went over to the still form of Bill, pushed him back up into a sitting position before embedding the needle into his neck. The blood flowed quickly down and into the bucket. "Blood is sacred, blood is life" Brenda chanted as the bucket filled. The noises of outside in the courtyard seemed a world away.

Forty Five

Xion was bruised and achy by the time the coach came to a halt at where she could only assume was Gatwick Airport. Scared that she would be arrested or worse, all she could do was pile as many bags and cases around and over herself as possible, trying to hide within an impossibly cramped space. She heard the sound of the driver climb down off the coach and then after a couple of seconds the opposite side of the baggage compartment opened up, letting in both noise and light. Quickly, Xion scampered back to the side she had got in from. She yelped instinctively as the back of her neck caught on sharp metal. Feeling the back of her neck, she felt a little blood from a scratch and felt the compartment door behind her. There were two small, crude holes where bullets had passed through. *How had they not hit me?!* Xion thought in amazement. She could only guess that the luggage had saved her life. The driver then started rummaging through the bags, pulling them out and shuffling them around.

Please don't find me, please God don't find me! she prayed to herself as his hands came ever closer to where she was hidden, but she was in enough shadow not to be seen. The compartment door came back down and she was once again plunged into darkness. Xion sighed, expecting the coach to get on its way again, but it just stayed there. She didn't even hear the creaking of the steps as he climbed back onboard. Instead, nothing. After what seemed like an absolute age, Xion decided that there was no choice but to try and slip out. First she carefully put her eye close to one of the bullet holes, trying not to cut herself. Through it, Xion could make out a kind of flashing light, red and blue. *Shit! Of course!* she muttered to herself, *the driver would have reported the shooting at the station and his lucky escape! And now they will find the bullet holes followed by me!*

Part of her so wanted to get arrested. But then, she didn't really know who these people were that were after her nor how far up the chain it went. If they had eyes in the police, Xion would be even more screwed and unable to escape. She would just disappear or be kept in a cell somewhere for these lunatic killers to collect her and deliver her to their employer. Or worse. Trying to stay calm, Xion realised that the commotion did seem to be coming from the side of the coach with the bullet holes. This made sense too as it was also the side of the bus with the passenger door. There was nothing else for it but for Xion to try and slip away from the other side. As quietly as she could, Xion pushed aside some of the bags that were shielding her. There would be fingerprints everywhere now, but this was the least of her worries.

Seeing a catch on the inside of the compartment door, she carefully turned it. The door was really heavy from the angle at which she was having to push, but   it gave enough for Xion to get a quick peek outside. A few people were milling around and there was also a small cluster of curious passengers looking at some kind of commotion on the other side of the coach. There was nothing for it but to try and slip out. If she waited any longer, the opposite hatch would open and she would be rumbled. As slowly as she dared whilst trying not to let the hinges yank the hatch away from her, Xion rolled herself out onto the tarmac, landing both feet down and then closing the hatch again.

To her relief, everyone seemed more interested in the almost maniacal ramblings of the driver as he audibly described the sheer terror of the station incident.

"Yeah, bullets flying everywhere there was. Had to escape as quickly as possible I did, worried these poor passengers would get hit. As you can see officers, two of them almost hit us where we sat!"

Xion smiled as she slipped into the terminal building. *Nothing like embellishing the truth a bit, eh mate?* she thought to herself, *got to do what you can if you want to get that interview on This Morning!"* She was shaking uncontrollably and realised that low blood sugar together with adrenaline was making her feel weak. The last thing she needed now, after all she had been through, was to pass out. So she made her way through the terminal towards the arrival section. Xion had no idea what her next move would be, but one thing for sure was that David would be going crazy right now after hearing her panicked voicemail. She had to compose herself and ring him back. Hopefully he had made it to Brighton OK and had remembered where they stayed the last time they were there.

She went upstairs and got a coffee and a pastry, before heading to the large window which looked out over the bus platform. A sizeable crowd had gathered now, with a few passengers giving their statements to the police. As she watched, another police vehicle pulled up. Three more officers added to the throng as they started to pull on white onesies. Two of the original gang started sealing off the area with police tape, much to the apparent disgruntlement of the crowd. Xion was glad to have escaped when she did. Of course now she had to think very hard about how to get to Brighton. The obvious route would be by train, as there were always plenty to choose from with regularity.

Finishing her coffee, pastry and feeling more like herself again, she got up and started to move away from the window. But then Xion was convinced she saw a couple looking at her from the other side of the road. It was just for a second and then they had disappeared, two figures with one wearing an expensive looking cream overcoat.

"Can I not get a single fucking break here?" she cursed out loud, far louder than she had meant.

"You alright my dear? Terrible business this isn't it? Were you meant to catch this too?" An elderly lady suddenly piped up next to her.

"Oh, err, yeah. Gonna have to try and find another route now. Good luck on your journey". Xion quickly fobbed her off and made her way towards the train station.

Now worried that she was being followed again, she went back into the coffee shop. There were too many people around to risk taking a jacket from a chair this time, so she took off the one she was wearing and turned it inside out. The lining was a dark grey and as with most puffer jackets did not look that different on the inside. It would have to do for now. She was so glad of her nefarious upbringing. Would others have been able to think on their feet as she could? Xion doubted it. She just hoped David was able to think like her. He had done so well thus far, that was for sure. But she also knew of that sensitive side to him. And then of course there was his goofy sense of humour, always playing tricks when they were working together in the warehouse. *When all this is over, if we get out of this, I need to maybe sit down and tell him how I feel*, she thought suddenly, then sniggered to herself. *Like he would be interested in someone like me!*

The ticket machines were not as busy as she thought and, purchasing a single to Brighton, Xion headed straight for the platform. It looked as if the next train would be arriving within the five minutes, much to her relief. The platform was jam-packed too which was even better. Moving along, she saw a group of exchange students all huddled together and chatting away in some Mediterranean accent. They were all sporting red baseball caps with some academy logo printed on the front and Xion had noticed one lying on the platform floor. Quickly, she picked it up, removing her orange beanie and placing the cap on backwards. Standing next to the group, her small figure meant she blended in perfectly and Xion took a deep breath as the speaker system announced the impending arrival of the train to Brighton. It was a direct one too, only thirty minutes until she was finally reunited with David. She could almost cry with a mixture of emotions.

As travellers bustled off the carriages, the exchange group started embarking and Xion held back as long as possible before climbing up at the back of the group, taking the baseball cap off at the last minute as what she could only think was a teacher looked up from a clipboard, ticking off names. Sitting down at a free window seat, she noticed the couple that were staring at her arrive on the platform, but just a few seconds too late as the doors shut. Then recognition flashed across her face. They were the killers after her! The woman had tried to disguise herself with a long cream coat, but there was no mistaking the hard look she gave as she argued with the conductor. Xion actually thought she was going to pull out her gun and shoot the poor bastard, but the man next to her put a hand on her shoulder, coaxing her back as the train started rolling forward. *I've beaten you again!* She thought to herself. But they knew where she was heading and would be right behind her, of that she was certain.

Forty Six

David was soaked through. The rain had got heavier still in the short time it had taken him to walk along the seafront and then left up a side street that took him into the heart of Kemptown. The sun was already beginning to set, not that he could see it through the dull white cloud. It seemed to envelope the world like an ominous layer of foreboding. The rain had also brought a chill with it that seemed to clutch at David's joints, constricting them into an inability to move properly.

There were very few people out and about, not that he ever really remembered there ever being many in this part of Brighton. David passed a big white block of dilapidated looking flats. A couple of lads in their mid-twenties were stood outside, hoods up and the scent of what he supposed was weed, but mixed with something else or just badly harvested, momentarily filled his lungs, making him cough as he passed. One of the lads laughed loudly, "breath it in bruv, it'll do you good you poof!"

He never understood why strangers such as these wanted to cause hostility at apparently nothing, wanting to start trouble with complete strangers. But then, they knew no one would confront them. They could say or do what they liked and no one would stop them for fear of having a knife shoved in between their ribs. And so they felt like kings of their rotten castles, all paid for by the taxpayer of course. It annoyed David that he had to work bloody hard, albeit perhaps not entirely on the right side of the law, to have part of his money go to scum such as these wasters. He sniggered to himself, remembering that he actually didn't pay taxes anymore, not since working for Adam in the shadows.

"What's so funny, faggot?" The same hoodlum spat, moving away from his spot by the wall of the flats and towards David.

"What? I wasn't laughing mate. Leave it alone will you" David replied, starting to walk away.

"Well, now, why would I do that, eh? You got any money on you?" The lad asked in an almost amused tone as he put a hand on David's shoulder.

Without even thinking, David grabbed the wrist and twisted it round, kicking the lad's feet away at the same time and sending him sprawled on the pavement. The other lad just looked on, realising it was not worth trying to interfere.

"Easy bruv, only messing!" yelped the first one as he got up.

David just looked at him with eyes that told the lad he was capable of anything. "You don't know me, nor what I am capable of, bruv" he simply said, before continuing away from them. They didn't try and follow him. Turning a corner, David suddenly took a deep breath, feeling his shaking body underneath the sodden clothes. *What am I turning into?* He thought to himself. His nerves were pretty much shot with everything that had happened and these lads were comparably nothing to him.

Looking up at where he was, David realised that he had made it to the address he was looking for. It was a red brick building with smart, high bay windows and a small front yard kept nice and tidy. A few steps led up to the white front door and he could see a few buzzers on a panel to the right. One of them said "Percy and Becks". These were the couple that both he and Xion had stayed with. *Great!* he thought, *at last, some normality*. David pressed the buzzer, then waited. After a few moments, he pressed it again. Still no answer. There were two other buzzers and he decided to press another. "Yep?" came a deep response.

"Hi, err, sorry to bother you. I'm looking for Percy and Becks?"

"Can't help you mate. If they're not answering, obviously they're not in" came the curt response. He wasn't angry but was clearly busy.

"If it's not too much trouble, could I possibly wait inside? They know me from way back and it's horrible out here".

"Why don't you call them then?"

"My phone doesn't have their number. Could you at least come down? Please?"

There was a pause, before the intercom clicked once. A few moments later, David heard footsteps followed by the front door unlocking. The door opened and a huge guy filled the space. Black dreadlocks flowed down almost to his knees and his dark skin betrayed his age. In fact, David had no idea how old this guy could be, only that he was definitely older than he looked. "Right," he started, "Here I am, now how can I possibly help?" After a few seconds of looking David up and down and clearly not seeing a threat, the guy pulled him inside and closed the door. "Bloody hell mate, you are like a tiny, drowned mouse, no offence. Come up and dry off".

David followed him up some stairs to the first floor. "Please, take off your shoes yeah?"

"Sorry, My name's Billy" David lied "And you are?"

"Oh, of course, sorry. I'm Aberash, or Abe for short. Now take off those shoes and come in. I can fix you a hot drink".

"Abe, you are an angel, thank you!" David almost cried with a sense of relief and kindness that he hadn't felt in so long. At least, that's how he felt as he removed his trainers, leaving them outside as he ventured into the flat. Beautifully lit with a soft glow, candles were burning atop thin cabinets that lined the hallway. The walls were painted a soft beige colour, almost like putty or faint mud. A scent of some sort hung in the air and David thought he could smell nutmeg mixed with something else.

"You have a beautiful home, Abe. But please, I would hate to offend by getting water everywhere from my clothes." He sneezed out the last words.

"Bless you, Billy" Abe simply said, pausing before saying his name with a hint of scepticism. "I tell you what, drink this…" Abe offered David a glass filled with what looked like whiskey but had that nutmeg smell in it too. "…and I will find a towel you can at least wrap around you. Then we will talk, yes?"

He left David in the hallway, going into what must have been a bedroom and retuning with a large orange bath towel, double the size of any David had seen. Handing it to him, Abe then beckoned David into the lounge and to an armchair by the bay window. There was a fire burning in a simple black cast iron hearth and David, warmed through by the toddy he had just downed, felt instantly like he could just curl up and sleep for a thousand years.

"So then, Billy is it? Strange, you don't look like a Billy. You don't have the energy of a Billy. But that is not important. What is more pressing right now is the whereabouts of your friend, Xion. Am I correct in thinking that?"

"Sorry what?" David blurted out "How could you possibly know about…?"

Abe smiled. "Ssh my friend. I am no enemy. I am a friend of Adam's. He put me in touch with Xion a few years back to help me with a rather embarrassing incident. She told me of one of her partners in crime, a slight, but handsome and kind man she called David". Seeing the look of bewilderment on David's face, Abe said simply "I have a gift too, but I am nothing quite like Adam".

"You have been waiting for me, I mean expecting me. So you know who I am then?"

"David, I know of you yes. You have been on the news and I am very surprised and impressed that you have made it all the way here from the North. You are not quite the slight man Xion thinks you are, are you? Nor kind, that seems to have been lost to you of late. You have had to be quite the opposite to survive thus far, am I right? And you carry the weight of death around with you".

It felt of a sudden as if every muscle, every tense fibre of his being was suddenly washed away and David burst into tears. "I'm so tired Abe! I've done, had to do terrible things. Things against my nature. Adam would be ashamed of me if he knew. And I've put Xi in terrible danger now too. If I hadn't have gone to that club, none of this would be happening. I don't even like sodding club music!"

The tears would not stop and Abe simply sat there opposite David, letting his emotions run their course. When David had finally subdued himself and was quiet, Abe said "Adam would actually be proud of you David, not ashamed. And as for the couple you came here to see, well, Percy and Becks haven't lived here for a while now. But this is a safe house. I use their flat for guests who need somewhere to lay low, trusted people. Now, what do you know of Xion? Is she on her way here?"

"She was hiding in the baggage compartment of a coach when she left me a few messages. I wanted to call her, but I think my phone was hacked and traced so I smashed it. Stupid I know. An IT guy that smashes his phone instead of simply removing the SIM and switching it off! I'm an idiot".

Abe smiled and David found himself instantly at ease under his gaze. *There's something strange about this guy,* he thought, *something under the surface. Is this why Adam knows him?* Abe got up and went over to a desk drawer, pulling out an old mobile phone that looked like something out of the noughties. "Use this", he said and he threw it to David. "Call her".

"Sorry I don't know her number, she has a new phone and might not even have that one now" David confessed, feeling suddenly very guilty.

"Look at the phone, David Jennings" Abe said and saying his full name made David almost jump out of his seat "Just look at it and dial. You'll remember".

As he stared at the display, a phone number suddenly entered his mind, a number he didn't recognise but one he was sure somehow was Xion's. He quickly dialled it, hearing it ring a few times before being answered.

"Dee is that you?" came the voice of Xion. For all David cared, it could have been the voice of an angel.

"Xi, I'm so glad you're Okay. You are Okay, right?"

"Yeah Dee, for now. I'm on my way to you. Are you at the safehouse?"

"Yes, I'll wait for you here." Not wanting to say too much or be on the line too long, David hung up.

"Good" Abe spoke softly, that deep resonance sending a wave of calming energy out filling the room. "She'll be here soon enough. In the meantime, I think it's time for another drink, don't you?"

Forty Seven

"Just stay behind me", Adam advised Janet, reaching around and pulling her back. He counted close to a dozen black cloaks spreading out around him. Although his wits were coming back to him now that the mandrake root was leaving his system, Adam still felt weaker than normal, but he tried not to give that impression as he stretched up to his full height. At over six feet he pretty much towered over all of the others, but there was something even more menacing in Hashaan's stature as the demon stood in front of him, reaching almost seven feet tall.

"I would never have thought one of mine would betray me. To my knowledge it has never happened before and to be honest it has taken me by complete surprise. And she has her humanity back too I see. I would very much like to study her, once I have drained you completely of course".

"Don't you want to chew on my bones? I mean, isn't that what you disgusting snake people do? By the way, you left a bit of a mess in the segregation wing, you may want to get all those bits cleared up. Someone could trip over the blood and guts and hurt themselves".

Adam needed to buy as much time as he could whilst his strength returned. Unfortunately, what he truly needed was to feed off someone, but the only human in sight was poor Janet, and he really didn't trust that what flowed through her system was entirely pure anyhow. A part of whatever she had become was still evident in her eyes. Until she was far away from this place, Adam had to think that she could turn back at any time. Hashaan seemed to have some kind of mental bond over his minions after all. Of that he was certain.

The serpent demon continued to smile as the other, smaller cloaked figures closed in, snarling or hissing as they did so. One suddenly pounced with a speed Adam did not expect, hitting him in the side and knocking him off balance slightly. But he simply reached out with one arm, grabbed the creature in a vice like grip around it's throat and snapped its neck like a twig. Falling to the ground in a crumpled heap of black material, the others retreated a few steps.

"Don't you feel all alone, a sad and utterly pathetic creature that has no purpose in this world?" Hashaan mocked, the stench of both his cloak and breath making Adam gag slightly. There were old, dried bodily juices on his worn robes still, and he was certain from the scent that bits of putrefying flesh were caught between fanged jaws. "Wouldn't it simply be a mercy to both you and the world if you died right here, right now? Surely you are tired of just existing?"

In a weird way, Hashaan was not wrong in what he said. It was in fact as if he could reach Adam's innermost turmoil, but there was no way he could let this race of demons continue their slaughter. Or could he? Hashaan laughed out loud, a guttural sound that did not seem natural at all, his head almost split in two as he threw his head back. His hood feel back too, revealing pointed ears and a scalp that had faint green veins running across it like old parchment weathered in the sun. "Ah, you still have feelings for these humans, don't you? They are insignificant, fodder to be manipulated and culled in order to serve. Cattle and nothing more. Only when we see fit can they be elevated, either by draining them or changing them into one of these beautiful servants, to serve me".

So he thinks he is a god, does he? Thought Adam, *Insanity makes him even more dangerous.* Again, Hashaan had read his thoughts. "Again, you fail to see the big picture here. In order to control, you must first cull those that have no desire to follow. These wretches that only want to kill, maim and abuse do not deserve life. But others that have potential do deserve mercy. I give them that mercy by healing them with the blood of the wretches. How is that not the perfect system? Cleanse the bad by pouring it into the good. You know we have been doing this for centuries. You were almost

upon us in Paris. I know you remember, Adam
Vaziri the Lonely Vampire".

Adam was biding time and maybe Hashaan knew
this. He seemed to be reaching into Adam's mind,
but for some reason his minions were not
advancing. It was as if they were simply an
extension of him somehow. That must have been
what Janet meant when she said she had ingested
his essence. But he needed to get out of here, and
time was running out.

As if on cue, the main gates behind them starting
moving inwards, revealing a large executive coach
with blacked out windows. It stopped halfway inside
the courtyard, unable to go any further for the
scene playing out in front of it. The coach door
opened and a handful of men dressed in black and
carrying pistols jumped down. Hashaan spun round
and in one motion his cloaked spectres rushed at
them. The men barely had time to let off bullets
before being overwhelmed by the swarm, blood
spraying everywhere as throats were ripped out
and limbs torn from their bodies as if they were
made of nothing. One of the men managed a few
shots from his pistol, aiming wildly at shapes that
darted from side to side like shadows and Adam
heard a yell from somewhere to the side. It seemed
to come from an entrance to a wing of the prison,
but he had no time to investigate as Hashaan used
the sudden distraction to his advantage, leaping

into the air and knocking Adam backwards to the ground. He leaned over him, pinning his arms to the concrete slabs and sneering, his eyes glowing like burning torches.

"Your blood is like a nectar I have never tasted. It flows through me and I cannot believe the extra life it has given me, nor the strength over you now".

"You think that by having a few drops of my blood you are now so much more superior to me. You will never be able to control what's inside you. Our two species do not mix".

"And yet here I am overpowering you". Hashaan replied, opening his maw wide revealing his rows of sharp fang-like teeth. "I'm going to chew on your bones now".

Adam reached into himself, to that part of him that he had spent so many centuries supressing for fear of being outed to the world. His eyes took on an ominous glow of orange, his own set of incisors stretching down. His body seemed to swell slightly beneath his skin and Hashaan struggled to hold him in place. Steadily Adam pushed himself up, easily lifting this serpentine being up with him without even having to try hard.

"Have you ever wondered why I am still here after all these years? You never asked the question why I came up here to this hellhole?"

As Hashaan let go of his arms, Adam slammed the creature's torso into the concrete, like a bolt of lightning hitting the ground, forcing a few slabs to crack under the force. Their positions were now utterly reversed as Adam gave in to his predatorial side, letting the rage and feral instincts take over completely, not caring who saw. This was now a battleground. Pushing as hard as he could, Adam felt ribs crack and the air filled with a shrill scream as yellow gunk starting pouring out of Hashaan's now ruined cloak, seeping into the floor.

"I have looking for you for a very long time, you disgusting piece of vermin. And now I have you. I have tried breaking your bones, so let's see if you survive this".

And with that, he grabbed hold of a slimy heart from within Hashaan's chest cavity and ripped it out, throwing it across the courtyard to explode against the outer wall. Hashaan had a look of utter shock mixed with fear, his last words being "But how can you beat me? You will never win, I am..." and then nothing. The glow disappeared from his eyes, and his snake-like jaws relaxed as his head lopped to one side. As Adam stood up, he looked down at the still, wretched form and growled "I'm a god amongst men, you just slither along the shit we excrete for you".

Janet pulled on his arm, bringing Adam back to the bigger picture around them. Hashaan's servants were reeling in pain, holding their heads and squirming over the bloodied corpses of the guards. It was as if some connection in their brains had been severed and they were shutting down. Janet too was holding a hand to her temple, but as she had already severed most of her link, the effect seemed not quite as severe. All of a sudden, shots started ringing out and one by one black cloaks crumpled to the ground. A guard that had been hiding inside the coach had found the courage to step out and, seeing an opportunity was taking them out one by one, easy pickings. Within less than a minute, all was silence, the faint whooshing sound of the ricochets dying out. Then Adam noticed the guard was pointing the gun at him. Pulling the trigger, Adam was quick enough to move to one side, the bullet passing through into the darkness of the room behind him.

Within a split second he was next to the guard, wrenching the gun out of his hand and sinking his teeth into the man's neck, not caring about the mess he made. This guard was a long needed meal and Adam had gone full vampire. As the last drop of blood flowing like silk down his throat, Adam let go of the now limp, empty body and it fell to the ground. He gave out a loud sigh, feeling the warm, sweet liquid fill him with utter euphoria. A quick bite here and there from unsuspecting victims over the centuries was nothing compared to draining a body completely and in this moment, Adam didn't care if he never supressed his dark passenger again.

Forty Eight

Charles was frozen in his seat, gripped by fear. He couldn't stop the same thought from spinning in his head, *how had it come to this?*

From the screams of guards being literally pulled apart, to gunshots reverberating off the courtyard, and now the gurgling sound of the last remaining guard being eaten alive right next to the entrance to the very coach he was trapped in, Charles', mind was near to fracture point. Farling however, *the slimy weasel,* seemed to be revelling in it all, smiling wide-eyed as he peered out of the windscreen. The maniac could almost have been munching on popcorn!

"Oh this is priceless. The Master is dead, his servants are dead, which puts us, well, me at least, at the top of the chain".

He turned to look straight at Charles, his eyes alight with a look of pure evil. "You can be my assistant if you play your cards right. But just remember, Julie and Alex are the reason you have to comply. Their lives are literally in your hands right now Charles". Even before finishing the last sentence, Farling was turning back around, as if to signify how insignificant in his mind Charles actually was.

The mere mention of his beloved wife and son being put back on the bargaining table seemed to snap Charles out of his trance and without even thinking, he jumped out of his seat, grabbing Farling's laptop from where he had left it and swung as hard as he could at the back of the man's head. There was an almighty crack, but not entirely from the screen breaking in its case. Farling fell over to one side and Charles kept hitting him, smashing his nose until it was a bloody mess smeared across his broken cheekbone, left eye closed and lips split. It was only the sound of Adam breathing heavily as he climbed up into the coach that made Charles come to his senses. Stopping with the laptop raised above an unconscious Farling, Charles looked down at a mass of blood and spittle, snot bubbles forming and popping out of what should have been a nose, but was now a mound of flesh just trying to get air in.

"Can you drive this?" Adam asked simply, looking at Charles with glowing orange eyes, and a strangely ageless face also covered with blood.

"Erm, yes I think so" came Charles' feeble answer as he dropped the broken laptop. "I mean, I've never driven a coach before, but I guess it can't be that hard".

"Let's hope it's the easiest thing in the world for you. We need to leave, and now!"

Charles looked back down at Farling coughing up blood and seeming to choke. Adam went over to him, lifting him up with ease. For a moment Charles thought he was going to eat another victim, but Adam merely threw Farling out onto the ground outside. "I know you, I've seen you on television haven't I?" Adam quizzed, not really looking for a response. Misdirection often gave renewed focus to a situation and that was what Adam needed of Charles right now.

"I'm Charles McNeil MP, Minister for the State of Prisons. And you are?"

Adam couldn't help but burst out laughing "State of prisons eh? Well, you're doing a fantastic bang up job, aren't you? I'd rip your throat out right here and now, but I need you to get me South. Now drive and don't give me another reason to rethink my plan, Okay Charles?"

Hearing these rhetorical questions, Charles got into the driver's seat while Adam stood next to him. There was a lever to Charles' right for the door and the automatic gears were next to the steering wheel, also on the right. They seemed simple enough for Charles and, putting the beast in reverse he found it relatively easy to ease the coach out onto the main street. As they straightened up, Adam quickly signalled for Charles to open the door. He jumped down and pulled shut the two wooden gates, sealing in from the world the carnage that had unfolded. Climbing back on board, Adam turned to Charles and muttered "There is some major bullshit you are now going to have to spin to cover this up. You understand that right, Mr MP?"

And that is exactly what Charles did. Moving steadily down the M6, Charles spoke with Victoria, Head of Scotland Yard. After a brief few moments of letting her spit and seethe down the other end of the line in utter contempt at his apparent lack of ability to handle any given situation, Charles cut her off and, under the watchful stare of Adam in the rear-view mirror, starting formulating the most wonderful bullshit story to cover up the atrocities. Once the call ended, Adam came back up from where he was sat calming himself down with half a bottle of scotch. "You really are all slimy bastards aren't you? In it all together like some elite, long-running swingers party. You know how each other tastes so much you can pretty much concoct anything together, can't you? All the while, society is none the wiser. Hashaan was right, humans really are nothing but sheep".

"Hashaan? You mean the Master?" Charles had never heard his actual name before now.

"Oh no Charles, that is not your Master. We are all but pawns here my slippery friend. All the world's a stage and all that. But I happen to like the world we live in, for the most part. Of course, whether or not this extends to you relies wholeheartedly on me finding my young friend David Jennings alive, well, and most importantly a free man".

"After everything that has happened, I have no idea if that is going to be possible! I mean, his face was on the news".

"But you're a master of bullshit right? A media magician surely?" Adam leaned in close, making Charles swerve slightly as he edged away. "You best make another phone call, Mr McNeil MP".

Charles dialled Victoria one more time, rapid scheming running through his head as he heard the ringtones.

Forty Nine

Xion woke with a start at the guard gently pushing her shoulder. She had been asleep the entire trip to Brighton, a much needed and somewhat dreamless recharging of her batteries. Receiving a surprise call from David was the best news ever, knowing he had made it to Abe's and would stay there until she arrived. Xion realised that she had been far more worried about her friend than she had for her own safety.

"Sorry to startle you Miss. We've arrived into Brighton, but police are questioning everyone that has embarked at Gatwick, as there was apparently some kind of terrorist incident that matched the one in London, shots fired into a coach or something. Apparently a taxi driver and a police officer were murdered close to Euston station in Broad daylight in his own taxi! Crazy days we're living in right?"

They had shot a police officer too?! "Hi, err, thanks for the heads up. Not sure what information I could give them though". Xion was visibly shaken at the thought of being grilled by the police. *What if they have me down as a person of interest? Like an E-Fit picture or something?* She was panicking and feeling tense all over again.

The guard noticed this and tried to calm her down "It's ok, I'm sure they'll only want to know if you were there and if you saw anything. Nothing to get worked up about".

But this did nothing to calm her down. Xion started crying. Feeling a little awkward, the guard sat down on the seat opposite her and patiently waited for Xion to stop, desperately thinking on his recent training in dealing with panic attacks and difficult passengers. *Shit!* He thought to himself, *if only I had actually paid attention to the bloody course instead of wishing it to end.*

"Is there anything I can do to help? You seem really shook up. Did you witness anything?"

Xion took a deep breath. This was a complete stranger. *Maybe I can tell him something and he can help me?* She thought. It was a big risk, but how else could she get out of this? "Look, I really can't talk to them. I was at Euston and it was a friend of a friend that was shot in the arm. Freaked me out so much I ran straight onto the coach. But I didn't see a thing. I flipping left my anxiety meds at the station and just need to get home".

"My sister suffers with really bad panic attacks, I know how debilitating it can be. I never heard that anyone else had been shot though! Not in the station anyway. There wasn't anything on the news about that. So you knew the person? Shit, that must have seriously been terrifying for you!"

"Oh my god, yes! I didn't actually know her, but I keep thinking it could have been me, you know? As I said, I just want to get home. I can pop into the station later to give a statement. I just can't do it now, not until I've had my meds. Please help me. Sorry, what's your name?"

Xion was feeling better as she thought on her feet. Problem solving was her job after all. This was what she did and what she was best at. And this young guard seemed to have a bit of a thing for her, it seemed.

"My name's Jakob, and yours?" he said with a big grin, feeling like he had properly scored.

"Jane, as in Plain Jane" she replied, mustering up the best and cheekiest grin she could. Jakob was actually quite cute, his short spikey blond hair perfect above a small ovel face that resembled an elf. He only looked to be in the late teens though, maybe older with these young looks. He had a tattoo of leaves and vines that seemed to snake down from somewhere up his right sleeve, finishing just passed the wrist and touching his right hand. Nothing too lairy, but enough to think that this was a lad that could think outside the box and also maybe even the rules on occasion. After all, only a few years ago he may not even have been employed in Customer Service with a visible tattoo.

"Look Jane, with that awesome pink hair you are most likely far from plain". *Easy there tiger* she whispered to herself "Listen, I could get into trouble for even thinking of the idea. But I can get you out through the back staff exit to the carpark. You will have to wear a hi vis and put on that red cap. But please go to the police station later okay? You know you could help them, right?"

Xion could not believe her luck. It had been so shit thus far, maybe things were finally changing for her and she could actually get to David without any further incidents.

She nodded and, following his cue by standing up, she followed Jakob to the back of the train. There weren't any other passengers still onboard and, once she had put on a hi vis vest Jakob had acquired from a storage cupboard they both slowly alighted onto the platform. The good thing about these trains from Gatwick and London was the sheer length of them. This particular one had eight coaches, which meant they were well out of sight of anyone milling about by the barriers, namely anyone in black and blue uniforms. Jakob kept going until they were back out in the open air, then hopped down onto the rails.

"Are you sure this is okay? Isn't there some kind of regulation saying we can't do this? Jakob, I really don't want you to get the sack!"

He held out his hands and with a bit of an awkward jump, Xion landed on the gravel. Looking back at her, he said simply "I'll not lie, this job is a bit shit to be honest. No one is particularly nice to you and as for the kids, all they want to do is try and get away with not paying. Some of the adults too come to think of it! And because I look young, I get zero respect off anyone".

But you ARE young! Thought Xion. Anyhow, he was her ticket out of here and the last thing she wanted to do was inadvertently change his mind. So she nodded again in a sympathetic way before they made their way across to the far edge of the end platform which ran adjacent to the car park. There was a locked gate leading to it and Jakob typed in a code before the gate buzzed and opened a crack.

"Wait here whilst I have a look to make sure it is clear okay?" Jakob whispered. Xion grabbed the gate, stopping it from closing automatically as he disappeared round the corner of the station building, returning a few moments later with a worried look on his face. "The whole of the back of the station is blocked by police. They are stopping everyone. I don't know how you are going to get out".

Looking around, Xion noticed some old pallets leant up against the wall. They were fairly small and, picking one of them up she motioned for Jakob to open the gate again. "They are all stored at the back of the car park. Just walk along the fence as far as you can go. You'll see the car park ramp going down. I don't know if the police are stopping people coming into the car park though."

"Then you pick up another pallet and come with me. Please Jakob, help me!" Xion pleaded with him.

"Okay, Okay. If we get stopped at least it will look better being the two of us and I can show them my ID. Just let me do all the talking ok?"

"Absolutely, sounds perfect to me" replied Xion and off they went, lugging pallets that after just a few moments felt a bit too heavy, forcing Xion to stop every few steps. There was indeed a police car blocking the entrance to the car park, but they did not seem too bothered about either Jakob or Xion as they propped the pallets up against a couple of Biffa bins and made their way out onto the street. Jakob showed them his ID anyway, but the two officers stood by their car simply waved them through. Xion couldn't believe her luck. She also felt a bit bad that Jakob would likely get into trouble for helping her. Hopefully the CCTV cameras didn't pick them up or no one was watching. He could slip back into the station at the front perhaps. Jakob had the same idea. "Right. I'm going to pretend I was on a break or something by getting back in round the front. With the station on lockdown I shouldn't get questioned much. You take care okay?"

"Thank you Jakob, you're a superstar" Xion replied. Shaking his hand vigorously and taking off her hi vis, Xion made her way across the street and down some steps which led her towards a large church with a huge roof. This area seemed full of small back streets which hid Xion well as she continued to cross one after the other, finally coming to a small park area by the side of another large church. Sitting on the bench, Xion took a moment to focus her breathing whilst she contemplated her next move. She knew she needed to ring David but was still worried that by doing so might put him in more trouble. *Fuck it,* she said under her breath and dialled his number.

"Xi! Where are you?"

"Hey Dee, I'm here, just making my way to you now. Bit of a shitshow at the station, loads of police. People want us so bad Dee. Never known anything like this!"

There was a pause before David responded. "Well, I'm about to add to the list of shite then mate. Did you know that Adam has gone up to bloody Stafford to collect me? What's with all that shit eh? Where is he?"

Xion did not want to answer at first, but with everything that was going on, she couldn't hide anything from her friend. "Dee, please don't be mad with me, but yes I knew he was heading up there. The plan was to get you out ages ago, but things have been getting so strange. Adam wouldn't let me go with him, but neither did he want to go at first. Something about him being spotted by some other creatures. I swear I would have come up to see you, but he had me busy on so many things and without you, I had double the work to do! Then he just up and left. He didn't tell me where exactly he was travelling to, but I could only guess it was to get you out".

"But I never saw him. And if he got caught in there, with those creatures draining every one of their blood… What if he's got himself caught and they've figured out who he is, who he really is?"

Flashbacks of his cellmate Billy gently swinging with a trickle of blood making patterns on a cold dark floor made David shudder. He had been so close to being slaughtered like a pig and so lucky to escape the way he had. Perhaps Adam would put a stop to it, once he figured out what was going on. Xion's voice quickly snapped him back. "Look, we really shouldn't be chatting like this, not until we're in person. I think I'm just twenty minutes' walk from you. Hang tight, okay?" and with that, Xion hung up.

She sat there a moment staring at the phone and feeling guilty. He had spent the best part of three months inside with no contact from either her or Adam. It was at Adam's request and she couldn't shake the feeling that he knew more than he had been letting on. But this was no surprise and certainly nothing out of the ordinary. Adam kept so many secrets, his head must be so full after eight centuries! And her feelings for this geek made it even more painful. She decided to ring him back quickly. To her surprise, at first it came up with an unobtainable tone, but then a high-pitched sound rang out, a sound Xion knew all too well from her job as a hacker. Her phone had been set up as a trace! Quickly, she switched it off and took out the battery. *Shit!* she thought, *You stupid idiot. They have been tracking you! And they must have been tracking David's phone too.*

There was no time to lose, she had to get to the safe place they had both visited up in Kemptown. Although It was just a fairly short distance from where she sat, it was mostly uphill. But at least there were plenty of backstreets where Xion could stay hidden along the way. She got up, putting the phone and battery in her pocket and started across the park, moving East towards a building she knew as part of Brighton University. Actually it was art studios owned by the University and behind were lots of small streets snaking their way up the hill towards Kemptown.

Fifty

Shayanne waited quietly in the car whilst Henryk got them both a coffee. Only moments before she had got the call from their employer informing them that both of the little shits' phones had successfully been hacked and that they would soon receive coordinates. After the chaos in London and then losing the girl at Gatwick, Shayanne was done with this particular assignment. Too many eyes and too many variables. She just didn't like it. At least the police had clearly been told to keep their identities out of the media. Shyanne smiled thinly as she thought of just how many politicians and other people high up in the chain were being controlled like marionettes. *You are all sheep, target practice for me should I so desire,* There had been nothing on the radio about the police wanting to find certain suspects. At least this was some good news. Her phone pinged a message and Shayanne stared at some numbers she knew to be a location. As she typed them into Google Maps, the location appeared to be Brighton seafront, but shortly after another message pinged, showing more numbers which gave a location next to St Peter's Church, not far from the back of the train station. They had not been able to get anywhere near Brighton Station as it was surrounded by police. But these second co-ordinates had to have been her! And as for the first set, these could only have meant they had both of their quarries very much in sight!

Henryk climbed back into the car, handed
Shayanne her coffee and waited for the good news.
"Well about fucking time! We can grab both of them
and be done with this shitty job".

"They would have moved already by now" Shyanne
cautioned him, "probably meeting up and so with a
lot of luck, we should get further co-ordinates
showing them close together. While we wait, let's
do a recce near the second set. Hopefully we'll get
lucky as the little bitch could only have just got off
the train. I'm impressed she made it out of the
station. We should think about hiring her instead of
putting a bullet in her head. She's a smart one,
that's for sure".

Henryk smiled as he turned to Shayanne "I thought
you wanted to take your sweet time with her. Hasn't
it been a while since you got to use your knives? It
is your signature after all, peeling them alive like
some delicious fruit. No?"

"Oh Henryk, are you flirting with me? If so you are
once again barking up the wrong tree. I'd rather
have a go at this little minx we're chasing. You can
watch if you like, hold the camera steady". She
punched him in the ribs and he let out a yelp,
almost spilling his coffee in his lap.

"Hey!"

"Go to St. Peter's Church, just up there. Then we'll just have to try the side streets leading up the hill. She would have gone that way using the quiet streets. But the police station is not far so be careful alright? Don't look too suspicious".

"Whatever you is think boss". Replied Henryk as they moved out from where they were parked, making their way slowly to where Xion had been sitting moments before and unaware of just how close they were to her.

Fifty One

Adam was back to his human self as he sat on one of the armchair-style seats halfway down the coach, having finished the bottle of expensive Brandy and was now on to the bottle of Whiskey Farling had kept next to him. Thinking of the sheer anger that went through Charles as he had launched himself at Farling, laptop in hand and rage in his eyes, Adam slightly admired this unassuming man driving them down the M25. The rage must have been building up inside him for a long time for it to erupt in such a manner as to practically take a guy's head off with a laptop!

This Farling character had still been alive when they had left him with the other corpses at Stafford, but only just. Hashaan was another story altogether. Adam liked to believe that he had successfully rid the world of this hideous snake creature. But something deep down inside was telling him a different story. There had been so many occasions throughout his long life where adversaries had unexpectantly popped up years after he had supposedly dispatched them. Fighting both the Germans and then the Russians during the 1940s and 1950s had made him slightly fearful of the resilience of the human condition and its determination to survive and conquer at all costs. What the nazi scientists left behind after the second World War, the Russians then took up and continued with results that were both phenomenal and terrifying in equal measures. It had taken the loss of many friends to put a stop to them, but even now Adam doubted he had really rid the world of their evil stench. And now he feared the same of Hashaan and his minions. This serpent demon answered to someone or something higher up the chain after all.

And what about this bloodletting business that the government were in on, not to mention the police and god knows who else? They should have burnt the prison to the ground, but that would have meant freeing all of the criminals onto the streets of Stafford. It was a real pickle, no doubt about that. And Charles was thick in the middle of it, as was he. For now at least. Adam got up and walked over to the front of the coach. Charles had been very quiet as he drove. Adam was again impressed with this man's skills. He had picked up driving a coach very well and looked like he had done it before.

"So when did you last drive a coach then?" he asked Charles testily.

"What? This is my first time" answered Charles with a start.

"No it isn't. I'm realising you have a few skills to your belt, like lying and manipulating, these are things a politician needs of course. But you have other, older skills. It seems that driving large vehicles is one of these. So tell me, where did you learn?"

There was an awkward silence before Charles, who was obviously weighing up whether he should lie or not, answered truthfully. "I was a driver for our local MP before I took the oath myself. I had to learn to drive all manner of cars and even a corporate bus. Not that hard really. It also meant I could listen to conversations and learn from them".

But Adam had stopped listening and was laughing uncontrollably "I'm sorry, did you just say you took an oath? To do what exactly? Lie, cheat and totally brainwash the public into thinking and doing what you want at all times and to keep them in the dark about what is actually going on in the world?"

"Well, we could of course have told them about your kind and others like you. How would that have gone down do you think?" Charles responded, a little too narky for his own good. Adam stopped laughing suddenly and looked at him with hard, brown eyes "That really would not have gone down well at all, for you".

After a few moments more of uneasy silence, Adam thought it time to bring up what had happened back at the prison. "So, I take it you had arrived at the prison to see how this project was getting on? Anything else I should know?"

"I was there to facilitate the opening of more centres in other prisons. It's a great and viable project. Innocent people are not dying and the public opinion is that most of these criminals are scumbags that shouldn't be let out anyway. We're doing society two favours here!"

"What kind of twisted reality do you live in here? How is any of this "doing the world a favour"?" Adam couldn't believe the words coming out of Charles' mouth. The man was insane.

"Think about it, we rid society of scum that would only recommit crimes once they were released anyway and at the same time solve a national shortage of blood. Donors never need to know where it has come from and if they need it they're not going to give two shits as to where it has come from, are they? It's a total win win".

"And I suppose you are selling this blood back to the NHS rather than donating it yourselves?" Adam asked, knowing full well the answer.

"Every enterprise needs money to keep going. The NHS strikes for better pay and the government raises taxes to give it to them. They then use some of that extra money to pay for the blood. So really it's the public fundamentally paying for their own blood donations. Without them knowing it".

"You're totally deluded. And anyway, it's over now. The police will be swarming in there as we speak, see all of the carnage and unexplained bodies and all of this shit will be blown wide open".

Now it was Charles' turn to laugh "Now who's being deluded? We own the police remember? Nothing will be on the news. In fact, I'm betting there will be a mass prisoner transfer happening as we speak. Let's turn on the radio and see shall we?"

He flicked a switch and, sure enough, there was a breaking story on most of the stations.

"…without a doubt one of the biggest prison shake-ups in recent history. We can see another prisoner bus exiting Stafford Prison now. This is the fourth bus to leave, confirming suspicions that this prison is to be shut down with immediate effect. As to where these prisoners will be taken is anyone's guess. The system is already at full capacity, with many people, rightly or wrongly I might add, asking the hard question of whether they shouldn't just disappear altogether and save the public tens of millions of pounds a year. And so, once again, the main story this hour is that HMP Stafford has been shut down following a surprise visit from Charles McNeil MP, Minister for the State of Prisons. He has promised there will be massive shake-ups in prisons and this is surely one of many to follow. We will have more on this as it unfolds, but for now I take you back to the studio".

Adam could not believe the sheer magnitude of the lie he was hearing "Well, I've been around a long time, but this has to be one of the biggest and quickest weaving piles of bullshit! How the hell did you manage this so quickly?"

"It wasn't me. But now that you have killed everyone involved there, it definitely seems my job is intact, doesn't it?" Charles couldn't keep the smile from his face. The threat on his family had surely been taken away now and he would be elevated. But this vampire was still a big problem that he couldn't solve on his own. Charles just hoped that the strange creature and leader of the cloaked freaks called Hashaan was not in fact The

Master himself, as Adam had hinted. He would need higher help if he was to insure Adam never spoke of what had happened. There was still these runaway delinquents David and Xion to care of still too. But perhaps Victoria had been made good on her promise to call off the search. They still hadn't heard anything about it yet, but if her idea of stringing a story together that he had been caught turned out, Adam should at least leave him alone.

"What's going through your scheming mind now?" broke in Adam, who was looking quizzically at Charles.

"I am just wondering if you are going to feed on me before this journey comes to an end?" Charles replied cautiously, but a little too confidently. Adam smiled at him, but there was no joy in his eyes. "You are useful to me for now Charles my friend. For now. Did this Victoria woman say where David was travelling to by any chance?"

"They think he is going to Brighton. But the news should soon say that he has been recaptured and that the search has been called off. For intents and purposes he is now a free man. The public will quickly forget and move on". Adam was worried that if this information did not flow directly down to David himself, his twitchy geek of a friend may do something stupid to put himself back in the spotlight. He had to get to him sooner rather than later. "Can this bloody bus not go any faster for God's sake?"

"You really shouldn't…" Charles started but Adam cut him off. "If you are going to tell me not take the Lord's name in vain, I tell you now I am your God and your Lord. I am your Master until I decide otherwise. Now get us the fuck to Brighton!"

And with that, Adam moved back to his seat, quietly seething at everything Charles had told him. There was no way to stop this bloodletting from happening and he knew it. It had been going on for so long, in so many different countries. And now it had set up shop here in his beloved England. He hadn't even cut the head off the snake, that was for sure. In fact, Adam couldn't shake off the feeling that Hashaan's heart would grow back soon enough, literally speaking.

Looking out of the window, he spotted a sign for the A23 and knew they were close now. He had several contacts in Brighton, one at the Royal Sussex Hospital and another at a safehouse close by in Kemptown. Aberash was an old friend. He had sentient gifts that came in useful from time to time and some kind of magik that had apparently been passed down to him through generations on his mother's side. A long line of wisemen and women flowed through his DNA, or so he said. Adam wasn't exactly a sceptic, after all, he had been around enough to see all kinds of unexplainable things. Hell, he was living proof of one of them! But Adam had learned to be overly cautious. He didn't trust people and refused to draw them too close. Everyone around him died one way or another anyhow, so what was the point?

Fifty Two

Janet wandered through the side streets of Stafford with only a minimal sense of where she wanted to go. Some distant memory of a house nearby that meant something to her. But there was another voice that clawed at her mind with wanton fury. A voice telling her to kill and feed. Then a picture of a man and a small girl came to the front of her thoughts. They looked so familiar, as if they meant something special to her. A strange and overwhelming urge to find them and another feeling. Was it love?

Janet looked up and realised she had stopped outside a terraced property that stood on the other side of town to the prison. She had definitely seen this red door before, with its number painted in white on a plaque with pretty yellow flowers around it. A brass knocker seemed to call for Janet to announce her arrival, which she did automatically, without thought. After a few moments the door opened and the small girl from a distant memory stood there, barely reaching her waist. "Mummy!" she squealed and wrapped her arms around Janet's mid-section.

"Janet darling is that you?" came a male voice followed by another familiar figure appearing in the doorway. He was taller than Janet, but not by much, with messy brown hair and spectacles that seemed to match the geeky look he was going for with a tatty knitted jumper and brown chords.

"Where the bloody hell have you been? Are you ok? It's been all over the news! We were so worried!" The barrage of words came out at supersonic speed and it was only after he took a breath that the colour drained from his face as he took in the sight of this cloaked figure in front of him. "What has happened to you Janet? You look terrible. And where's your hair gone? Come in, come in, before the neighbours see you" he added quickly, pulling her in with the girl still attached like a belt.

Once Janet was safely inside, Robert closed the door behind her and then proceeded in taking off her dirty cloak that hung like rags over her frame. He almost yelping in shock at her naked, skinny frame and Matilda the small girl seemed confused and a little worried. "Mummy, why are you not wearing any clothes? And where is your hair? You look very pale. Are you sick? Daddy, mummy is sick".

"Yes, precious, mummy is sick. Why don't you go and play in your room for a bit while daddy gets her dressed, then we can make mummy better. Okay?" Robert was feeling a little scared now. This was not entirely the wife he had said goodbye to early this morning. She was not making any sounds other than a rasping-type breathing. Thankfully, Matilda went upstairs to her room without any fuss and Robert led Janet into the living room, sitting her down on the sofa. Closing the curtains to any possible nosey neighbours outside, he wrapped one of their patchwork throws over her shoulders, then knelt down in front of her.

It was then that he took in for the first time the lack of colour in her skin. She was skeletal too and Robert immediately reached for the phone. He was about to dial for the doctor when Janet suddenly grabbed his hand, hurting him a little as she snatched the cordless receiver from his fingers. "No, don't do that". She said simply and quietly.

"But my love, you are really sick and something has happened to you. We need to get you to a hospital, like now and find out what it is. Can you at least tell me what happened today at the prison? Why are they shutting it down and moving all of the prisoners away? Please my darling, tell me something! Don't just sit there!"

He was about to get up just enough so that he could sit down next to her, but something inside Janet seemed to take over. A pounding sounded in her head that smothered her husband's pleading and an insatiable thirst overwhelmed her. Without warning she hit him hard on the head with the phone. It was a blow that defied her slight stature and blood started trickling down the side of Robert's face.

"Wha…?" was all he could muster before she brought the receiver down hard again, knocking him out cold. Seeing the blood forced the other voice in her mind to come forward, whispering "drink, you must feed". It had the same tone as her master, but how could that be? Janet seemed to lose all sense of herself and instinctively jumped on her husband. Her jaw opened and stretched wide, her teeth elongating to sharp points, like those of a snake. With a loud crunching sound, she took a large bite out of her husband's head. The lack of nerves and vessels meant that there was no spurt of blood, but instead red jelly-like matter simply fell out of the open skull to the carpet. With Robert simply twitching uncontrollably, Janet then went down further, this time severing several arteries in his neck and drinking up the fast flowing blood that shot out. It covered everything and even sprayed above the foot of the stairway, dripping off the family portraits hanging there.

Matilda had not been able to play with her doll house, as she was too worried about mummy. It wasn't until she heard a weird munching sound that she made the decision to go back downstairs and see what was going on. Reaching halfway down the stairs, she was hit with a warm liquid that touched her forehead and cheeks.

"Daddy? Mummy? What's happening?" she cried, not wanting to go any further and suddenly scared. Instead, she turned and ran back up the stairs, rushing into her parents' room and quickly climbing under the big king-size bed. She laid there for what seemed like an eternity, before the sounds of creaking stairs stopped her breathing, eyes wide as saucers. Then nothing again. She almost had time to take breath before bony hands grabbed her ankles and pulled her out from where she thought was a safe space.

Deirdre and Norman had been enjoying a nice game of Scrabble when they heard it from next door, a high-pitched scream that made their blood run cold.

"Dear Gods! Was that little Matilda?" Norman gasped, dropping the letters he had in his hand and was about place. "I think it was Norman. Quick, call the police!" Deirdre replied as she too dropped her letters and reached for the phone. As she dialled the number, Norman physically shook, looking down at the poor 3 letter word he was about to place:

RUN

Fifty Three

As the last of the prison buses exited the big gates, officers could finally close off the scene and start to usher the press away from the cordoned off areas either side. They had managed to block off most of the pavement area outside, with camera flashes snapping blindly at the small blackened out windows hoping to get a glimpse of this hot story. There were so many unanswered questions and a few of the locals had actually showed up with placards that read:

KEEP THE PRISON OPEN!

PRISON SYSTEM 0   REOFFENDING 1

Victoria had arrived shortly before and was trying to placate both the public and press as she had half a dozen microphones as well as phones and Dictaphones shoved in her face.

"Firstly, I want to thank everyone for both their patience and also for their sensitivity and understanding in this particularly difficult situation. I can only apologise on behalf of the Metropolitan Police and Prison System for the exceptionally low standard of care found within these walls, but I can assure everyone here and at home that we are doing everything in our joint power to ensure prisoners are treated both fairly and as is deserving of their crimes. They have been segregated accordingly and will be rehoused in appropriate category prisons as per their relative sentences. No one need worry about them being freed early or undeservedly. Stafford prison will be put under thorough review with major changes being made before it can be reopened. As we speak, other prisons will also be looked at, with appropriate actions being taken should issues and concerns be unfolded during this process of reform. Thank you for your time. Now please, if I can urge everyone to disband and let these officers and investigators get on with their important tasks. Your safety is our upmost concern after all".

There were a few disgruntled mutterings from amongst the crowd as Victoria turned and walked through the smaller door inset within the large wooden gates. As this was closed behind her, she could just make out the officers' tones change to one with more authority. The crowd raised their voices still as a few officers in completely unnecessary riot gear (purely for a show of power) went about moving everyone on from the scene, with many shouting "It's my God given right to stand here if I want! You can't make me move!" Victoria smiled as she walked into the centre of the courtyard, *Oh you have no idea what we can make you do, little people* she thought to herself.

The bloodletting project had gone without a hitch for so many years, way before she joined the force almost twenty years ago. But these last few days, the system had become an absolute disaster. She looked at the state of the courtyard. Although all of the bodies had now been cleared away and stored in the central brick building, there were still red stains everywhere which gave away secrets of a massacre. It looked like the remnants of some battlefield. An officer approached her and saluted stupidly. "Why are you saluting me you dumb idiot?" she barked at him.

"Sorry Ma'am. I'm just not sure how to address you is all".

Victoria looked hard at him, a young spindly character that looked a bit too fresh faced and pimply for her liking. "You don't address me. You just explain and then get the fuck out of my face. Got it Constable?"

"Yes Ma'am, sorry Ma'am."

"Good. Now take me in there". She pointed to the round building. "Show me this shitshow".

Together they went inside the building, where the walls were lined with black body bags. Tripod spotlights had been set up flooding the room with light that it had not seen in decades. It really was a filthy place, and the smell made Victoria want to gag. At the back in the middle was a kind of raised platform made out of the same bricks as the walls. Chains dangled from the ceiling on a pulley system, with the ends attached to hooks either side. Piles of large buckets were stacked up and a few crates with white rubber tubing. Blood stains were everywhere, but mainly all over the floor. The throat-catching metallic smell of blood seemed to draw in all of the oxygen, making it feel very heavy and opposing.

"Have these bodies been checked and identified yet?"

"Not yet Ma'am. Some of the forensic team have attempted to identify a few of the bodies, but they said it has been hard to piece some of them back together. Some of them, they said, don't even appear to be entirely human looking. I haven't had the stomach to look myself Ma'am".

Victoria suddenly turned on him "And nor should you Constable! It is not your place here, do you understand? Your job is to show your superiors, which is pretty much everyone other than you, around and not ask questions but answer them. And where's my cup of tea?"

The young officer blinked slightly at this strange end to her tirage, but then simply nodded and darted towards the exit, with Victoria shouting after him "Two sugars, Constable!"

Once he was out of her sight, Victoria searched the room for someone who looked to be in charge. She found a tall officer with disposable clear plastic coverings over his police cap and uniform looking at one of the body bags and marched over to him. He quickly stood up. "Detective Sergeant Trigger, Ma'am. Very nasty business this, very nasty".

"What the hell happened here Detective?" She asked, with her usual hint of venom on the tongue. These past few years, Victoria had woken up most mornings wondering if it was time to hang up her cape, so to speak. She had started to despise everyone she worked with, and this malice was seeping into her tone and mannerisms. As Chief Inspector she could get away with it, as most were highly afraid of her anyway and would never dare confront her or report her to HR, but things were changing. Society was becoming too soft and fluffy, with everyone getting offended by the simplest things. It had become a world she was pretty sure she did not want to be on the top rung of anymore. But she had got herself too deeply embroiled in the seedy secrets now binding this country together, to simply pass on the mantle and walk away. *Far too deep*, she thought to herself as Detective Trigger gave his impression of what had gone on.

"From what we could ascertain from both the ground and CCTV, a tall man appeared out of this room into the courtyard followed by one of the cloaked figures. Some kind of cult we think that has been performing rituals here in secret for years from this very room. Some kind of blood cult, probably satanic of nature. They were met by other cloaked figures and a fight started out but was interrupted by a coach entering either at the right or wrong moment, depending on how you want to look at it. Bodyguards got off the coach but were immediately ripped to pieces by these cloaked figures. They managed to get a few rounds off first and one or two stray bullets killed a prison guard, shot through the neck over there".

Trigger pointed over to the entrance of the Vulnerable Prisoners' wing before continuing. "Quite unnatural how these cloaked figures managed to kill the much bigger security guards, given the difference in size and stature, not to mention the force needed to rip limbs apart with the bare hands. Then what appeared to be the leader of the cult attacked the lone man and pinned him to the ground. Just as he did that, the man seemed to change somehow and killed this leader, ripping out his heart or some other body part. Hard to tell that particular detail exactly from the CCTV Ma'am".

He paused again for dramatic effect, expecting Victoria to be shocked at what she was hearing.

But she simply held her hands out, muttering "And then? Come on man, spit it out".

"Err, right Ma'am, well, there was another bodyguard still on the coach and he then opened fire, killing the cloaked figures. But the lone man ran to him with incredible speed and ripped his throat out it seemed, drinking him! Never seen anything like it Ma'am! He then got on the coach and after a few moments a small unconscious man was thrown out and the coach backed out. We believe this unconscious man to be the Assistant to Charles McNeil MP, Farling, but there appears to be no sign of him. Nor is there sign of the cloaked form that came out of the building with this lone man, animal, character."

"And what of the leader of the cult? Where is his body?" Victoria asked, a hint of impatience now in her tone that seemed different to the irritancy of before.

"Oh yes, he is over here". And Trigger led Victoria over to where a few of the body bags were stacked up. He pulled the top one down onto the cold dank concrete floor and unzipped it. "Sorry Ma'am, but this is not for the faint hearted".

"You really think me of faint heart, Detective? You really don't know me do you?"

Trigger looked at her with unsettling eyes and backed away slightly. There was just something about her tone he suddenly didn't like. Victoria opened the bag and took in the sight of Hashaan with a gaping wound in his chest, an empty cavity where his heart should have been. Standing up, Victoria spoke quickly to Trigger. "Get everyone out Detective. But I need you to stay. There is something I need to show you, something for our eyes only. Do you understand?"

Feeling a sense of importance, Trigger ordered his team out, closed the door of the room and then came back to where Victoria was standing over the corpse of Hashaan. She beckoned him close and crouched down as if to show him something, but as he lent over a glint of steel rang through the air, severing Trigger's throat wide open from a dagger she had been concealing in a sleeve. Blood poured into the empty body cavity of the Serpent demon and his eyes suddenly opened, a yellow glow that fixed on Victoria.

"Give me his heart". Hashaan's practically inaudible voice muttered. Victoria rolled the lifeless form of Trigger over and, slicing open his chest to reveal his ribs, she broke them apart one by one, grunting slightly at the task. Then, taking her knife once more Victoria carefully removed the still heart and placed in the chest cavity of Hashaan. It immediately started beating once more, the arteries and veins binding with those from within him and skin started to meld together. Hashaan slowly rose to a sitting position and turned to Victoria with a thin smile that reached the far sides of his skeletal pale face "Well done, my dear".

"My Lord, we need to get you out of here. This place is no longer safe. I have a car ready for us".

As she started to lift the demon up onto his knees, the main door to the room suddenly opened, letting in both light and sounds of arguing from without. "But I was told to get her a cup of tea Sir! You know how scary she is, I can't disappoint her!" It was the young constable returning with her drink. Victoria admired his determination to do well. Hashaan spoke louder this time "Bring the young man here to me". She was a little confused, but beckoned the constable in, ordering everyone else to stay outside and close the door. He made his way slowly to them, holding out the cup of tea in a shaky hand as he ventured "Erm, what is going on Ma'am? Who is this?"

Before she had a chance to answer, Hashaan practically leapt on him, pulling him down to the floor and sinking sharp teeth into his neck. Blood sprayed everywhere and Victoria shuffled back so as not to get any of the spilt hot tea, or blood on her. There was a horrific munching sound as the demon ate through the poor unsuspecting man's neck completely, his unblinking head falling to the floor whilst Hashaan was still holding the torso.

Dropping it and standing up to his full height, with a face covered in a shimmering scarlet, he smiled wickedly before looking down at Victoria. "Young fresh meat is simply the best meat of all. Now we can go my dear".

And so, holding Hashaan up, Victoria ushered him through a side door, out into the courtyard and then through another door that led to the utility room of the prison. There was a door at the far end that led onto the street, the same door in fact that David had escaped through almost a week before. A Black car was waiting with blue lights flashing just behind the radiator. And then they were gone.

Fifty Four

Gareth sat quietly in his little plastic booth in the prison van as it rumbled down the motorway. He had no concept of where they were going. No one had been told anything, but seeing so many inmates jostled into the vans couldn't be a good sign. He had heard so many strange noises the last few days. And these last few hours had been like something out of a movie. Gunshots and screams, then sirens and shouts from officers. At first, as he had sat on his bunk, Gareth was sure one of his dickhead compatriots had the TV on at full volume, but after he had scoured all of the channels on his own box and found no such film playing, Gareth started to get a little scared. He was a low level gangster after all.

The thought of guns and murder were not things that happened to him. He just had to get drugs from point A to point B. Of course he clearly hadn't been very good at it or he wouldn't be sitting here in the prison van, but the system of abuse he was brought up in gave him very few chances in life. His family were scum, his friends were worse and he always saw himself as such too. And so here he was. And yet this did not seem right.

After a relatively short time, the van appeared to slow down slightly and pull off to the right a bit. He felt a rough gravel surface beneath the van as it lumbered along some uneven path, before coming to a standstill. A few moments passed with Gareth wondering what the heck was going on. A few of the other inmate passengers started yelling to each other, demanding to know where they were and what was happening. Then he heard the van door open, followed by one of the "cell" doors. And then another. Silence filled the van, an eerie echo of sound being stamped out instantly that felt almost louder than the sounds themselves. Finally he heard the lock click on his own pod and the door opened to reveal two tall figures dressed in black cloaks, hoods covering most of their pale features. One reached in and grabbed Gareth's arm, the strength wholly unnatural and he was unable to pull back. A hood was placed over his head blocking out any light and he was forced out of the van and along a dirt path. The air seemed to change and turn cold all of a sudden and the hood was pulled off, revealing a huge warehouse with cages lining all of one side. As his eyes adjusted, Gareth could see inmates filling the cages, all seemingly fast asleep.

He then felt a sharp prick on the side of his neck and, as darkness enveloped him for the final time, he could just make out a thin, hissing voice say "Good, this is the last of them. Prepare the first for draining. We need to get of it out into the market as soon as possible. The bodies can be burned round the back of the building and buried together".

"Yes Master" came the reply, "Blood is Sacred, Blood is Life".

Fifty Five

By the time the police had arrived, Janet had long gone. The front door to both her and her neighbours' properties were left wide open and the scenes inside turned the stomachs of every officer attending. There was blood everywhere, some of it coating pieces of body which lay strewn across the floors. With everything that was going on in Stafford prison, it had been all hands on deck trying to assist the transfer of over a hundred prisoners and so everything else had taken a backseat. They were short staffed even before the sudden announcement of the immediate closure of the prison, let alone now. But as each officer entered the horror scenes in Oxford Gardens, they soon ran out again vomiting their lunch up. Training had prepared them for most things, but to see the heads of an elderly couple placed opposite each other on a dining room table, eyes still wide as if they were thinking about their next scrabble moves on an already started game, this was something else entirely. It was hard to make out which pieces of ripped flesh went with what body. But as sadistic as this seemed, the true terrifying scene was next door.

PC Barbara had a young family of her own and so found the scene all the more gruesome. The still and pale body of a small female child was positioned next to what she could only think was her daddy, both looking at the television. Except half of the back of the man's head had been chewed off and his neck still leaked blood from the vicious wound inflicted. His eyes were closed and he looked to be sleeping almost, from the front anyway. The girl looked as she was cuddled up to her daddy, with some cartoon playing on the screen in front of them. It wasn't until forensics arrived, dressed in white overalls that the full horror showed itself. As one of the team lent in close to examine the girl's face and neck, she lopped to the side and her torso fell away from her sitting legs.

"Fucking hell!" the officer yelled, pulling away as the poor child's intestines were made visible. But PC Barbara noticed only one thing, her stomach stronger than most, "where's the blood?"

"Erm, hello?! Flipping look around you, yeah?" came the response of a young male officer standing in the doorway, his lunch gone from his stomach and more of pretty much nothing in danger of following. "Where isn't there blood, Barbs?"

"No, I mean the child, look at the girl! There's no blood on her. No other wounds than the obvious separation of her torso from her legs. Her clothes are clean. All this other mess looks to be from the father's body, not hers". Sure enough, they noticed for the first time the strangeness amongst the terror. Barbara shivered as a thought came to her. "The dad, it was eaten by some huge animal, but the girl was simply drained of her blood and then positioned like this post-mortem".

The young officer sniggered, albeit a little unconvincingly. "You telling me we have both a vampire and a bloody werewolf here in Stafford? What? They escaped from the bloody prison?"

"No, not them, something much, much worse" Barbara responded darkly. The officer stopped smiling, realising that Barbara was not joking in her words, a deadly serious expression on her face. Walking out into the street, she nodded at a few officers out there, including a forensic officer who was wiping at his mouth. "You chose this job Bill, grow a pair of balls will you!" She then picked out her phone and dialled.

"Hello Ma'am, sorry to bother you as I know how busy you are right now. I could be wrong, but I think we have an escaped Afeaa Shaytan".

Fifty Six

The hug that met Xion as she stood there on doorstep of Abe's property was one of those embraces you never want to end. The kind of hug that fills your soul with love and safety, an invisible blanket that tells you everything is going to be okay. That was the hug she got from David as he opened the door to her. After what felt like an eternity of tears and unspeakable emotions flowing through each other, they finally broke free and stepped inside. Abe was waiting in the hallway and greeted Xion with an even stronger bear grip, almost breaking her ribs in the process with his large, empowering form, dreadlocks scratching her cheeks slightly as she fell into his arms.

"Xion my beauty, we have been waiting so long. It seems like an absolute miracle you are here at all. Either of you in fact, after what David has told me of your adventures up to now".

"Xi, I am so, so sorry for getting you caught up in all this" came David's soft reply, tears still streaming down his face. It was amazing how many tears of grief a body could produce over a relatively short period of time. And it felt to David that you could pretty much bathe in the sheer quantity of tears he had shed these past few days, if not weeks.

Abe made them all another drink, with a few of his special ingredients that calmed the mind and soul.

They then sat down in the living room, Xion curled up on the sofa, both David and Abe in the two armchairs facing her. The daylight was gently fading outside and as Xi and Dee took turns trying to describe their journeys, Abe watching the light mute and the streetlights switch on. When they were both caught up with each other, silence filled the room. It was Abe that broke it, feeling he needed to express a sense of foreboding running through him.

"My beautiful young friends. I am overjoyed that you have both made it here and I can assure you that you will be safe within these walls. However, I feel that the adventure is not yet over. Xion, have you seen these contract killers since you came here to Brighton?"

"No, I was very careful getting here, using all of the back streets up to Southover Street. From past Queen's Park, I cut up behind the General Hospital. No one would have known where I was since the park outside St Peter's Church, I'm positive".

"And yet my lovely, they will not just give up. Too much is riding on them finding and either capturing or killing you. Just look at the lengths they have gone to silence you both. David, if this Green Eyes character on the train is also part of the killer group, you are still not safe either".

"Can't we just wait for Adam to get here? He'll know what to do. I mean, he could just kill them before they even blinked. Especially now it's getting dark!" David did not think he could handle any more excitement. He was so tired and as he looked over at Xion, he could see she was totally spent too. *But where else can we go? We have to finish this somehow.*

"Look, I totally get that we can't just stay here. And I also get that we have no idea what Adam is up to, where he is or if he even still alive? I mean, he is almost impossible to kill, but with everything I have seen up there in the prison, anything is possible!" David stood up at the window, looking out over the street below. He then felt it too, something unspoken, unseen that was telling him it would only end with them taking the offensive.

"We have to draw these killers out, don't we? They will just keep looking for us otherwise. Xi, this doesn't have to be your fight anymore. I can do this".

"Like fuck you will Dee!" Xion piped up angrily. "You've been lucky is all. You have never been built for any of this, no offence. I've lived on the streets and grown up with shitbags all my life. I know this world and these people, you don't! if anyone should sort these bastards out once and for all, it should be me. We just need a solid plan, and a solid place to execute it".

"You don't know me! Not anymore. The shit I've had to see, had to do these past few days. I've been to prison for Christ's sake! I've had to stand in the docks and get sentenced. I've run, killed, watched a friend get killed, hidden naked. You can't sit there and tell me I'm not built for this! How fucking dare you Xi". Xion was totally taken aback by this tirade of anger. She had never seen this side of David before. And she was pretty clear from the expression on his face, David hadn't seen this side of himself either.

It was Abe's turn to stand now. "My friends, this is not something for one of you to do alone. If we are going to finish this, it has to be all of us, perhaps even Adam too. He knows to come here if he has been told you are here David. Xion, he has no reason to think you are here too, but if he does then there are two very important reasons for him to get here as fast as he can. You are as much family to him as anyone has been. But we cannot wait. Xion, can you still use your phone?"

"Of course, but it has been hacked and is being used as a tracker". Then the penny dropped. "Oh, Abe, good idea mate! Give them co-ordinates to where we will be hiding, then be ready for them.

But we don't have weapons, we'll be slaughtered, picked off like fish in a barrel!"

Abe smiled "You know the bushes up on the seafront, not too far from here actually?" he asked simply. David looked disgusted "You're talking about Dukes Mound right? Filthy place that, not a place to wander at night unless you're desperate for a quick fondle or more without a care of what you might catch!"

Xion looked at him curiously "Dee, I never knew you were into that. All these secrets someone can have eh?"

Sniggering, tension now diffused, he responded "Up yours Xi, I'm not like that and you know it. But I've heard of Dukes Mound. Full of dark bushes and winding paths with very little light. It would be a good ambush point for sure. Possible collateral damage though if people are wandering around there".

Xion went serious suddenly. "There will always be collateral damage with these thugs though. I saw that all too well in London. These wankers really don't give a damn who they kill to get to me, or you it seems. They are completely blasé about how they go about things. It's as if they are not scared about getting noticed or caught".

"They have definitely been, or are being protected, that's for sure" cut in Abe. "Or else they would have been caught by now. And so I suggest we make our way to the bushes once it is dark and then activate the tracking signal. Then we wait. Oh and as for weapons…" Abe went over to small side cupboard and pulled out a couple of metal rods. "Tasers. Strong ones. I don't believe we should kill them, but these will incapacitate them for sure. Then once they are unconscious, we tie them up and wait for Adam. I'm positive he is on his way here."

"And if he doesn't come? What then? We can't let them get free, and if they are being protected, we can't simply hand them into the police!" Xion really wasn't sure of the plan, such as it was. None of them were trained in anything like this. Well, she didn't know much about this Abe character and he certainly looked like he had secrets, but could they really pull this off? Sensing her unease, David went over to the sofa where she was curled up and plonked himself down next to her, wrapping an arm around her shoulders affectionately. "Xi, we can't let this carry on. We have to get the upper hand on this. We've been on the back foot for days and now, finally there is a way, however small, to get ahead."

She laid her head on his shoulder in return. "Yeah, I guess. Can't just stay hauled up here can we?" she admitted meekly, then looked up into David's eyes "We can do that later". Xion then pushed away and punched David playfully in the ribs. "Now, I'm going to take a shower. You should too, you stink!"

David nudged her playfully and she smiled up at him. Something seemed to pass between them and Xion almost wanted to invite him to join her but she held back. It could well have been adrenaline. A discussion needed to be had later, if there was a later.

She got up and, looking at Abe who gave her a gentle nod, made her way to the bathroom. "There are some clothes in the bottom drawer that should fit you I think. They might be a little big, but I would go for dark colours". As he heard the bathroom door close, Abe then turned to David "David, David. You know this might be a good chance for you to say how you feel right?"

David looked down at the floor. "I can't Abe. I like what we have. I don't want things to get stupid and awkward after everything. I love her too much".

"If we get through this night, then you will know it is time, my friend".

Fifty Seven

It was dusk by the time Charles rolled the coach down passed Preston Park. He was anxious to stop and be rid of Adam so that he could make his way back to London, or better still park up somewhere and arrange for the coach to be collected whilst he relaxed in the back of a government car that took him straight back to his family home, back to Julie and Alex. He had really missed them and wanted to see Alex's beaming face. Being an important MP meant too much time being spent away from his beloved and Charles wished he could change that.

Perhaps once he was properly elevated to replace Farling, he would have more of an authoritative voice and could demand that he spend more time with them. The main thing was that they were no longer in danger. Had Charles known from the get-go that Farling was the one holding them ransom, he would have taken matters into his own hands ages ago.

Charles sniggered to himself, *yeah right! Like I could. I'm a lying coward, but I'm also resourceful and can make the most of opportunities when they appear.* From back in the coach, he heard Adam stirring from a slumber and he couldn't help but wonder what kind of dreams someone like him must have, if any. *All those centuries of adventures, of happy times and absolute torturous times. How can you block all that out or compartmentalise them?*

"It's not easy, but after centuries of having them, you also learn to filter". Came Adam's sleepy voice, making Charles jump and swerve the coach slightly. "Jesus Christ! I didn't say anything! How did you know what I was thinking?"

Adam stood slowly and moved up to the front of the coach. "Compartmentalising my many daring adventures isn't too much of an issue. I don't sleep much these days". He stroked his chin, still only slightly stubbly as he had no need to shave. His hair didn't grow any longer and if he shaved, it would almost instantly grow back the same length.

"All that action has left me rather drained of energy". He smiled that wicked smile Charles' way. "It's almost as if I could do with another snack".

Charles audibly gulped. "You still need me, remember how useful I can be. You must know that from reading my bloody mind, right?"

Adam sighed. "One of my gifts, or curses. It's actually surprisingly unreliable most of the time, as thoughts tend to constantly change. And I have to filter out all that annoying singing people do in their heads all the time. But you Charles, your head is simply brimming with chatter isn't it?" It came out as intended, a rhetorical question. "If we had more time, I would very much like to listen to the scheming voices in your head, but alas I think are time together is finally coming to an end".

He made it sound particularly menacing and Charles shivered despite himself, pulling the coach into a layby. "You do know that killing me won't stop the wheels from turning don't you? They are very big wheels, far bigger than me!"

"Oh stop whining Charles. I think your blood would taste rather sour anyway, don't you? What with all your lies and manipulation. Liquid shit runs through your veins my weaselly friend. But I also think you could be useful. Letting you live means you may be of use to me from time to time. You owe me".

Placing a hand on Charles' shoulder, Adam leant in close, smiling once more and showing teeth that were slightly too long and sharp for his mouth. But he simply reached across and pulled the lever to the right of him, opening the door of the coach. "Thank you for your help with David, Charles. You get one favour from me, if and when you need it. But we are far from friends, remember that".

As he stepped off the coach, he paused before turned back. "I wish you, Julie and Alex well. But be very careful with what you do next. You think you know what you are getting yourself involved with, but you don't. Being elevated, as they phrase it, may not be all you think it is. Well, I have warned you and I will do no more than that".

And with that, Adam started walking along London Road. He turned once and saw that Charles was on his phone. *Probably arranging that lift back to London and also for someone to come and pick up the coach*, he thought. He was a good driver and Adam wished he would not take the promotion that would be offered to him by these demons. He still had a chance to come back from the darkness that was slowly choking the good out of him. And then he smiled sadly. *You can only but lead a horse to the water. He may still decide of his own choosing to die of thirst.*

And then he heard a deep sound from somewhere within, as if a voice had come into his mind. It was Aberash, indistinct words but the energy and tone were crisp enough. Turning back, Adam ran to the coach, but Charles had obviously thought he had changed his mind about feeding on him and closed the coach door before he could reach it. "Charles, let me up you bastard!"

"No way! We made a pact, you and I. you can't go back on that now! You said we owe each other, you said that!"

"Oh shut up! I need a phone. Grab me a phone from in the coach. Do it now you arsehole!"

Visibly sighing with relief, Charles went to the back, returning with one of the bodyguard's smartphones. He then opened the door and threw it to Adam, closing the door again. Adam didn't bother thanking him. Instead he turned back towards the town and, switching on the phone waited for it to ring. When it did and he answered to the voice of Abe, Adam laughed down the line at his old friend. "With everything I have seen and experienced; all the people that have come and gone from my long life, your gifts still amaze me Aberash!"

"Adam, good to hear your voice my friend. David and Xion will be thrilled and relieved to know you are safe. They still don't seem to believe that you are unkillable I think". There was a jokiness to his tone which relaxed Adam as he walked past St Peter's church, turning left to start the steep hill which would take him to Kemptown.

"They're both with you? Are they okay? What is Xion doing there? She was not meant to be a part of this". Adam was slightly puzzled. He had no intention of drawing them both into this predicament. After all, had things gone the wrong way, he would need Xion to continue helping him, train someone else to help even. He felt bad thinking like this, but it was the way of the world, a world that moved a hell of a lot faster than he did. Abe started to explain what had happened in short version, ending with their plan for catching the contract killers.

"Aberash!" Adam continued, "What are you thinking letting them do this! They are geeks, techie nerds. They're not up to this! They'll be killed!"

"My friend," interjected Abe, "you underestimate them as they do you it seems. They have survived through so much already, but they are still being hunted. These killers will not stop. They can't as they too are also in too deep now. David and Xion need your help. Everyone is now in the same place, as if the Gods meant for this to happen. Xion and David have gone to the Mound on the seafront already. They left a short while ago. On my cue, she will put her battery back in and signal her whereabouts". Before Adam could interrupt, Abe added "It is her choice to be used as bait, with David waiting nearby and we are to also be there, lying in wait. Together we can do this and the bushes are a perfect stalking ground".

"Shit, I know they are but not for those reasons! Okay, I'm on my way there now. You best catch up with them Aberash and hope they haven't already come to harm".

"I'm leaving now boss". The line went dead. Adam was still a good 20 minutes away at least. He only hoped he could get there in time. *What are they bloody thinking!* He shouted inside his mind as he started jogging up the hill.

Fifty Eight

"You know it's trap boss, yes?" pleaded Henryk to Shayanne as they headed east along the seafront towards new co-ordinates that had just pinged on her phone.

"And you know that they are nothing but untrained, scared little shits, yes?" mimicked Shayanne in a deliberately bad Eastern European accent. "If they think they can play with us and try to make us the prey, they are in for a sodding rude awakening, I can tell you! And besides, even if this David and the little bitch are together now, they are still only two hopeless, homeless and utterly idealess geeky twats that just don't know when they are dead already!"

Shayanne was seething. Inside she knew that they were now playing a dangerous game. The co-ordinates were not random this time, they were at a specific place on the seafront, up by the Marina. Why would Xion go there, if not to try and trap them? Or was she really quite stupid and had switched her phone on waiting for a call from her boyfriend David? No, she didn't think the latter for a second. "Have you heard from Grant or Freddie?" she asked, changing the subject.

Henryk shook his head "No boss, they have all but disappeared. I reckon they were caught at station. Why else wouldn't they call?"

"How can three out of the five of us have been screwed on this?! On what was supposed to have been a simple snatch and grab mission? Something else is at play here. Either we have totally underestimated these little bastards, or there's another party in play that we don't know about. I don't like it, and yes it's probably a trap, but what choice do we have? We can't turn back now. You want to explain to our employer that things haven't gone as planned? You want to hear that rasping voice of something entirely unhuman tell us how he will rip us apart? Or worse? I certainly don't. To hell with that! I quite like my limbs and blood where they are, exactly where they are, thank you very much!"

"Totally get you boss. We're here. Best park up here on top road and walk down. Good to get a scope from top".

As Henryk parked up at the side of the road, they could make out a single entrance down into tall, bush-lined paths, dimly lit by sporadic streetlamps that cast a seedy glow in the damp air. The rain appeared to have stopped for now, but there looked to be an imminent threat of more along on the way. Shayanne opened the glovebox in front of her and pulled out both a silencer for her revolver and also two extra cartridges of bullets. She slipped them all into the holster hanging just under her right breast and, climbing out of the car, she took off the stolen jacket and pulled on a black beanie. There was no mistaking the intention of her outfit. She was done pretending or hiding. If they wanted the real assassin, they would surely get her now.

Reaching back to the rear seat, Shayanne grabbed her knife belt and fastened it around the waist. On it were her favourite selection of knives, mostly small blades that we perfect for throwing or for close contact work, like flaying or disembowelling. *Oh how I hope it comes to that!* She almost drooled. Pulling on a short black coat that covered the weapons, Shayanne glanced over at Henryk. He was more old school, settling for two pistols strapped to his thighs and brandishing a long, lethal looking machete which must have been close to a meter in length.

"Is that really necessary? Not very subtle there are you Henryk?" commented Shayanne.

Henryk merely shrugged. "You have your ways, I have mine. You take the skin, I like to take limbs".

Shayanne sighed, "I mean, what if there are local police patrolling these bushes. It looks very much like a dirty gay cruising ground to me, being in

Brighton and all that. If they catch a glance at you walking down with a fucking machete in hand, I think any kind of stealth will be pretty much blown wide open, don't you?"

On that note, Henryk reached in the car and pulled out a long scabbard, in which he slid the giant knife, sliding it over his shoulder. He then nodded simply to her before turning to make a start down the path.

"For God's sake man! At least put on your black jacket over the top! Jesus, have you totally lost the plot?!" hissed Shayanne. She had a mind to slit his throat and dump him in the car. These so called professionals she had hired on good faith were turning out to be liabilities, no doubt about that. Throwing the long black overcoat to him, Shayanne stared impatiently as he fumbled to pull it over himself. Once he was finally suitably dressed, they both walked slowly down the path. Then they stopped and turned back up, deciding instead to first walkalong the top wall that spanned the paths.

It wasn't a great view of what went on down below, but maybe they could get lucky without having to go down into the cruising ground. Shayanne pulled a small night scope from her belt, a simple one-eyed affair that would normally fix to the gun as a sight. Looking through it from a vantage point halfway along the top wall, she could make out two guys kissing on a bench, one with his hand down the other's trousers. She quickly moved along, only to see a guy come out from behind some bushes doing up his fly.

"Fucking hell, this is not what I signed up for. I think you'd get off on this though, maybe you should take the sight". And she passed it to Henryk, who was curious at what was making her gag.

As he moved the sight along slowly, he couldn't help but snigger "This is nothing. You should see what happens in Albania. Everyone thinks we are against the gays, but it just makes them more inventive in private. We have some of the best pornos, you know that? I make money from them before".

"You had your finger in all the pies, I know. You see anything other than the sharing of STIs?"

"No boss. Wait. There! She is sit on a bench along the bottom path. She is alone. You see. Must be her right?" He passed the sight piece over to Shayanne quickly.

"Jackpot! There she is the bitch. We've got her!"

"Can you see anything?" David asked from the bushes behind where Xion was sitting. "It stinks back here. Made worse because it's soaking wet!".

"I really wouldn't touch anything, or look around too much if I were you Dee. Not sure it's all water". Xion giggled, much to the displeasure of her friend.

"Where's Abe? We need his eyes up the top. They'll park up there right? They have to". David was so nervous and really didn't like the idea now they were doing it.

"Just calm the hell down alright? Shit, someone's coming, but I don't think it's them!" and sure enough, a tall skinny guy probably in his late forties came walking confidently down towards Xion.

"Not really the place for you this, hun" he commented, standing in front of her. It was then that he noticed David peering out from behind the bushes. "Oh I see, pimping out your friend are you? Want me to come in there do you darling?"

"Please, this is not what it appears to be okay? Just walk away, please!" pleaded Xion, but the guy was having none of it. "Oh my sweet, we are all here for something, and nothing ever turns out as it should. But I love that. You can watch, even film if you like". And he started towards the back of the bench, making his way into the bushes to the side of where David was.

"Mate, seriously, you need to fuck off okay? This is dangerous". Hissed David, backing away as far as he could, his back now up against the trunk of a thin tree. They were in pretty total darkness and he felt a hand grab his crotch. "Whoah! Stop now, mate".

Suddenly the hand fell away and the man fell forwards into David's arms. The weight was pushing David to the ground with the man on top, a limp form.

"What the fuck?" he could just about say before falling forwards out of the bush into the light. There was blood all over his front, but David knew it wasn't his. A vicious exit wound had appeared on the forehead of the man, parts of his brain starting to seep out down his lifeless face. David yelped and clambered over the bench, almost into the lap of an equally startled Xion. There was a whooshing sound and something hit the tree right where David had just been. They both fell off the bench, hiding with their torsos flat to the ground as more bullet rebounded off the bench.

"Shit, we are bloody sitting ducks again! And lit up like Christmas trees to boot. What are we going to do now? And this floor stinks!" Looking ahead, David could make out some more bushes that had an entrance inside, as if they were purposefully hollowed out. "We need to make a run for those bushes there. It's pitch black and we might be able to get out the other side to the bottom road. It's our only chance!"

Before they moved, Xion quickly dialled the number for Abe. He answered after just one ring "Xion? Are you in place?"

"Oh Abe, it's gone to shit quickly here! They've killed a bloody cruiser and now we're pinned down. We're going to make a run for it. We need you here now! Where the heck are you?"

"I'm at the top road. I think I can see them, but they are hiding well behind a wall. No, hang on, they are starting to make their way towards you I think. I'm on my way. But you might have a chance now they have moved. Go!"

And so, not bothering to hang up, Xion pushed David and together they leapt towards the bushes on the other side of the path.

Fifty Nine

Adam ran along the top sea road with unnatural speed, drawing more than a few looks from people walking. But he didn't care at this point. He was so close to ending this. Dukes Mound was just up ahead, with paths leading upwards towards the top road above the arches. The marina lay directly ahead of him. There were a few guys walking in various directions along the paths, disappearing into bushes or sitting on benches. It was a very seedy affair, but Adam could also see the logic behind meeting here. There were many hiding places, places where one could easily sneak up on another without being either seen or caught. All he had to do now was find Xion and David. Aberash was on his way too, but maybe Adam could find these assassins first and put an end to this.

He decided to keep to the lower road first, hugging close to the trees and bushes as he made his way slowly along and keeping to the shadows. Drawing the attention of a few single guys, Adam simply smiled and shook his head. One of the guys made a pouting face in mock sadness. There had been a time when Adam would have indulged himself a little. He liked to experiment and had done so much for so many years with his maker and once lover, Leofric. Snapping his mind back immediately, he berated himself. *Now is not the time to reminisce!*

Then, up ahead he noticed some kind of commotion. Moving closer, it looked as if some guy had collapsed and others were trying to sit him up. Even in the darkness, from here Adam could clearly see that part of the man's forehead was missing. He had been shot! Which meant David and Xion were close by, as were their pursuers. And then he spotted them. A woman and a man, both in black working their way slowly and deliberately down one of the paths.

They approached the commotion and as the men tried to push them away, Adam saw the glint of steel fly through the air three times and all men fell to the ground. *Okay, my turn now,* he thought and came out of the shadows, approaching the couple with a speed that knocked the woman off her feet and into the bushes. The man swung the machete blade viciously his way, but Adam easily swerved out of the way. He then grabbed at the man's arm, snapping it like a twig and forcing the blade to drop to the ground. Blood spurted from an arterial wound at the elbow and a spray hit Adam in the face. Tasting the sweet, warm liquid made him lose total control for the second time in a matter of hours and he bit into the man's neck, practically ripping it apart and drinking his fill. Just as he was about to finish, Adam suddenly felt a sharp pain in his side and looked down to see Shayanne pushing one of her knives deep between his ribs. It was a pain he was used to from many battle years. It meant nothing to him. He simply grabbed her wrist and pulled the knife out, her hand still attached. Shayanne yelped at the twisting of her arm as Adam forced her away from him, dropping the lifeless form of Henryk to slump in the middle of the path.

"You have failed", he muttered, the deep growling of a voice resonating from the predatory side of himself.

"And what about you, you monster? What about all the lives you have taken? You think you have won, but you will always fail. How can you save these pathetic lives and yet take so many more?" She retorted, her words spitting into his face as he held her fast, the bloodied dagger still hanging from her wrist.

"Every day is a punishment for me, but you don't need to see another one. I am your judgement". And with that, he twisted Shyanne's neck with his free hand, spinning it round to face the opposite way. It was a loud crack that rang in the air and was still dissipating as she too slumped to the ground, lifeless, on top of her dead partner.

After a long moment, both David and Xion appeared from where they were hiding in the bushes. They stared at Adam as if seeing the real him for the first time, blood dripping down his beautiful face and orange eyes glowing like terrifying beacons in the seedy darkness of this forbidden landscape. Adam then wiped his face on a bit of clothing ripped from one of the dead bodies lying at their feet.

"As always Adam your timing is something to behold in itself! What are we to do with these bodies?" Xion stammered, not really able to fully process what she had seen. The last few days were becoming too much for her and David could see it in her wild eyes.

"We need to go, and now!" he said and Adam nodded in agreement. Together, the three of them moved down onto the sea road, just as a car pulled up. It was Abe. Within minutes, they had left the scene behind them and were making their way back to Kemptown. As they got out of the car, the town seemed alive with fresh sirens bouncing off the walls of the houses and streets.

"Looks like you are all staying with me for a while". Abe commented as he let them into his home once more.

Sixty

Charles sat at his desk and stared at the file in front of him. The cover simply said:

Prison Reform Program, North England

He knew what this really was. This was the opportunity to set up further sites across prisons, maximising output and, more importantly, making him very rich in the process. He had sold his soul for this opportunity and he was not going to waste it. He had come too far and seen too many terrible things to back away now.

His desk phone rang, a high shrill that cut through his racing brain. Charles picked up the receiver, "Charles McNeil MP?"

"Charles, do you know who this is?" came a fainting hissing voice. Charles knew. Blood drained from his face and he downed almost a full glass of brandy before answering. "Yes, my Lord. It is good to hear from you".

"Are you sure? You don't seem very pleased to hear from me. It is almost as if you are surprised I am still alive". As the sentence was finished, Charles knew what was to follow, and he wanted to cry. "You see," continued the voice, "I am a man down, which means for now you will take his place.

What you thought would set you free has now put you deeper into the scheme of things. How ironic. You are to continue your reform of the prison system and set up more rooms for my project within the prisons listed in the file on the desk in front of you. If you do well, you will be rewarded beyond your wildest dreams".

"What is the time scale, my Lord? I was hoping that I might have a bit more time".

"Time is a precious thing none of us really has control over, Charles. Get it done as quickly as possible. Oh and Charles?"

"Yes my Lord?" he replied meekly.

"Say hello to your lovely Julie and adorable sone Alex for me, won't you?" Then the line went dead, leaving Charles holding the receiver. It fell from his hand, thumping onto the table. As he picked up a family photo of Julie, Alex and himself playing on Brighton Beach, Charles was unable to stop the tears from falling onto it like rain. He poured another drink, the only thoughts hitting his brain being *I'm right back where I started. No, so much worse than that.*

Epilogue

They had all stayed with Aberash for a week to let things calm down. Charles had been true to his word, as there was no longer any more news about David circulating anywhere. With access to a computer, both David and Xion were able to scour the internet and erase any and all traces there. Xion was worried that any images or headlines might ping back as they had before, but interest seemed to have been lost finally. The whole country was now more concerned on the whereabouts of nearly a hundred prisoners that had never made it out of Stafford to their transfer prisons. HMP Stafford itself, it appeared, was not reopening any time soon and Charles was back visiting different establishments around the country.

Adam couldn't believe how society just believed whatever rubbish was fed them as they went about their lives in any direction they were led. But this had always been the way.

Pouring hot water onto a teabag in his mug, he looked up and smiled as Xion entered the kitchen wearing a shirt he was convinced he saw David wearing the previous day.

"About bloody time my dear" he smiled as she opened a cupboard door, pulling out another two mugs. David then entered too and gave Adam a sheepish look.

"Morning Adam. Looks like we can head back up to London in a day or two. The police are weaving some bullshit story about terrorists having gone back to some country other another. The threat level has been dropped and headlines are pretty much focussed on this Charles MP character now and his stupid prison reform."

Moving behind Xion, David wrapped his arms around her as she made them both a coffee.

"We have indeed overstayed our welcome. But I'm afraid we cannot go back to London just yet." Adam said softly, looking them both straight. "I'm sorry to ask this of you both, but I need your help in the field once more." And with that he pulled out a letter that had been keeping in his jeans pocket. Letting go of Xion, David opened the envelope and slid it out. He gasped as he read, before passing it to Xion, the colour drained from his face. She read it out loud:

> Adam, my beloved,
> I am sorry to have taken so long to contact you directly, but I have tried to let you know of my existence and whereabouts these past years. I think you have seen my markings and so I am sure this has not come as such a surprise. I have been tracking the demons known as the Afeaa Shaytan

across the globe. I know you have recently had a run in with one of the High Masters in the North of England and so I now ask for you to come back up, but to Scarborough. They appear to be coming together here for something and I do not know that I can handle them all on my own. I have some reinforcements; a nurse you remember from Brighton hospital as well as a few other brother and sisters I have made. But you are by far the strongest of my children, my love. I have missed you and I need you now to help me put an end to this race of filth once and for all. Your friend Aberash can send me a message with your answer and keep us in contact until we meet. I very much look forward to sharing a drink with you again Adamis. It has been too long.

Yours eternally,

Leofric.

P.S. Please bring your helpers David and Xion with you. They will be of use.

"Adam, what the hell is this? You can't seriously ask us to do this after everything we've just been through?!" Screamed Xion, unable to control her emotions.

"Xi, we have to help. We've no choice, we're a part of all this whether we like it or not" David said softly trying to calm her down. He reached out and took the letter from her before she could tear it up, handing it back to Adam. "I know what this Leofric means to you Adam. But seriously, after all this time, can you trust him? He has been so good at staying hidden all these years, we've not even been able to get a whiff of him other than the odd letter scribbled in blood on walls, like the one here in Brighton a few years back".

"Yes, I've always felt him. Abe has also helped me to keep a track of him, but you're right David, I'm not sure I can trust him. However, we have no choice but to go. This Hashaan is still out there, I'm sure of it despite me ripping out his heart. And Charles happens to be planning to go to Scarborough in the coming weeks. Everything is pointing there".

"Well then, best pave the digital highway for us, hadn't I?" remarked Xion bitterly and, picking up her coffee, she stormed out of the kitchen, bumping into Abe as he too entered. "Sorry", she mumbled under her breath.

Adam felt suddenly like a father of petulant teenagers. He sympathised with them but needed them to focus. "David, go and calm her down please. You can help her too. I need a word with Abe".

As he left the kitchen, Abe spoke gently to Adam "Well, they make a lovely couple. Their energies are aligned perfectly. But I don't think they are ready for such another adventure my friend".

"None of us get to choose I think. Now, we must formulate some kind of plan".

The story will continue with Blood Oaths.

Printed in Great Britain
by Amazon